For Mum, who encouraged [illegible],

For Wolf, my only other big dream, and

For Lee, without whom, I couldn't have realised this dream.

Chapter One

They first met at the library when they were fifteen. Actually, that's not true. They first met when they were eleven, and they both attended the same secondary school. They were vaguely aware of each other, but they were in different forms and different ability sets, so they barely knew each other's names until year 9 when they had one lesson together; Craft and Design Technology. Bryony's worst subject and Isaac's best. Even then, they didn't mix. Their reputations had proceeded them, but to be fair, Isaac was not quite the playboy idiot that Bryony had been led to believe he was. He was fairly attentive in class and only occasionally played the class clown. He was beautiful, though, and as such, he had a constant gaggle of people around him. Bryony was not one of them. She recognised he was more attractive than all the other boys in the school, and in her unguarded moments, she did allow herself to fantasise about what it would be like to be his friend, not even a girlfriend, just one of the group who seemed to find life so effortless. She, on the other hand, was the major stress head that her reputation, if she were interesting enough to have such a thing, said she was. This was accentuated by this particular lesson. Mr Gabe insisted that they allow their creative ideas to flourish. Bryony's creative ideas were actually excellent in her head, but converting them into an artist's rendition on paper was a completely different skill set that she simply did not possess. And that was only part one of the mission. From there, she had to somehow make her drawing of a birdhouse, yes, that was a birdhouse, into a 3D piece of woodwork. Needless to say, it didn't get any less stressful for her in that class. Therefore she had little time to think about Isaac or the beautiful and ornate magazine rack he had made for his mother and had landed him a well-deserved A.

They first spoke, as in had a proper conversation between just the two of them, in the library. Not even the school library. They were in the very small, barely used by anyone other than the elderly or the very young, town library. This was one of Bryony's very favourite places in the world, other than her own bedroom. But her mum and dad had decided to renovate the kitchen and the bathroom at the same time, and so for the past three weeks and undoubtedly the next month at least, her bedroom was not the quiet sanctuary it once had been, and she simply could not study with all that noise. So, each Saturday morning, she sought refuge in the quiet, dusty library. It was on one of these Saturdays that, from out of absolutely nowhere, Isaac appeared at her table and sat down. Surprised and confused, she pulled her earpods out and stared at him. He was wearing grey joggers and a nondescript black t-shirt with a sweater wrapped around his waist. His hair was a mess, and there was a splattering of dirt across his sweaty face and neck.

'Hey, Bryony. What are you doing here?'

'Erm, hi Isaac. I'm studying. What are you doing here?'

He grinned adorably, and Bryony felt her stomach do an unexpected flip.

'I bet you thought I didn't even know what a library was, huh?'

'No, I think I remember you were on the same school induction tour as me in year 7, and we went to the library then.'

'Right, yeah, damn it. I've been here, to this one before too. Even got a book out. The very hungry caterpillar. Pretty sure I've still got it at home somewhere.'

'You know that's not really how it works. You're supposed to return the books when you've finished them.'

'Yeah, but I've not finished it yet. No spoilers!'

Bryony giggled, surprised by how easy it was to talk to him.

‘So are you looking for another book? Can I suggest The Gruffalo? It’s got an awesome twist in it.’

This time Isaac laughed and leaned forward conspiratorially.

‘Actually, I’m not here for a book. I’m pretty sure I’m on the librarian's hit list.’

‘Wow, that’s pretty brave of you to show up here then.’

‘I know right.’

‘And trust me, these librarians are relentless. If they catch you, you may not make it out alive. They’re known for their torture methods, you know. You’ll have to spend the rest of your days in the old lady romance aisle.’

Isaac really laughed this time, then looked at her intently as though surprised by her. Bryony tried to keep herself from blushing. ‘*I’m a strong, independent, and bright young woman. I will not melt because the boy is cute.*’ Her internal monologue raged. Still, she smiled her sweetest smile at him.

‘We’re playing hide and seek.’ He announced.

‘Who, you and the librarians?’

‘No.’ He chuckled. ‘Me and Charlie and Leo and Mo. We got bored of footy, which is to say, some older kids came along and kicked us off the field, so we decided to go old school and play hide and seek. Will’s on, and we’re allowed anywhere on the main high street. As soon as I saw this place, I knew no one would look for me here. I almost didn’t come in because the thought of having to read something was terrifying, but then I saw you through the window over there, and I was saved.’ He nodded his head in the direction of the large ornate but dirty window that got none of the attention it deserved, either from the library visitors, or the cleaners.

'I've never considered myself a saviour before.'

'How does it feel?'

'Surprisingly fitting.'

They grinned at each other, and once again, Bryony felt her cheeks getting hot, and she tried, in vain, to calm the butterflies having a party in her stomach. She dropped her gaze to the books open on the table.

'So, do you come here often?' He asked, leaning back casually on the hard, wooden chair, pushing it onto just the back two legs, looking like he'd been there a thousand times.

'Isn't that a chat up line?' She asked sharply.

He immediately sat up straight, bringing the chair back down to all fours. The grin that slowly began to spread across his face was both knowing and mocking. She felt herself blushing again but refused to look away.

'Normally, I'd say yes, but I swear that's not what I meant. It was a genuine question. Why? Do you want it to be?'

'No, no. Sorry.'

The crimson in her cheeks darkened to a very unattractive lobster shade, spreading right up to her hairline and then down to an ugly, blotchy rash effect on her neck. She was so mortified she couldn't speak. Fortunately, Isaac was unexpectedly gallant in the situation.

'If I was trying to chat you up, I would definitely not use some tired, old chat up line. I'd go with something far more original like, erm ….'

He thought for a minute, his handsome face somehow even more beautiful with frown lines across his forehead. The reprise gave Bryony a chance to calm down and regain a little decorum.

'Okay, I've got it; are you a parking ticket, 'cos you've got "fine" written all over you.'

'Oh my god, that's dreadful.' Bryony managed to say with a little chuckle, her colour returning to normal.

'Hold on, I've got more. What about this? See this shirt – it's made of boyfriend material.'

'No, no, no. That's definitely worse.' She shook her head, smiling.

'Yeah, well, Eamonn, my older brother, swears he managed to pull a girl by saying, "Well, here I am. What are your other 2 wishes?"'

'Wow. Well, he must be full to the brim with confidence.'

'That or he's too stupid to know how dumb he sounds.'

'My older brother Steven claims that chat-up lines are modern society's way of herding together the unintelligent masses to filter out the available and desirable potential mates.'

'Oh. Right.' Isaac said.

The silence stretched out for an age.

'He's a dick. None of the rest of the family like him very much.' She added, then grinned just a little bit wickedly.

Isaac roared with laughter so loudly, two librarians appeared to look at him sternly, and Bryony had to hush him before he got them kicked out. He was unapologetic for the noise he made or the fact that he had caused a bit of a scene. In fact, he barely seemed to notice. But he did notice her. He looked at her squarely, unhesitant and without any embarrassment. Bryony would have felt uncomfortable, and indeed she did a little bit, but if she was being honest with herself, it gave her a chance to look at him properly too.

'Quick, hide.' She said suddenly, her attention drawn to the window.

'What?'

'Under the table or behind my chair. Quickly!' She insisted, reaching across and grabbing his arm, pulling him around the table so he could crouch behind her chair. As soon as he did, he understood her motive, and she heard a mumbled expletive as he ducked down behind her.

'Just pretend like you are working, you know, like you were when I came in.'

'I wasn't pretending. I really was working!' She exclaimed, turning to look at him.

'Don't look at me, you'll give it away.' He grinned at her. 'Are they looking in?'

As casually as she could, Bryony raised her eyes to look outside onto the high street. She could see Will and Mo standing outside, both had their back to her, but she couldn't see Charlie. She whispered this information to Isaac.

'You don't have to whisper, they can't hear you.' He pointed out, and Bryony could hear the smile in his voice, as well as feel some heat from his body; he was so close to her.

'Actually, you do have to whisper. This is a library!' She whispered back. She was staring at the book in front of her that not half an hour ago had dominated her attention, but now she could barely even see.

'Where the hell is Charl…'

'Shh.' She hissed, kicking her leg back more forcefully than she meant to, hearing a muffled groan from behind her.

The boy who had just walked in was in shorts, a muddy T-shirt with a hoody wrapped around his waist, and a plastic bag containing a football slung over his shoulder. He stomped past them to the end of the aisle, where he quickly glanced left and right before pulling his phone out of his pocket, turning around, and stomping back out again, texting all the time and not even noticing her, let alone Isaac. When he was gone, the two of them remained motionless for a minute or so more. Only when Isaacs's phone buzzed to let him know he had a new text did they move again. He stood up and stretched before returning to his seat and pulling out his phone to read the text. His grin was broad, and he turned to her.

'They have no idea where I am.' He told her and showed her the text.

Charlie - Dude, I give up already. Come out so we can go to Mo's for COD

'So, you win?' Bryony asked.

'I win.'

'You'd better go and soak up the glory then.'

'Yeah. And you've probably got loads of work to do. Why else would you be here, right?'

Bryony desperately hoped that she wasn't imagining the sense of hesitancy about his departure that she felt was coming from Isaac.

‘Yeah, exactly.’ She agreed reluctantly.

‘Right.’

He stood up and pushed the chair under the table. He hovered for a moment.

‘See ya at school, I guess.’

‘See you then.’ She said, looking up at him, wondering if they would ever speak again.

He turned and walked off.

She picked up her pen and tried to read the notes she had been making, determined not to watch him go, though that was all her mind was actually focused on.

‘I should probably get your number.’

Bryony jumped, almost out of her seat. She’d been so preoccupied with thoughts of Isaac, she hadn’t noticed him come back and stand right next to her.

‘Sorry. I didn’t mean to startle you. I just… Well, I think you should give me your phone number.’

‘You do. Why?’

‘Idiot girl, why didn’t you just say okay and give him your number.’ She mentally chastised herself.

‘Because this is an excellent hiding place, but I don’t want to come here alone. If we play hide and seek next week, which I’m going to insist upon because I’m awesome at it, I will want to know you are in here before I step foot inside and open myself up to a librarian attack.’

'Well, you could always just look through the window. I always sit here when I come.'

'Oh my god, Bryony. Just give the cute boy your number. What is wrong with you?' Her fluttering butterflies screamed at her.

'That's good to know and a very good point.' He said, seeming stumped. He hovered again, and just as it was almost getting awkward, Bryony's brain kicked into gear.

'Although,' She began, and Isaac's face perked up. 'You may think of another cheesy pickup line between now and then that you need to run past me.'

'Yes. That. Exactly. I don't want to embarrass myself.'

'So I'd be doing you a favour by giving you my number.'

'Consider it charity work.'

She laughed and enjoyed his smile as he noted her number on his phone.

'This time, I really am going. No more ninja tricks this week.'

'Save them to protect yourself from the librarians.' She replied, and with one more grin, he was gone.

Chapter Two

3 years ago

Isaac – Hey this is Isaac

Bryony – Hey

Isaac – So I had fun at the library today

Bryony – That sounds like an oxymoron!

Isaac – Your mum's an oxymoron

Bryony – ??

Isaac – Sorry. That's just something me and my mates always say

Isaac – Well this is awkward

Isaac – Shall we start this whole thing over again

Isaac - Hi

Bryony - Hi

Isaac – So do you wanna come to the carnival with me tomorrow night?

Bryony – The carnival? The old abandoned fairground? Isn't that place boarded up? And dangerous?

Isaac – Yeah but me and the boys worked out how to get in and it can be kinda cool

Bryony – You want me to come to a death trap and hang out with you and your friends tomorrow night?

Isaac – Erm no. I want you to come to a death trap and hang out with just me tomorrow night. Sounds far scarier don't you think?

Bryony – Just you?

Isaac – Yeah. You know. Like on a date

Bryony – A dare?

Isaac – What? No

Bryony – Sorry typo – Did you really mean date?

Isaac – Yes. A date. You and me. Tomorrow night at the carnival. What do you think?

Bryony – Idk

Isaac – Ok no probs. I just thought I picked up on a flirty vibe at the library. Did you?

Bryony – Me? Flirt? I didn't flirt. I don't know how to flirt. Did you think I was flirting? I didn't mean to

Isaac – Oh. Then sorry, I guess

Bryony – I do want to

Isaac – want to what?

Bryony – Go on a date

Isaac – You do? Who with? Anyone in particular or will anyone do?

Bryony – Oh, I meant you. But if you have changed your mind then that's fine too

Isaac – Yes, I have changed my mind in the last 2 minutes

Bryony – Oh. Ok. Sorry

Isaac – I'm going to really enjoy teasing you mercilessly in our future. I'll pick you up at 7

Bryony – Okay. Thank you

Isaac – Hahaha. You are welcome

Bryony – shut up. I didn't mean that

Isaac – you are so polite. Please pass my regards on to your parents for raising such a polite daughter

Bryony – Well in case you didn't realise this before, you should know I am really not cool. So I will understand if you want to change your mind

Isaac – No you really are not cool

Isaac – You are adorable

Isaac – I'm still picking you up at 7 tomoro

Isaac – nothing you can say can change my mind

Isaac – I'm bringing a book of chat up lines

15 months ago

Isaac – Babe what are you wearin?

Bryony – my school uniform you perv! Why?

Isaac – sounds awesome but I need you to change into something sexier

Bryony – What? Why?

Isaac – So many questions – don't you trust me?

Bryony – Not at all - I've known you too long. Tell!

Isaac – I got your bday pressie

Bryony – My birthday is four months away. What's going on?

Isaac – we are going for a romantic date

Bryony – babe I'm not getting dressed up to go to the Carnival

Isaac – that's not where we r goin. Wear something sparkly

Bryony – What?!! I need details

Isaac – it will ruin the surprise

Bryony – if you don't tell me where we are going I cannot dress appropriately and without the details I will turn up in joggers and your old nasty sweater – and you know I will

Isaac – Babe your killin me. I'm trying to be romantic

Bryony – And I won't shower

Isaac – fine

Isaac – I won tickets to the premier of the new Tom Holland film in Leicester Square in London! We are walking down the red carpet baby! xxx

Bryony - Oh My God! Really? I love you so much right now. Why didn't you tell me b4! What the hell am I going to wear?

5 months ago

Isaac – Hey Babe r u awake?

Isaac – Babe?

Bryony – Isaac its 3:10. Whats wrong?

Isaac – Do u fancy goin for a picnic?

Bryony – Yea defo. After school tomoz?

Isaac – No Babe I mean now. Let's go to the Carnival and do a picnic under the stars!

Bryony – Babe! It's like 3:14 am!!

Isaac – I no. It's a pyjama picnic. I'll pick u up in 15 mins

Bryony – I need to function. Gotta brush teeth. May need longer

Isaac – I'm outside waiting. Got evrythin we need. Just need u. Be quick

Bryony – God I love U xxxx

Isaac – Love u too. Hurry xxxxx

5 days ago

Bryony's phone – 15 missed calls from Isaac

Isaac – Baby answer your damn phone

Isaac – Bryony you HAVE to talk to me

Isaac – Monroe is lying –she's just trying to break us up. She's jealous of us babe

Isaac – Bryony if you don't answer your phone I'm coming to your house

Bryony – I have nothing to say to you. Don't you dare come here

Isaac's phone – 6 missed calls from Bryony

Bryony – Where the hell are you? I'm trying to call you so you don't drive. You've been drinking Isaac. Don't get in your car. I'll talk to you ok

Isaac's phone – 12 missed calls from Bryony

Bryony – Isaac! I am getting worried now. I don't forgive you but I will talk to you

Isaac's phone – 22 missed calls from Bryony

Bryony – Isaac. I'm sorry. Please baby answer the phone. I'm so scared. I love you xxx

Chapter Three

'Bryony. You *have* to get up now,' her mother's voice bid shrilly, even into her duvet-covered ears. 'We have to leave for the church in two hours, and you must shower.'

Bryony didn't even grunt in response. When the duvet was unceremoniously ripped off the bed, leaving her exposed to the elements and shivering, she still couldn't summon the necessary strength to move. She just lay there, foetal position, not sleeping, not talking, barely breathing. She just couldn't.

Time passed. She was unsure how much, not that she thought about it much, but all of a sudden, her mother was there again. This time, not shouting. She stood in front of her, talking in her "we-have-guests" voice, though Bryony couldn't tell what she was saying. She was aware, though, that she had retrieved or, more likely, had been given back her duvet. Her eyes flickered over her mother, looking very demure in her formal black dress. It suited her. There was a time when Bryony would have told her so. With an almighty effort, she made herself concentrate on what her mum was saying.

'… is here to see you. Isn't that wonderful of her to come and talk to you? On today of all days.'

She was indicating to the corner of the bedroom that was directly behind Bryony, meaning that if she wanted to find out who was there, she'd have to turn over.

No chance.

She felt her eyelids get heavy from the exhaustion of listening and began closing them. The sharp jab of her arm being surreptitiously pulled, forced her to keep concentrating. Her mother 'helped' her sit up, and finally, Bryony saw her visitor. Melanie. She practically shone with angelic light in the corner of her room. Her hair was done, her face impeccably made up, and she was wearing a beautiful navy dress with heeled shoes. Bryony gawped at her, suddenly acutely aware that she hadn't left her bed for five days. Not even to brush her teeth.

'May I have a few moments with her, Victoria?' Melanie asked, her voice quiet but strong. Victoria (never Vic, Vicky, or Tori) managed to keep the indignation off her face, but barely and Bryony knew she would be severely put out by this; nevertheless, she left the room, leaving Bryony with Isaac's mum.

As soon as the door closed, Melanie crossed to the bed, sat on the edge, and gently grasped one of Bryony's cold hands. Melanie's hands were not much warmer, and when they looked into each other's eyes, pain was reflected back like an infinity mirror of heartache and grief.

'How are you, darling?' Melanie asked, all the warmth missing from her hands was there in her voice, full of unselfish love and compassion. It was more than Bryony could bear. She immediately felt her eyes burn, and the tears started to fall hot and fast whilst her throat constricted and the sobs burst out of her aggressively. Melanie wrapped her arms around her and held her almost painfully tight, but Bryony didn't care.

'I know, I know, darling.' Melanie comforted her, allowing her to cry as much as she needed. Bryony had cried almost constantly for four of the five days she'd spent in bed. She had thought she had dried up and that there were no more tears left in her, but apparently, with just a comforting word from Isaac's mum, the floodgates had reopened. Her stomach and shoulders hurt from all the shuddering sobs she'd expended, but she hadn't the capacity for constraint now. The ache inside was far, far stronger. She had no idea how long she cried for. Melanie, unlike everyone else, didn't seem to be on a time schedule. She didn't think that by wiping away the already-spent tears, she could stop the others from falling. She just let her be. In the end, it was Bryony who pulled away. She quickly wiped her face with the duvet, noticing for the first time all the other stains that were already there, and was mortified. She hoped that Melanie hadn't noticed them too. Especially in that beautiful outfit. Oh God!

'I don't understand. How are you up and dressed?' Bryony asked. Her voice was croaky and thick from disuse.

'Because, my darling girl, today we have to be. Today is not about us. The funeral, the wake, and the few days after, they are for everyone else who knew him. It is to allow them to grieve and get over their loss. Their grieving period will be so much shorter than ours will, but they will need to show us how much they cared, how much he was loved. So, just for today, we are going to get up, get showered, put our big girl pants on, and be there – for all the others. Once it's over, it will be our time again, for as long as we need. Are you with me?'

Bryony stared in awe at her. She was so strong. After all, she had just been through, and there she was – still thinking about everyone else.

'I don't know if I can.' She stammered so very weakly.

'Bryony, you have managed to get up and get dressed every single day I have known you. Make today just like those days, okay?'

'I... I… I'm just not …'

'Bryony, please. I need you. I need your help with all his friends. I can cope with all the adults, but I don't think I can… please.'

And there it was. The mask had slipped, only ever so slightly, but Bryony saw that Isaac's mum was hanging on by a thread, and that is what gave her strength. If Melanie could act strong and look so convincing when inside she was raw as skin on a cheese grater, then so could she. She grasped the older woman's still-frozen hands and looked her deep in the eyes.

'I'll be there.' She promised.

The mask re-installed itself, and Melanie smiled kindly at her before leaving swiftly. The moment she was gone, Victoria came back in, her face tight from the effort of not saying something even though she felt very aggrieved. One look told Bryony all she needed to know about her mother's mood, and she didn't have time for it right now.

'Mum, I'm going. Will you help me? Please.'

The expression changed immediately, and Victoria sprung into action. She raced to the bathroom to turn the shower on and then guided Bryony, as though she were a hospital patient, down the hall into the steaming room. She probably would have helped her clean herself if Bryony hadn't indicated that she was fine to take it from there. When she returned to her room 15 minutes later, feeling slightly better than before, or at least stronger, now the first part of the job was done, she found that her bed linen had been stripped and replaced with fresh, clean covers. There were about five different black outfits that had been laid out across the bed for her to choose from; the ones her mother was less keen on were furthest away. Suddenly she felt weak again. The pressure of choosing an outfit for the worst day of your life was just too difficult.

She collapsed onto her dressing table stool and rested her head on her hands.

She couldn't do this.

She could. She had to. For Melanie. For Isaac.

She inhaled deeply and lifted her head. Her mum was hovering. Nervous.

'I can't choose, Mum,' she said quietly. Unable to even look at the clothes so carefully arranged on the bed.

'Do you want me to choose for you, honey?'

Bryony nodded. It didn't matter what she wore. Who the hell would care or remember anyway.

Monroe.

Oh, bloody hell. Monroe would be there. She hadn't seen her since…

The party.

Her head dropped to her hands again, and her whole body sunk in despair just as her mother was approaching with just two wardrobe options, including a floor-length, every-inch-of-the-body-covered black dress that looked like it was from the seventies.

She couldn't do this. She couldn't do this.

She felt a too-hot hand on her bare upper arm, and she looked up. Her mum was crouched in front of her.

'Do it for Melanie,' she said quietly.

Whilst the sentiment itself was lovely, it was the knowledge that it must have cost her mother so much effort to say it that reinvigorated her. She nodded and took wardrobe option number two, the pencil skirt, blouse, and cardigan, from her mother and stood to get dressed whilst Victoria put the other outfits back on their hangers and in her wardrobe.

Once she was dressed, she felt exhausted. She sat at her dressing table, staring at her pale, gaunt face in the mirror. Her mother brought her a cup of tea.

'Shall I do your hair for you?'

Bryony nodded, smiling weakly but gratefully.

For someone who had had short hair for her whole life, it was incredible how very gently but effectively Victoria managed to brush, dry, straighten and put up all of Bryony's long locks into a neat and demure French pleat. It was surprising to her how very much they looked alike when she had finished, especially when, with Bryony's blessing, she added a touch of makeup to her face just to hide the dark circles and ashen cheeks.

'I've used waterproof mascara, so you don't need to worry about anything.' She said as she finished up by spraying a little perfume onto her neck and wrists. 'Now we are all ready to go, and we even have five minutes to spare. Would you like to try something to eat? Just something small, like some toast or something?'

Bryony stared longingly at the bed. Every fibre of her being wanted to be back in the dark, warm, safe haven of her freshly laundered sheets and completely ignore the rest of the world, but instead, she followed her mother downstairs. Her body ached. She had barely moved it for nearly a week, and it felt like it had rusted over. If only she were so lucky as to be mechanical. She eased herself into a kitchen chair with all the grace of a drowning cat, feeling alien and unreal. Had she really managed to get up and get showered? How had she done that? Was she really going to his funeral today? *His* funeral?

'Hey, how you doing? Nice to see you up and about.' Steven said. He sat opposite her at the breakfast bar, eating cereal like always. He had come home from uni, but Bryony couldn't remember if it was just for the funeral or if he was meant to be home anyway? She stared at him as he looked increasingly more uncomfortable. Her brain felt unconnected to her body, and she couldn't seem to make it work any faster than dial-up speed.

'Um... I'll finish this in the front room.' He stammered, taking his cereal and practically running from the room. A piece of toast had been put in front of her, or maybe it had always been there. She stared at it for a while.

'Try and have a bite, love – go on,' Dad encouraged. He pushed the plate even closer to her with his free hand, the other clinging to the ever-present coffee mug. The smell of strong coffee felt familiar to her, warming, and she tried a bite of toast. It was so dry. She chewed and chewed, trying to make it smaller in her mouth, trying to make it small enough to swallow, but it just stayed there, absorbing all the moisture and refusing to budge. She spat it out into the bin when her mum wasn't looking.

The five minutes were up. It was time to go. Once again, she was ushered like a hospital patient. Supported on both sides by her parents to the car. Mum let Steven sit in the front for this unique journey. She sat by her youngest. Her only girl. Her baby. Bryony stared out the window at all the familiar sights as they began to pass by.

Her own driveway where she and Isaac spent endless hours talking because she had a curfew of eleven, but the driveway was home, so she was allowed to stand out there and talk for a while.

The local shops where she and Isaac would argue fruitlessly about which chocolate bars would be the best in a zombie apocalypse. Bryony knew it was either a Snickers bar or the peanut M&M's because the protein, healthy fats, and nutrients from the nuts were far better for you than any other item, but Isaac was adamant it was the Mars bars – not just because they were his favourite but because they help you 'work, rest and play.' She'd have given anything to have the argument with him again, and this time, she'd let him win, even with his outrageous logic.

The Carnival, mostly hidden from view of the road, where they had their first date, plus many, many more since then. The arguments, the makeups, the first kisses, the first 'I love you's', and the first of so much more.

'Bryony, are you okay, honey? You're shaking.'

Bryony turned away from the window to face her mother. No amount of makeup could have made her look good in that moment. A fraction of a second later, the seatbelts were off (the law be damned), and Bryony was wrapped up in her mother's warm arms.

'I am so sorry you have to go through this, love.' She whispered into her ear. 'I would give anything, anything, to make this easier for you, my darling girl.'

Bryony rested against her mother's warm body until the shaking stopped, and her ragged breathing managed to return to normal. She clung to her mum's arms like she was three years old all over again. With trepidation, she turned her eyes back to the window. No more painful memories. She couldn't face them, or rather, she couldn't face that they were all she had left of him.

They didn't speak again for the rest of the journey. When they pulled into the overflowing car park of the church, her dad had to park along the grassy verge, almost back to the entrance of the long driveway because of the endless stream of cars. Bryony recognised a few of them from college as they walked back up to the church, especially Monroe's bright red beetle bug, which she had been in many times, and Mo's, or rather, Mo's mum's ten-year-old Vauxhall Corsa in which she and Isaac had been caught, almost naked, in the backseat by Mo's very religious father.

Her head went woozy, and she struggled to keep her balance. Her mother steadied her. She felt like she hadn't seen all of her friends for years rather than just a few days, and they were strangers to her now. She couldn't relate to them anymore. She didn't know them anymore. It was as if Isaac had been the bridge upon which their friendships stood, but now that bridge was gone, and they were all back on opposite sides again.

'Breathe, Bryony. Just breathe,' her mum said so quietly, only she could hear. It was an old technique her mum had taught her when she was a little girl, and had begun to have panic attacks because the world had overwhelmed her. Her big brain learnt so much stuff, her sensibilities hadn't the wisdom to make sense of it all yet, and it sometimes got too much. 'We always go back to step one, don't we, darling? And all we do in step one is breathe.' Her mother continued in that low, deep, calming tone. Despite the day, Bryony couldn't help but smile slightly and squeeze the arm she was leaning on. Their relationship had been more than a little strained for a while, but regardless of all their personal drama, her mother came through for her. They set off again after a moment or two, and the only time she faltered was as they approached the large group of her school friends, no, Isaac's friends.

They were all hugging and crying ostentatiously in front of the main entrance. It was the usual crowd; Charlie, Mo, Leo and Jordan, Emily, India, Billie, and Monroe. The moment she saw her, Monroe only had perfectly made-up eyes for Bryony. She launched herself at her, nearly toppling her over, and her mum and dad had to support her from behind. To Bryony, Monroe felt too strong, too alive, as though she was mocking the death of Isaac with her overpowering vivacity.

Still, through some automatic response, Bryony hugged her back though she tried hard not to breathe in too deeply; the unique perfume Monroe always wore threatened to make her gag

‘You absolutely must not blame yourself,’ she whispered in her ear. When she pulled back to look her squarely in the eye, she seemed completely oblivious to the horror and outrage etched all over Bryony’s face. In her head, Bryony screamed, *‘I don’t blame myself, you utter cow!’* but somehow she was shocked into silence, and the words were never verbalised. Instead, she just stared back at Monroe, noticing the perfect makeup beneath the carefully dabbed tears. The healthy glow emanating from her only seemed to highlight the sallow complexion and shrunken frame of Bryony. As always, she felt inferior and vulnerable in Monroe’s company. Of course, Monroe knew how to mourn better than she did; she did everything better than Bryony.

Once she was released from Monroe’s toxic embrace, the other girls came over to console her. Billie at least had mascara stains on her cheeks, and she just kept repeating, ‘It’s awful. Just terrible,’ under her breath. India got to her next. Her squeeze was limp and a little awkward. ‘At least you’ve lost a load of weight ‘cos of it.’ She said with a small, sad smile. Bryony blinked at her but was saved from having to make any further response by Emily. Bryony had always preferred the more thoughtful and reserved girl in this group of people, but somehow they had never become close.

‘How are you holding up?’ She asked gently after a warm hug. Bryony suddenly felt overcome with grief again and found she couldn’t force any words out. ‘Sorry. Stupid question. I’m sure you’re barely holding it together at all.’ The surge of gratitude she felt towards Emily enabled her to give her a bleak smile, and she returned it, placing her hand on Bryony’s arm, looking as if she was about to do something else, but Monroe spoke over her. Emily removed her hand.

‘I just keep thinking like, none of this real, it isn’t really happening, you know. And then it just hits me, like, WHAM! Zachie’s not here anymore, and he never will be again, you know,’ She covered her face with her bejewelled acrylic nails. Her shoulders heaved dramatically, and she leant into Will's chest. The boys, Bryony noticed, looked like little lost sheep, their leader no longer around to model the correct behaviour. Suddenly she was aware of what a monumental loss Isaac was to the rest of the world, not just her. She took a moment to look further afar than her family and peer group. Isaac's mum, dad, and four brothers stood close to the door, along with a vicar. Just behind them stood some of his extended family. She recognised his aunt and cousin, Riley, who were huddled together, looking bereft and unsure. Stood a bit further back were some of their teachers, including Isaac's football coach/P.E. teacher. He had been the one who had suggested that Isaac go to the local stadium for tryouts with a scout for the under-21s. They hadn't heard back yet, they hadn't been especially hopeful, but still. He looked weird in a suit, Bryony thought, or maybe it was because he looked grey, which was unusual for the normally pink-faced coach. Isaac had been one of his favourites.

As she scanned the grounds, she realised pretty much everyone from their year group at school had come, plus lots from the other years and some university mates of his older brothers, with whom they all hung out last summer.

Even Dana, Ash, and Jorgia were here. Her former best friends before Isaac came into her life. Dana saw her looking and smiled cautiously in greeting. Bryony looked away quickly. She still felt awkward around them since she had so completely dumped them when she'd gotten a boyfriend.

Someone else caught her eye up on the hill. They stood on their own and too far away to be seen clearly, but they were moving closer, slowly. There was something so familiar about his gait. Bryony was transfixed, staring as he came closer, determined to identify who he was. She felt someone's hand on the small of her back, trying to encourage her to move, but she resisted, determined to see who he was. She was aware of voices talking to her, but she ignored them, her attention only on one thing – the figure still so slowly heading their way. The hand on her back became two hands on her upper arms, becoming more insistent, but again she refused to move. He was almost close enough for her to identify him, although she could feel, deep down, she knew who it was. She would know him anywhere. He was cupping his hand over his eyes because the sun was so bright, too bright. He looked almost translucent.

The hands on her arm became vice-like, and she heard her mother's voice in her ear.

'Darling, we cannot stay out here all day. We have to go inside. Everyone else has gone in.'

Reluctantly Bryony nodded, tearing her eyes away and succumbing to the inevitable. Still, as she moved towards the building, she couldn't help but take a sneaky glimpse back. When she did, she froze in shock, making her father nearly fall over her. Her knees became jelly-like, and it took two of them to keep her upright.

'Bryony darling, I know you're scared, but we just have to keep going. It won't last long, I promise.' Even though she never tore her eyes away from the impossible figure ambling down the hill, somehow, her family managed to manoeuvre her into the church. When seated, her mother gripped her hand and tried to surreptitiously mop the cold sweat off her face with a tissue.

She chattered inanely under her breath the whole time, a thing she did when she was nervous, and she was nervous, more than nervous. She was deeply concerned. Her daughter's face was suddenly grey. She was shaking uncontrollably, and her clammy hands were limp and lifeless in her own. She suddenly looked as though she had seen death itself.

The funeral began, but Bryony didn't take in a word. Her attention kept drifting back towards the door, but nothing troubled the door. It happened when Mo, Charlie, Leo, and Jordan were standing on the plinth. Not one of them was dry-eyed as they choked their way through their well-rehearsed eulogy, none of them having correctly anticipated how hard it would be to talk about their bestie, their lifelong pal, their fallen hero in front of practically everyone they had ever known. Bryony's attention was still on the door, so she didn't notice it straight away. In fact, it was the coldness that drew her attention first. The room seemed to suddenly drop ten degrees, as though the air conditioning had been put on full blast. It had jolted her from her reverie, and she faced forward, looking up towards the four boys. And there he was.

Isaac.

She gave a tiny gasp and stared at him. He was standing in front of his parents and brothers; his face was so heartbroken it almost didn't look like him at all – except that it was him. It absolutely and undeniably was him.

'Bryony, you're frightening me, what's the matter?' Her mother whispered urgently. Bryony stared, bewildered, at her mother, then back at Isaac. Her mother followed her gaze for a moment but still searched her expression for an explanation.

'Isaac,' she managed to croak, though her voice felt rusty and raw. 'He's right there.'

'Oh honey, I know he is, but it's just his body Bryony, that's all.'

It took her a few moments to work out what her mother was talking about, but when she did, she shook her head emphatically and gestured, less subtly this time, to where Isaac was still stood.

'No,' she said, above a whisper now, 'He's right there.'

Victoria pushed Bryony's hand down and glanced around to see if they'd drawn any attention to themselves. Bryony would hardly believe anyone would be looking at them when Isaac was stood right there, but a few people had started to glance at them uncomfortably and whisper amongst themselves, and no one, absolutely no one, was looking at Isaac. Not his parents, his brothers, his friends, or anyone else in the whole room, Bryony realised.

'Bryony!'

His voice rang out loud and clear through the quiet room, sending chills through her whole body.

'Bryony – can you see me?'

This time she had to force herself to look at him, terrified of what she might see or, possibly worse, what she might not see. She lifted her gaze, and they locked eyes.

'Bry? You can! You can see me, can't you?' He took two steps towards her, and she screamed, then clambered over her mother and ran out of the door as fast as possible. She hadn't gotten far when she had to stop and catch her breath, then sit down on the grass because she felt dizzy and faint. She put her head in her hands, breathing hard.

'You can see me, can't you, Bryony?'

His familiar voice sent hot and cold shivers all down her spine.

'No,' she shook her head vehemently, refusing to look up. Her dizziness increased.

'I knew it! I knew you could. I wonder why no one else can? Oh, Baby, I knew we were perfect for each other.'

He sounded excited and was jumping around in front of her. She could tell by the way the ice-cold air was moving around her. He began to talk again, but he was cut off by her mother.

‘Bryony honey, are you okay?’ She crouched in front of her, unwilling to plonk herself on the grass like her daughter had, but her warm hands were a welcome sensation on her goose-pimple-ridden skin.

‘Mum, I can see him. He’s here, Mum.’

‘Oh, sweetheart, of course he is. He will always be with you, and it’s only natural that this will be overwhelming for you, he was such a huge part of your life.’

‘No, Mum, I don’t mean like seeing his body in the coffin. I mean that I can see him walking around and hear him talking to me, right here, like I’m insane or something. I can see him – right there, as clear as you are. Like a hallucination or something.’ She pointed to where Isaac was stood, listening.

‘A hallucination! You think I’m a hallucination?’

‘Sweetheart, you’re tired, and it’s been a really emotional day.’

They both said at the same time.

Bryony covered her ears and hid her face in her knees for a few seconds.

‘Don’t talk at the same time,’ she addressed no one in particular, then realised that no one else could see Isaac, but he apparently could see everyone, so the remark was a direct order to him and one he wouldn’t be pleased about. When she looked up again, she could tell he was cross, but she felt too overwhelmed to care too much about his dejection right now.

‘Of course, I think you’re a hallucination. What else am I going to think? That you’re a ghost? I don’t believe in ghosts,’ she shouted at him.

When she turned to face her horrified mother, she felt her energy sap and her shoulders sagged.

'Mummy, I think I need help,' she whispered, her voice so small it was barely audible.

'Of course, darling, don't you worry, we'll get you an appointment with someone. Until then, I think it's best if you try not to interact with your hallucination.'

'Oh yeah – of course, you think that,' Isaac growled as Victoria helped her daughter to her feet. 'Come on, Babe. You know your mum has been trying to break us up pretty much since we got together.'

'Can we go home, please, Mum?'

'She's always hated me, Bry.'

'No darling, we have to go back to the Spencer's for the wake. It won't be for long, just an hour or so, to show support and be polite.'

'She's probably glad I'm dead!' He yelled as they began walking down towards the car park. The tears began to fall fast and heavy down Bryony's face, and she was grateful for the support of her mum's arm as they hurried away.

'Bryony! Babe! Please,' the desperation in her dead boyfriend's voice made her look back. She longed to run back up to him and stay with him here in this sunny graveyard forever, and if she had been stronger, maybe she would have. However, in her weakened state, her mother was easily able to guide her onward instead.

Chapter Four

When they pulled up outside Isaac's house, Bryony became frozen again. The reality of being so close to all of his possessions and his bed and his laptop, and all the memories of spending most of the last few years in this house rather than her own, seemed to have filled her body with liquid nitrogen. The effect was instantaneous. She felt numb again. The funeral, the hallucinations, the people, all of it was just too much for her brain to take. Her heart was already obliterated into non-existence, and now her brain was being destroyed as well.

'Darling, your hands are freezing. Turn the heater on, Michael.'

Her father silently obliged, silencing her brother's objection with a glance whilst her mother began rubbing her ice-cold digits between her warm palms. They were all sitting in the car outside Isaac's house. They were the first to arrive, thanks to Bryony's early exit. Everyone had seen her. She realised that now. At the height of her confusion with the hallucinations, all she had thought to do was run. Run away as fast as she could. She hadn't thought about how it had looked to other people. She'd made a fool of herself. A spectacle.

She knew what they would all be saying. Even on the day she was burying her long-term first love. People would still judge her behaviour. The adults would think she'd been inappropriate, disrespectful, and selfish. The kids would call her a drama queen and an attention-seeking diva. Even those who wouldn't voice their opinions would still think it. But none of them had seen what she'd seen. None of them had seen Isaac. Seen him trying to be seen, to be noticed by his nearest and dearest, and for none of them to acknowledge his presence. It must have been so awful for him.

And she'd left him there.

‘Can you see anything?’ Her mother whispered so only she could hear. By “anything,” Bryony knew she meant Isaac.

She felt her heart begin to beat more erratically as she contemplated averting her gaze from the headrest of the passenger side seat in front of her. She inhaled slowly, shakily. Her mum squeezed her hand.

She could see the front porch steps where he’d first held her hand but no Isaac. She could see the gap in the fir trees that lined the left-hand side of the garden, where they had stood so close to each other as he had tried to prolong their first date, but no Isaac. The wall at the front of the garden was there too, steady and strong as it always had been when they sat on it together and planned out their future; the names of their kids, the holidays they’d go on, if they’d have a dog or a cat; but no Isaac. His absence was like the loss of air. She felt like she was suffocating.

She turned her head back to face the headrest, shaking it slightly for her mother’s behalf.

She felt her mother’s encouraging, relief-filled squeeze.

‘It must just have been the stress of the church, darling. You won’t see him again, I’m sure of it.’

Her words were supposed to be reassuring. Her mother had no understanding of the relentless pit of anguish that churned within her.

She kept picturing Isaac’s face as he begged her to stay. Her head hung in guilt and shame, not in relief as her mother supposed.

Her concept of time had been an unexpected loss alongside that of her boyfriend, albeit a less impactful one. So, she had no idea how long they had been waiting for the others to arrive. Long enough to test her mother’s patience certainly. And enough for both her father and brother to feel the need to get out of the car and stretch their legs. Bryony didn't move a hair. She felt an odd sort of calm by her stillness, and it almost felt as if she were a mere porcelain statue, and if she were to move a limb, it would simply snap off.

Still, when the Spencers and the rest of the mourners arrived, her mother barely spared a thought for her daughter's clay features, and she ushered her out of the car as patiently as she was able to. Bryony, though stiff, numbly did as she was told, and after a polite enough time had passed for Melanie and the rest of the family to prepare for their guests, Victoria marshalled her family to join the others and, as a procession, they slowly marched into Spencer's home.

They were all greeted by Melanie, who still looked pristine, her makeup had been no doubt touched up, for her eyes were red-rimmed. She greeted them all warmly and thanked them for coming whilst ensuring they quickly moved on into the house. Bryony was a few paces behind her mother, and when she reached Melanie, the older woman grasped her hands, pulling her aside. She indicated for the queue of people behind to make their way into the front room whilst she gently guided Bryony toward the kitchen at the back of the house. Victoria stood awkwardly in the hallway, unwilling to move on without her daughter but equally unwilling to impose herself in a private conversation. She tried to look busy in the hallway and took up the mantel of directing people coming in.

Once they were out of earshot of everyone else, Melanie grasped Bryony's upper arms and looked at her very seriously. Bryony couldn't tear her gaze away, Melanie's eyes were so like her dead son's.

'I heard you had a bit of a wobble at the church,' she began gently, 'Oh, my sweet angel, I'm so sorry I bullied you into coming today. I should have known it would be too much for you. I just thought it might do you good, you know? Offer you some closure. I'm so, so sorry, Bry.'

'Mel, I'm fine, honestly, don't worry about me,' Bryony amazed herself with how solid, and sure her own voice was. But she knew Melanie would have to deal with her husband's and her other sons' grief before she could even begin to deal with her own. She did not want to be another thing she had to worry about. 'I did have a wobble, but I'm glad I went. It was helpful,' she lied and smiled tightly, but Melanie bought it, and she released a long sigh of relief.

'Are you sure? I'm so glad. It's meant to be good for us. I mean, I know it was awful, but that should be as awful as it gets, right?'

Melanie always took Bryony by surprise when she sought vindication from her kids as much as other adults, treating them as equals. She liked it, though, and she nodded confidently but offset it with a shrug. Melanie shrugged, too, and unbelievably both girls laughed. It was a sad, bittersweet laugh, just a little chuckle, really, but it was the first one since Isaac. Small steps.

'I have to go and be out there,' Melanie said, indicating toward the front room, 'But tell me you're staying for a while and that you'll come and find me later. I need a proper cuddle with you.'

Bryony confirmed she would definitely be staying a while, masking the sinking feeling of dread at the prospect. Melanie dropped a kiss on her forehead and rushed off to play host. Left alone in the kitchen, she had a quiet moment to herself. The kitchen didn't look the same as it usually did. The Spencer house wasn't much bigger than hers, but with five massive boys in it, it had always felt so cramped and messy and busy and loud and chaotic and fun. Nothing was ever put away properly, there was always a massive pile of washing on the side, waiting for someone to take it upstairs and put it away, and there were always shoes, trainers, soccer boots, and sports equipment hanging around. Now everything was neat, clean, ordered, and quiet. It felt sterile. Maybe the house was in mourning too. There were stacks of catered food on plastic trays on the breakfast bar, and the smell of them made Bryony feel sick, so she made her way back to the hallway where her mum was still waiting.

'I've promised Melanie I'll stay here for a while if that's okay, Mum.'

Her mum looked surprised for a second, but then she smiled.

'Of course, honey. That was good of you. Come on, let's go and find the boys.'

When they went into the front room, they were confronted with a sea of black and white. Black dresses and white shirts, relieved of their black blazers due to the unseasonably warm weather and the large crowd in the room. The separating doors between the front room and the dining room had been opened creating one large room. This very rarely happened except for special occasions, and Isaac's wake apparently qualified. Even so, the double room was not big enough to contain so many people, and yet somehow, it was eerily quiet. Anyone who spoke above a whisper would be heard by the whole room. It was oppressive and uncomfortable, and Bryony fought the compulsion to giggle.

Victoria had to tiptoe to see over a few shoulders before she could locate the rest of their family, and she found them at the far end of the dining room, by the window to the back garden, standing in awkward silence. They linked hands, and politely "excuse-me'd" their way across the room. A few people looked to say something to Bryony, probably well-meaning and kindly, about her outburst at the church, but Victoria didn't let her hang around long enough, which she was truly thankful for. When they re-joined the boys, they all stood in silence. The room felt unrecognisable to Bryony. Just like in the kitchen, the neatness had sucked out all the comfort of the room.

Noises of the living reached Bryony's ears, and it took her a few moments to work out where they'd come from. Outside. Her classmates and peers were all gathered in the glorious September sunshine of the vast back garden. They were hardly being raucous, but simply by talking normally with each other, they were attracting a lot of attention.

'Oh look, Mr Greaves is here. We should go and say hello, don't you think?'

'Oh no, Mum, let's not bother him,' Bryony answered a little too hastily.

'Nonsense, look, he's stood all on his own. He'd be glad of the company, especially from his favourite student,' her mother beamed at her, clearly refusing to take no for an answer. Bryony felt her insides squirm and her face flush. Her mother had no idea that Bryony had fairly quickly gone from being one of Mr Greaves' favourite students to his absolute worst in recent months. Her brain fumbled helplessly for an excuse, a reason not to go over, but other than the truth, which absolutely would not do, she couldn't think of anything.

So they went.

The slight breeze immediately cooled them as they stepped outside, but the absolute silence that fell as people realised who'd arrived sent icy shivers through her spine and burning flames across her cheeks. For a moment, they all stood completely still, like a rabbit caught in the headlights of a car. Amazingly, it was Monroe who saved them, in a fashion.

'Bryony, you poor darling,' she gushed loudly as she crossed the lawn, 'How are you doing now, after your little… erm… moment?'

She hugged her hard. Too hard.

'Come and join us. We're doing a…'

‘I’m sorry, Monroe, ‘ Victoria interrupted, ‘We were just going to speak with Mr Greaves.’

‘Oh, don’t worry Mrs D. I’ll send her back to you in just a tick,’ Monroe insisted. Defying adults with charm and confidence was second nature to Monroe, but Bryony’s mother despised being called “Mrs D.” as she had told Monroe, Isaac, and most of the others many times before. ‘It should be Mrs Duglass, Monroe, or at a push and with my permission only, Victoria.’

‘Rightio, Vicky,’ Monroe called back to her as she was already pulling Bryony away. She looked back over her shoulder at her mum and shrugged apologetically but did nothing to stop Monroe.

‘Jeez, Mr Greaves! I take it your mum doesn’t know about any of that? You can thank me later,’ she whispered to Bryony. She had linked their arms together and continued to whisper conspiratorially. ‘Listen, don’t worry about all that, what happened back at the church earlier. No one thinks you’re a drama queen or anything. I’ve had a word with everyone already and explained that some people just aren’t emotionally strong, so we’re going to be super supportive of you, ok babe,’ she gave her arm a quick squeeze, then dropped her a few steps away from their group. Bryony stood for a second, glaring at Monroe’s back. Somehow, indignation and a bitter resentment managed to filter into her diluted emotional state. She and Monroe had never been close, and as they got to know each other better, so they disliked each other more and more. Bryony was aware that Monroe thought she was standoffish and self-important and considered herself to be superior to the rest of the group because she was a nerd. She knew this because she’d overheard them all gossiping about her in the girls' toilets about six months ago. In turn, Bryony thought Monroe was a shallow, condescending bitch. It also didn’t help that Monroe flirted relentlessly with Isaac, well, with everyone, really, but especially Isaac. He always said it was harmless and it was just her way, but she was convinced that Monroe was obsessed with him and wouldn’t think twice about trying to sleep with him, even though she knew he was in love with someone else. Her.

She wondered if she had the energy to rise to Monroe's snide comments, and she decided that she didn't, so she ignored them and focussed her attention on the rest of the group.

The boys still looked like they were in a bad way, and there were definitely some red-rimmed eyes amongst them, but at least they were all able to talk a little easier, although they all shut up the moment she joined them. The silence was awkward and uncomfortable, and she began to wonder if Mr Greaves wasn't a better option.

'Are you okay, Bryony?' Emily finally broke the silence, and she attempted to smile, realising she'd asked the same inappropriate question as earlier. Bryony attempted to smile back, but it felt forced and pained, so she stopped and simply shrugged.

'No, but then, none of us are, are we?'

She glanced around at them all, and they all shook their heads in agreement.

'No, we aren't,' Charlie announced, looking grim but determined. 'And now that you're here, Bryony, I'd like us all to honour Isaac with a toast.' He pulled out a silver hipflask and a stack of plastic shot glasses from the inner pocket of his suit blazer.

'Dude, we can't do that,' Mo protested, 'All our parents are here.'

'I don't care,' Charlie argued, setting his jaw defiantly, 'Isaac was our very best friend, and we all miss him. We will toast to that, whether our parents like it or not because Isaac would have appreciated the gesture.'

Bryony smiled supportively at Charlie. Isaac would have been delighted that they were all doing something risky under their parent's noses, in his name.

Charlie began pouring measures and passing them around. Bryony was very aware that she literally hadn't eaten a morsel for about five days. Plus, she felt really queasy anyway, and the dark, plum-coloured liquid smelled strong and sickly sweet, making her want to gag.

'What is it?' Mo asked.

'Dark rum. I found it in my Dad's bar, right at the back, so he won't miss it.'

Charlie's dad kept his home bar well stocked; they all knew that from parties that had been held there in the past, but then they'd really only taken beer and cider, none of the harder liquor in the dusty bottles at the back.

'To Isaac.' Charlie said, holding up his tiny plastic cup. They all did the same before throwing the foul-smelling liquid down their throats. Many of them started coughing and gagging straight away, but surprisingly Bryony quite liked it. The fire seemed to burn all the way down her oesophagus, but once it was in her stomach, it just felt warming. She'd felt frozen for so long, it was nice to feel some heat on the inside. She also felt a rather dark pleasure at seeing the ugly puce colour Monroe had gone from her coughing fit.

'Guys, keep it together. Everyone will know what we've been up to.' There was a rising panic in Mo's expression as he realised the rest of the garden was watching them curiously.

'Another?' Charlie suggested.

A chorus of “no” and “hell no” rang out from the group, but Bryony shocked them all by confidently saying yes and holding up her small, empty receptacle.

‘Good girl,’ he poured a larger measure into both their glasses.

‘What shall we toast to this time?’ She asked.

‘This one is for the people who loved him most,’ he said quietly. He wasn’t trying to make the others feel bad for not doing another shot, but it was a bonding moment for the two of them. She smiled at him, and they tapped their cups before, once again, downing their drinks. Again, Bryony relished the fire feeling going into her. She and Charlie had barely uttered more than a few sentences to each other over the years, even though he was Isaac’s best friend. How strange that it was this moment that encouraged a kinship between them. The moment was over a second or two later when she felt a vice-like grip on her elbow.

‘You will come with me now,’ her voice was quiet and low in her ear, but it was immutable and fierce, so without another word, Victoria ripped her away from all of Isaac’s friends.

Bryony stumbled, partly from the unexpected tug on her arm and partly something else, but she managed to stay upright, just. Her mother was forced to drag her away more slowly, and whilst she managed to keep her expression neutral, her quiet tone betrayed the anger and disappointment.

‘Drinking! Really? This is his wake! Your teachers are here! Your father and I are here! Have you no respect? Moreover, you haven’t eaten a damn thing in goodness knows how long. You have nothing in your stomach to soak that up. What were you thinking, you silly girl?’

‘Five Days.’

'Excuse me?'

'I haven't eaten in five days because my boyfriend, the love of my life, has been dead for five days. And I was thinking that maybe I don't care that I haven't eaten or that you're here or my teachers are here. I was thinking that this is my boyfriend's wake and actually he would have thought it was funny that I was drinking in his honour and do you know what else – I liked it. It made my tummy all toasty and warm.'

Her mother's grip loosened, and they stopped walking to look at each other. Bryony was not expecting to see the softness in her mother's expression, and she relaxed a little.

'My darling girl, you do know that drinking won't help you, don't you? I mean, in the long run. Alcohol will do one of two things; either exasperate your current feelings and the mood you're in, making you feel so much worse, or it will temporarily numb your feelings but then hit you with the mother of all hangovers on top of your sadness. Either way, it's really not good. Look, I know at this moment you are throwing caution to the wind because you're going through hell, and you don't care about the consequences because nothing could be worse than this, right? But darling, even though getting through this is the hardest thing you've ever had to do, it could get worse, and one way would be to have to go to the hospital to get your stomach pumped. So let's just try not to make this awful time any worse, okay?'

Bryony nodded glumly, and this time she walked willingly over to the rest of the family, who were still standing with Mr Greaves. Her stomach gave an unexpected jolt of shame and guilt.

'Hello, Bryony, how are you?'

Mr Greaves greeted her genially, but she couldn't bring herself to meet his eyes. She nodded dumbly.

‘Oh, that’s a stupid question. I’m sorry, of course, you’re not okay, but listen, Bryony…’ he paused, and she felt a warm, gentle hand on her upper arm. She was forced to look at him. ‘I’m truly sorry that this has happened, and if you need anything at school, like... erm... I don’t know... maybe some time to yourself or someone to talk to, I’ll do whatever I can. And I know the school will organise grief therapy sessions at first, but after that, my door will always be open to you, no matter what, okay?’

Bryony felt winded, floored by confusion. She had been awful to this man, really recently. She had betrayed the trust they had built up since she first began senior school, and she had caused him a lot of hassle, aggravation, and undoubtedly hurt, and now he was being nice to her. Still being kind after all she had done. She was flabbergasted. There was no irony in his eyes, no resentment about his features, just the same old, gentle, clever, kind Mr Greaves. The tears came before she could stop them and dropped like rain down her face. Mr Greaves smiled a sad, sympathetic smile at her, gently squeezed her arm, and tapped her shoulder. He would not hug her, obviously, but Bryony wouldn’t have refused if he’d offered.

Her mother took over, she pulled Bryony into her and held her tightly, saying over her daughter’s shoulder, ‘That’s very kind of you, Mr Greaves, honestly. I know you’re Bryony’s favourite teacher; she’s clearly very touched by your kindness.’

Her mother had no idea.

She wiped her face and blew her nose on the tissue that had been placed in her hand, and finally extracted herself from her mother’s embrace.

Mr Greaves said nothing more to her, and the adults began to make small talk about how lovely the service was and what a wonderful turnout it was. Bryony’s attention drifted to where the friends were, but they had been disbanded and were now standing with their own families. She looked back at the house where she had spent so much time in the last few years. She allowed her eyes to travel to the small window of Isaac's room, almost feeling a sadistic compulsion to torture herself with the endless memories of being in there. Her gasp was audible, but the adults were now discussing the curriculum and UCAS forms, so they didn't hear her. Nor did they notice all the colour drain from her face or the absolute stillness of her body.

He was there.

In the window.

He didn't wave. He didn't smile. He just stared at her. He looked so devastatingly sad. The moment seemed to drag on between them. Both locked in each other's expressions.

'Bryony darling, are you okay? You've gone as white as a sheet.'

Bryony blinked, seemingly breaking the connection, but he was still there. He put a finger to his lips, telling her to keep quiet about seeing him, then beckoned her up to him.

She needed him. Needed to be with him. She tore her eyes away and looked at her mum and all the others who were looking at her with great concern.

'Actually, I erm... I don't feel too well. I shouldn't have... I probably just need to…will you all excuse me for a minute, please?'

'Of course, darling, I'll come with you.'

'No.' She said too quickly, she calmed herself, 'Honestly, Mum, I'm okay. I just need a few minutes alone.'

'Oh. Right. Yes. Well, don't be too long, darling. Your father will be wanting to get off soon.'

'What? No, Mum, I said I'd stay, remember? I want to stay, but that's okay. You guys can still carry on. You go whenever you want. I'll come back later.'

'Bryony, you're seeing things, you've been drinking – you're not acting like yourself. I'm not going to leave you on your own. Not today.' She said quietly.

'Mum, listen,' all Bryony wanted to do was go upstairs and see Isaac properly, and that would be so much easier for her if her family went home. However, in order to get them to go home, she knew she would have to play this cleverly. 'You have been brilliant for me today. You've really helped, and yes, I know I've had my ups and downs throughout the day, but I absolutely promise you I will not be drinking any more alcohol today. This was Isaac's home. I don't know if I'll get a chance to spend much time here again, so please, you guys, go home whenever you're ready. I'm going to go and spend some quiet time in Isaac's room and then help Melanie one last time, okay? I love you. I'll be fine.'

Her mother kissed her forehead and clasped her hands.

'When you're ready to come home, just text me or your father, and we will pick you up right away, okay? And I want you to try and eat something whilst you're here. Oh, and,' she leaned forward and spoke barely above a whisper, 'If you're going to be sick, make sure you get to the bathroom in time and that you clean up after yourself.' She kissed her again, and Bryony made her way back inside the house, glancing up one more time to the bedroom first.

He was still there.

Her heart began to pound double time, and she noticed her hands were shaking as she reached for the handle of the back door. The crowd inside had thinned a little, but it still took too long for her to get through to the hallway. She stood at the bottom of the stairs feeling a thousand emotions. Terror, excitement, worry, sick, anxiety, faint.

She took a couple of deep breaths and then ran up.

Upstairs was deserted, and the landing looked dark and claustrophobic for some reason. It took a moment to understand why. All the doors were shut. That never happened. There were five doors on the landing: the bathroom, the parents' room, Isaac's room, the twins' room, Anthony and Alex, the youngest Spencer's, and the door to the second floor, which housed another bathroom and two more bedrooms for the eldest two brothers, Eamon and Oscar. Usually, the only two doors that were ever closed were the bathroom when someone was using it and Isaac's room when they were having some "alone time." The whole house felt so alien to her now, like she didn't know it anymore. She quickly opened the door to Isaac's room and went in.

She almost screamed out in surprise, not at the sight of Isaac, who was in the same position only had turned around so his back was to the window now, but at the sight of Alex, the youngest of the twins, who was lying on his bed.

'Whaa!' Alex exclaimed, frightened by the sudden appearance of Bryony. 'Oh, hi, Bry.' He said, quickly wiping his face and sitting up. Isaac had the box room, which was the smallest in the house. So to save space, he had a cabin bed. This was like a bunk bed, except that instead of a lower bunk, there was a desk, a chair, and a shelving unit. Isaac had removed the desk some time ago to make room for a small settee that fitted snugly under his bed and had a large telly on the wall opposite, with his gaming system and paraphernalia on a small white table below the telly. The only other furniture was a tall chest of drawers and a laundry basket. He had a few band posters with corresponding tour t-shirts and the tickets adorning the walls beside his bed, and he had a collage of photos of him and Bryony that she had made him for his birthday last year.

Whilst Alex pulled himself together, Bryony glanced at Isaac. He was uncharacteristically sombre and sad.

'He's been crying his little heart out in here for the past twenty minutes. There's nothing I can do.'

He sounded so pained, so frustrated. So real. Her heart leaped. She wanted to look at him forever, to focus only on him, but she knew she couldn't, not with Alex in the room.

Alex sat up and swung his legs around, so they were resting on the ladder, his elbows resting on his knees, his head in his hands. Bryony approached him cautiously and placed a hand on his knee. Funny, they all thought Ant was the sensitive one of the twins. Alex was always more cocky and confident. It was weird to see him like this. Not as weird as seeing your dead boyfriend, but it was on the scale.

'Hey, Alex.' Bryony said, employing her deepest, gentlest tone. 'It's okay to miss your brother. We all do. You don't have to hide your tears from me,' she gave his knee a little shake.

'This is the only room that still feels like him. The whole house feels weird now, except this room.'

He was right. Bryony had felt it too, and she didn't even live here. But whilst the rest of the house felt clean and cold, this room remained comfortably unmade. There were chocolate wrappers that hadn't quite made it into the little bin, half a glass of flat cola was on the dresser, and his laundry basket still housed his dirty clothes. The room still smelled of Isaac.

'Yeah, I noticed that too. Don't worry, it's just temporary. Once the wake is over, things will start to get more normal,' Bryony said, having no clue if that was true or not.

'Dad cries all the time, and Mum hasn't shed a single tear. She just cleans endlessly. I don't know which is worse.'

'Everyone grieves in different ways, I guess' It was a horrible cliché and didn't help him in any way, but she didn't know what else to say.

'Weird. I always wanted to have this room. Couldn't wait for him to go off to uni so I could move in and wouldn't have to share with Ant no more. Now I don't want it. I just want Isaac back.'

His voice broke, and Bryony could barely make out his last sentence, but she knew what he wanted, and her heart broke all over again for him. 'Oh, Al,' she said, reaching up and trying to hug him, but he was too high up, and his knees were in the way, so she had to just ruffle his hair instead and place her hands as far around him as she could reach.

Isaac paced the small room, his hand tugging at his own hair.

'I'm still here, kid. Bryony tell him. Tell him I'm still here and that you can see me.'

Bryony hesitated. She was still not convinced that the figure of Isaac she could see and hear so clearly, so solidly, wasn't a hallucination or figment of her imagination or symptomatic of her mental collapse. Either way, she was unwilling to tell anyone what she could see, especially if no one else could see it.

'You know,' she began diplomatically, 'In a way, he is still here. He always will be. Maybe having this room could make you feel closer to him, but you don't need to rush. Stay in your room with Ant until you're ready. No one's saying you have to have this room anytime soon, are they?'

He didn't respond for a while, his face hidden in his hands. Bryony kept her hand on his knee but stared at Isaac. He stared straight back.

'God, sorry, Bryony.' Alex said suddenly, 'You probably wanted some alone time in here too, didn't you? Let me get out of your way.'

He jumped off the bed easily and stretched out his lanky body. Even at fourteen, he towered over Bryony's five-foot-four frame. In two strides, he had reached the door.

'Thanks, Bry. It's freezing in here, by the way. Help yourself to one of Isaac's sweaters in the drawer,' he said quietly before exiting. Bryony and Isaac stared at each other in bewilderment.

'Jeez, talk about mood swings.' Isaac joked, shaking his head.

'Kids.' Bryony replied, smiling.

'Hi.' He said.

'Hi.' She replied.

'Weird, huh?'

'Very. I mean... are you actually here, or are you a ghost?'

'I can't be a ghost, can I?'

'No, of course not, there's no such thing.'

'So what am I? I mean, apparently, I did die and all that, but here I am, and you can see and hear me.'

'Yes, but am I really the only one?'

'The only one here or at the Church.'

‘So if we look at this logically... no one but me has any awareness of you... and we know there’s no such thing as ghosts, so therefore,... the only explanation is that... you must be in my head.’

‘What like a hallucination or a figment of your imagination or something? No way.’

‘Can you affect anything else?’

‘What do you mean?’

‘Like, can you touch anything, like make it move or leave an impression on anything?’

He reached out to touch the bed, but his hand went straight through the wooden frame.

‘No, doesn’t look like it. But wait – maybe I can touch you. I mean, you can see and hear me – touch is just another sense, right?’

Bryony nodded, feeling her stomach turn somersaults. Isaac held up his right hand, and she held up her left one. They bought them close, just millimetres apart. It felt like putting her hand in a freezer.

‘Ready?’ Isaac asked. Bryony didn’t trust herself to speak. If they could touch, then she would have to develop a new theory of the existence of ghosts. Plus, she’d be able to touch her boyfriend again, which would be just awesome. She nodded.

They held their breath and closed the gap between their hands.

Bryony sighed deeply, unsure if she was disappointed or grateful, she hadn’t gone completely insane. They hadn’t touched. She couldn’t feel Isaac except for the cold coming off him, and his hand had pushed straight through hers.

‘So what does that mean?’

‘I guess it means that I’m having a mental breakdown.’

They stood close to each other in silence for a minute or so.

‘Wait. Hang on,’ Isaac finally said, breaking the silence, as Bryony knew he would. ‘If I’m only in your head, then how can I be experiencing things when you’re not here?’

‘What things?’

‘Like this morning. I was here all morning whilst my family was getting ready for the church, trying to get one of them to notice me.’

Bryony thought about it for a moment or two.

‘You’re absolutely sure no one else had any awareness of you?’

‘Babe, I was absolutely screaming my head off.’

‘I guess, I’m sorry, Isaac, but I guess that maybe my subconscious or whatever it is that is creating you would need to make you as believable as possible, and therefore I have given you supposed memories to make sure you are a well-rounded character.’

‘A well-rounded character,’ Isaac repeated gloomily.

‘I’m sorry, babe, but losing you has broken my heart and my mind,’ Bryony felt her eyes burn with tears as though the realisation that he wasn’t actually back and that she was just insane was like losing him all over again.

‘Oh, babe,’ he whispered, moving closer and looking like he longed to cuddle her tight. ‘Babe, you’ve got goose pimples all over, and look, jeez! Your lips are turning blue! Alex was right, it is freezing in here. Get a jumper.’

‘It is freezing in here, but it’s like 28 degrees outside. And Alex felt it too,’ Bryony said slowly; her usually lightning-fast brain was slow to make the links. She exhaled deeply, watching the clouds of her breath disappear in the room.

'So why the hell is it so cold in here? I'm not cold. I can't feel a thing. And this room is usually hot as all hellfire. Maybe it's cos my computer isn't on. Switch my computer on, babe. I'll teach you how to play GTA.'

'Oh, my God! It's you! You're making it cold. And if it is you, if you're having an effect on the temperature in the space around you and people other than me can notice it, then you're not just in my imagination.'

'Woohoo! Not just a figment of the imagination. Hashtag winning'

'Hang on a second, let me think.'

He was bouncing around silently, like a puppy trying to be good. Bryony couldn't help but smile. There was a creak on the stairs meaning someone was coming up. She opened the bedroom door and saw Isaac's Uncle John coming onto the landing. He started when he saw Bryony standing there staring at him.

'Hey, kid,' he said. She knew he recognised her; they'd met several times before, but he could never remember her name. 'I was just coming upstairs for a whizz. Someone's in the loo downstairs. Sorry were you going to…' he indicated toward the bathroom.

'No, no, you carry on,' Bryony said brightly, a plan forming in her mind. 'I was just sitting in Isaac's room,' she added, adjusting her tone and expression to something more sombre.

'Yeah, yeah... of course… right. Awful thing. He's so young.'

They stood in awkward silence for a moment.

'Right, I'll just…' He pointed to the bathroom.

'Yep, and I'll...' Bryony said, backing into Isaac's room and shutting the door. 'Go in there after him,' she whispered to Isaac urgently.

'What?'

'Go into the bathroom and stand as close to Uncle John as you can. That way, we'll know if he can feel your presence or not.'

'But Bryony, he's having a wee!' Isaac protested.

'Just go. Quickly,' Bryony insisted.

He disappeared, and Bryony stepped out onto the landing again, waiting.

What felt like five hours but was probably only five minutes passed before the bathroom door opened again.

Bryony looked up expectantly. Uncle John emerged, rubbing his hands. She could see Isaac over his shoulder.

'You again!' He said, grinning, then seeming to remember why they were here, he dropped the grin. 'I only had a wee, so feel free to use the loo straight away if you need it. You might want a jumper, though. It's bloody freezing in there.'

He shut the door behind him and then turned to look at her. His expression immediately became tight with concern.

'Are you okay, kiddo? You've gone as white as a ghost.'

'Excuse me,' Bryony said, stepping around him, 'I'm going to be sick.'

Chapter Five

When she woke up the next morning, her first thought was that Isaac was not dead. Not completely, fully dead. Her second thought was to check the time. They'd agreed last night that he would come over to her house at 09.30. Her phone told her it was 08.37.

She jumped out of bed and into the shower. Once she'd cleaned, dried, and dressed herself, she tried to put a little bit of makeup on, but it was useless. Her usually fairly ruddy complexion was too drained of colour, and her foundation looked ridiculous, so she cleaned it off and went barefaced downstairs into the kitchen, where she was met with the shocked faces of all three family members.

Crap, she thought, suddenly remembering she was meant to be all sad and depressed.

'I'm really, really hungry,' she told them, trying to look ashamed but not really knowing why.

'That'll be the booze,' her father remarked, returning his attention to his kindle. Her brother also lost interest pretty quickly and went back to his social media and cereal.

'Well, I, for one, am delighted that you've got your appetite back, irrespective of why that is. Did you manage to eat much at the Spencer's yesterday? You were back much later than we expected, and Dad said you didn't say a word in the car on the ride home. How was it after we left? Do you want toast or cereal, darling? Or shall I whip you up a full English?'

As ever, when back on form, her mum asked a series of questions without waiting for a reply to any of them.

'Toast is fine,' Bryony began cutting off both her brother and father as they looked up at the mention of a full English. 'And don't worry. I'll make it,' she added, knowing that time was a factor and that she wouldn't be able to explain that to her mother. 'Yeah, last night was alright, actually. You know, really sad, obviously, but kinda nice too, you know?'

'Don't say "you know" twice in one sentence, darling,' her mother interjected. Bryony rolled her eyes but managed not to retort nastily. She continued recanting the events of the evening before. 'Anyway, I stayed right till the end to help Melanie with the cleanup. You know, just having the five boys there, they're utterly useless when it comes to thinking about these things.' Bryony rambled. What had actually happened was that after her initial shock and subsequent vomiting, she and Isaac had spent all evening chatting together up in his room. For much of it, they people watched out of his bedroom window, trying to get used to each other in this new dynamic. They had always been a very affectionate couple, in company and of course, alone. It was strange being so close to him and not touching him or feeling his hand, his chest, his lips. Though neither of them said anything, Bryony knew he felt the same way. So they distracted themselves by listening to the snippets of conversation down below, which Isaac adored as it was just people gushing about how wonderful he was.

Mr Singh, their headmaster, had almost cried when he was talking to his mum, which was insane as the guy very obviously hated Isaac's guts - everyone knew it. It was also amazing how many kids from school had turned up and cried. Some of them, Isaac couldn't even name! He seemed to enjoy almost every single moment of it, especially as Charlie had gotten progressively drunker and drunker and louder and louder as the night grew on. At one point, he had tried to start a chant of "We love you, Isaac" to the tune of "can't take my eyes off you," which Isaac found hilarious, but as the drink turned him melancholic and he began sobbing loudly, his father was called, and he had to be bodily carried out. Neither of them found that funny. Still, they listened to others as they recounted tales of Isaac's heroics, antics, and general shenanigans, and the whole evening played out like an Isaac Spencer's greatest hits. But they both struggled when people started getting emotional, and when they heard Eamon, Isaac's super cool and much hero-worshipped oldest brother, falter and cry, everyone joined in, including Bryony, who cried enough for the two of them. However, without the release of tears, Isaac grew restless, frustrated, and angry. That was when Bryony had decided to call it a night, thinking it was still fairly early, so she was surprised by how late it was. She was one of the last guests to leave, and she suspected many of those remaining had actually forgotten she was there. She didn't see Melanie on her way out, but she noticed the twins were also absent, so she assumed she was busy.

She hadn't said anything to her dad in the car because once she had gotten out of Isaac's cold radius, the warmth of the evening cuddled her, and she felt more exhausted than ever before. She could barely keep her eyes open on the journey back home. It had been the strangest, most emotional day of her entire existence.

'It'll just be the four now,' her father said suddenly, jolting Bryony out of her reverie, and she hurriedly continued to butter her second piece of toast, taking a huge bite out of the first one.

'What will Michael?'

'The boys. It'll be just the four boys she's got now.'

The atmosphere in the room thickened and froze, and everyone stopped what they were doing to stare at Michael Duglass.

It took him a moment to feel it, but when he did, he put his kindle down and looked at them all in surprise.

'What?' he asked innocently.

Bryony spat out her half-eaten toast.

'Oh my GOD, Dad!' she exclaimed. She stormed out of the kitchen, furious at her bewildered father.

'What?' he asked again, completely non-plussed. 'I was just pointing out a fact.'

Bryony could hear her mother's exasperated, whispered scalding on the landing, and she slammed her door behind her, letting everyone know she would not be appeased easily. She paced her room, incensed by her father's insensitivity until she turned and saw Isaac swoop in through her closed bedroom window.

The shock nearly made her scream out loud. She had been expecting him but had thought that he would come in through the front door, not actually float up – like a real ghost.

'Hey, babe,' he said, catching her shocked expression and grinning.

All thoughts of her father melted into non-existence as she took him in. It was the weirdest thing. He looked so normal. His grin was utterly infectious, and she was still surfing the joy wave of him not being really, properly dead, so she grinned back at him, stupidly happy.

'So, we're floating now?' She leaned casually against the wall with her arms folded against the cold that Isaac bought with him.

'Pretty awesome, huh?' He replied, wiggling his eyebrows.

'When did you learn to do that? How did you learn to do that?'

'I dunno. It's easy, really, like I look at where I want to go, and I just move there.' He demonstrated by floating over to stand right in front of her, just inches of cool air between them. Bryony's teeth began chattering, but she barely noticed as she stared up into those deep brown eyes.

'I just wish I could touch you,' Isaac said quietly, his voice deep and soft.

'Me too,' Bryony managed to mutter. Their physical relationship always had, in equal measure, terrified and thrilled her. She'd never had the confidence to instigate anything, so she left it to Isaac to dictate how far they went and when. He'd always been respectful and gentle, and if they went further than she was ready for, he could usually sense it and stop. When he asked why she didn't tell him to stop, she felt too ridiculous and shallow to tell him it was because she was so intimidated by his beauty, so she'd just shrug stupidly. He still, even dead, had the power to render her speechless.

'Maybe if I try really hard, I can Patrick Swayze us up a moment,' he continued, leaning so close, she would have been able to feel his breath, if he had any.

'I don't get that reference,' she said quietly.

'You know, like in the film Ghost.'

'I've not seen it.'

'Jeez, babe!' he stepped back from her and threw his hands up in frustration. 'You've never seen anything I reference. I'm bloody wasted on you.'

'You know I don't really watch films or telly.'

'Too busy studying, my little nerd.'

'Not so much these days,' she half smiled.

'Wait! This is perfect. I've had a great idea. We can finally sit and watch all those films and TV shows I need you to watch so you can finally get all of my awesome jokes. And your parents can't even moan about it cos you're all sad and stuff.'

'You think the universe bought you back as a ghost so that we can watch TV?'

'No, babe. The universe bought me back because even death can't break our relationship. It has to be, right? Why else would I be here, and with only you being able to see me? It must be because our love is so strong. Don't you think?'

'Yes baby, I do,' Bryony replied, her heart feeling full to bursting and warming her frozen skin. 'Still, it would have been nice if we could touch.'

'Hell yeah, it would. We wouldn't be wasting our time on telly if we could touch!'

Bryony giggled. Actually giggled. She hadn't even smiled in the past week and five minutes with him here, and here she was, giggling.

'Maybe we can find a way, you know to Patrick Swayze it, but you just need to learn how to master touch or something. Maybe you need to start out real small and build up to it.'

'Yeah, like how I learnt my amazing ninja skills.'

Bryony burst out laughing.

Isaac often claimed to have amazing ninja skills and demonstrated them with outrageous king fu, roly-polys, and dreadful hiding behind things that didn't disguise him at all, such as lampposts and tree saplings. It was so ridiculous and silly, but it made her laugh every time.

'Yeah, maybe,' she conceded, still grinning.

'Bryony?' Her mother called quietly through the closed door, and she tapped it timidly.

Both Bryony and Isaac jumped apart and stared at each other in a moment of horror, knowing full well that Bryony wasn't allowed to have boys in her bedroom before Isaac came to his senses.

'She can't see me! Tell her to come in. She'll just think you're on your own.'

Bryony put her finger to her lips, telling him to talk quieter.

'She can't hear me either, Bry, I can swear like a sailor to her face, and she wouldn't have a clue.'

'Don't do that!' she warned him in a barely audible whisper. Louder, she said, "Come in."

Her mother entered, a strange expression on her face.

'Oh, hi, Mum,' she said, aiming for casual but sounding awkward and forced. 'What's up?' She added, instantly regretting it.

'Are you okay?'

'Erm … yeah … you know.'

'It sounded like you were talking to someone.'

'What? Oh no, no, just erm... voicing my thoughts.' Bryony refused to even glance at Isaac. He was being good, standing still and not talking, but she could hear the giggle he was trying to hold in.

Her mother looked at her, concerned for a long moment before sighing and perching on her bed.

'Don't be too cross with your father, darling. You know how tactless he can be. And it's not because he doesn't care; he just doesn't think sometimes, that's all.'

It took Bryony a moment to recall the scene in the kitchen earlier then it all came back to her quickly enough, along with her anger.

'That's just semantics, Mum. If he really cared, he would take the time to think before speaking.'

She couldn't argue with that one, and they both knew it, but Bryony knew she would still defend him.

'Oh, darling. If I got offended every time your father put his foot in his mouth, well, we'd have never even got married! Men, well, sometimes, men are just idiots. We, women, have to rise above and humour them for the sake of the human race,' she smiled and put the plate of toast she had bought up with her on the bedside table.

Isaac couldn't help himself.

'Whoa, whoa, whoa. Men are idiots! How very dare she! Your mum is a jerk, Bry. You'd better hold me back 'cos I'm going to take her out.'

He began jumping around, loosening up his limbs as though preparing for a fight.

Bryony fought to keep her expression neutral. At any other time, she would have been cross with her mother for attempting to abate her with feminism, but she was too distracted by Isaac to care. Instead, she shrugged and mumbled, 'Whatever.'

'Right then, if you're not going to fight for me, I'll have to do it myself,' Isaac said. 'I've been waiting for this moment for three years. Your mum has had this coming a long time.'

He began punching her mother, her arms, and her head, varying between uppercuts and jabs, accompanying each hit with a "pow."

Bryony bit her lip to prevent the smile from showing.

'I bought you more toast up.'

'Pow, pow, pow.'

'You should eat it whilst it's hot.'

'P-pow, pow,'

'You're going to need to eat.'

'Pow, pow, pow.'

'To build up your strength, especially now you're up and out of your bed.'

'P P P P POW,'

'Thanks, Mum.'

She stood up to leave.

'Yeah, you'd better run.'

Bryony snorted, and her mum turned around. She tried to pass it off as a cough.

'Actually, Mum…'

'Okay, maybe not run in the conventional sense, but you look scared.'

'…I was wondering if I could have the little TV in here?'

'Don't you think she looks scared, Bry?'

Her mother frowned.

'See – that frown means fear, for sure.'

'Darling, if you want to watch TV, you can sit in the snug.' Bryony's family didn't really 'do' telly. They had a moderate screen in the backroom downstairs, affectionately named the snug, but made a point of rarely going in there and ensuring the furniture in there was hard and uncomfortable, putting all the cosy sofas in the front room with all the books and the board games. They had another small TV that was kept in the airing cupboard and only moved if someone felt too ill to read. In truth, Bryony wasn't overkeen on the telly either. She found it annoying that Isaac would become distracted by it when they were in the middle of a conversation, or worse still, if she herself got distracted.

'Yeah, I know, but Steven is home, and he'll want to watch it without me blubbering beside him. Besides, I just want it as a distraction, really.'

Her mother considered it for a few seconds, and even Isaac was quiet.

'Okay darling, I'll ask your dad to bring it in later.' Bryony agreed, and her mother left.

'Yes!' Isaac danced around the bedroom idiotically. Bryony smiled indulgently at him.

'Now we have an excuse for talking noises coming from my room!' she told him.

'Well now, aren't you a clever sausage!'

'Yes, but that won't help at all if you keep distracting me when people are in here!'

'What?! Come on, she totally deserved it!'

Bryony grinned and felt overcome with the urge to kiss him again. Instead, she stuffed her face with the buttery toast her mum had bought up, realising how ravenous she was.

'Oh, you're definitely not mourning me anymore, I see.'

'Shut up! I reckon I lost about a stone when I thought you were gone.'

'Well done, babe, but I'm not going anywhere now.'

They smiled at each other, but it wasn't long before Bryony had to rummage through her drawers for another jumper.

'Don't you think it's amazing, though, Bry?

'What?' she asked, her back to him as she tried to find her scarf and gloves too.

'Us.'

'What do you mean?' she stood up, looking pleased with herself, her hands full of winter warmers.

'I mean, I'm dead. I'm dead, and literally, no one else in the whole wide world can see me except you. Surely that's a sign from God or the cosmic universe or whatever the hell you want to believe that we, you and I, are destined to be together forever. Our love is bigger than faith, than science, than death even.'

Bryony felt all the air leave her body. Sometimes Isaac was so romantic, she simply couldn't breathe.

She stared at him, feeling the warmth spread throughout her body, despite the icy chill in her bedroom.

'It's amazing, don't you think?' He added.

'Completely and utterly,' she replied quietly. They were still and silent for a time, just being with each other.

'How is it that after being together for three long years, you still have the power to turn me to mush?' Bryony said quietly.

'Because babe, love forever!'

She grinned. They had initially started saying "love forever" as a joke, taking the mickey out of Jordan and India, another couple in their group who were always on again, off again. Now it had become their sort of catchphrase.

'So what are we going to do with our forever?'

'Hmm, I dunno. I wish we could touch. I've got loads of touching ideas.'

Bryony giggled.

'Hey, do you reckon we could touch if you were a ghost too?'

Bryony choked on her giggle. She looked at him, absolutely horrified at the suggestion, but before either one of them could respond, her bedroom door flew open.

'Mum said you wanted the little telly in here,' her father announced. 'Where shall I put it?'

Isaac tried to sign a "time-out" to her but forgot he was a ghost, and his vertical hand went straight through his horizontal hand. Bryony glared at him furiously as she cleared the stuff off the dresser for her dad.

Isaac shook his hand in front of his throat, trying to indicate that she should forget what he'd just said, he didn't mean anything by it; he was just thinking out loud. But, if anything, Bryony looked more annoyed. She turned her back on him and glared at her father.

'Er.. hem. I know you're cross with me, Bryony,' he said, sounding stiff, formal, and very uncomfortable. 'I am very sorry I was so tactless. I did not mean to be cavalier with your feelings. I will endeavour to think more carefully before making comments. It was not my intention to upset you further.'

Bryony didn't really know how to respond to her father's robotic apology, so she just nodded.

'You still look very angry,' he pointed out.

'Well, that's because I am angry but not with you. I'm angry at... the world. The world is asking me to make sacrifices I'm not willing to make.' She turned and stared pointedly at Isaac as she said this, so she was surprised when she felt the warmth and weight of her dad's hand on her shoulder. They were not unless, in exceptional circumstances, an affectionate pairing; Bryony couldn't remember the last time her father had even touched her in any way other than a playful shove or a back slap, so she turned all her attention to him in this unprecedented turn of events.

'Oh, Bryony,' he began, looking at her so kindly she felt her eyes swim. 'The world is a cruel, cruel place. It will break minds, bodies, and hearts but remember one thing; it doesn't have favourites, it doesn't choose, and it isn't biased. Try not to take the bad times too personally, my dear.'

He tapped her arm and then kissed her forehead lightly.

'It's bloody freezing in here. Have you got a window open?' He added, sounding more like himself. Bryony shook her head.

'I'll bring you in the fan heater,' he disappeared through her door, and Isaac began to speak, but she raised a hand to silence him. Her eyes on the open doorway.

Sure enough, a minute or two later, her father returned clutching the small rectangular fan heater. Bryony reached out for it.

'Do you want me to set it up or the telly? Plug them in, link up the internet, and whatnot?'

'No, it's okay, I can do that!'

'Rightio then,' he handed the fan heater over to her and smiled awkwardly before he turned to leave.

'Dad!' she called after him. He turned back. They stared at each other for a moment. 'Thanks, Daddy,' she said quietly. This time he beamed at her and pulled the door shut as he left, giving her a little wink just before it closed.

'Bry?'

'I am not going to kill myself for you, Isaac Thomas Spencer,' she hissed.

'No, I know. Of course not… I didn't mean… I just say stupid things… you know that… I'm actually brain-dead over here. I'm sorry, Bry. I don't want you to do that, like, at all. You know my mouth always says stuff without permission. Please don't be mad at me. You're the only person I can talk to.'

She softened as they both knew she would.

'You still love me, babe?'

'Of course, I still love you, Isaac.'

Love forever, right?'

'Love forever,' she agreed.

'So shall we get the telly sorted?'

Bryony nodded and was about to plug it in when she stopped.

'I have an idea. Actually, I have a proposal.'

'Oooh, will you get down on one knee?'

'No, idiot, listen. I know what we can do with all this time. You want me to watch some of your favourite films and TV shows, right? Well, if I do that for you, then I want you to read some of my favourite books.'

Isaac groaned.

'Read?!'

'Yeah, remember all those times you said how you would love to read but never had the time? Now you've got all the time in the world. Plus, then we'll have more things in common to talk about.'

'Erm, yeah, I think I was just saying that to get you to like me more.'

'Oh, come on, Isaac, please. There's so many books I'd like you to read so that we can talk about them.'

'Yeah, but babe, I can't even touch you, so how could I turn the pages?'

'Oh yeah, rubbish.'

'I know, gutted.'

'Shut up. You're not gutted.'

'Actually, I am. You're right; it's not like there's anything else I can do, especially when you go to school. I can't even touch the buttons on the remote.'

'Audiobooks! You can listen on my Audible app!'

'Yay! But to be clear, I prefer watching television.'

'Ugh television smelevison. Books are so much better.'

Isaac laughed. 'Did you just say television smelevision?'

'Maybe.'

'You, Miss Bryony Doris Duglass, who's on the fast track to Oxford University, said television smelevision!'

'Well, I'm hardly going to Oxford anymore, am I? But yes, I did say television smelevision, and I'll say it again a thousand times over because television simply cannot compete with a truly good book.'

'Okay, that sounds like a challenge, so I'll make you a deal. I will read one book of your choosing for every series I choose for us to watch.'

Bryony thought about it for a second, but it was just for effect.

'You're on,' she said, holding out her hand to shake it. Isaacs passed straight through hers.

She smiled at him, then had a realisation that made her start laughing.

'What? Bryony, what are you laughing at?'

'Oh my goodness, I'm such an idiot!'

'You are? Why?'

'So when Dad was in here, you went like this to me,' she repeated the time-out motion he'd failed to do.

'Yeah,' he said cautiously.

'Were you trying to say time-out?'

'Yeah, but, you know, ghost issues.'

'I get that now, but at the time and in that circumstance, it looked like you were making a cross, you know, like what Jesus died on!' She demonstrated for him how it had looked to her. Isaac looked aghast.

'Oh, babe – no!'

'Yeah, but then you did this,' Bryony demonstrated the waving at the throat move he had done, 'Which obviously, now I know, you meant "forget it," but I interpreted to mean an execution or something!'

They both couldn't help but laugh at their own stupidity.

‘Okay, Bry, just so you know, I want to be very clear now – I absolutely do not want you to kill yourself.’

‘Good, because honestly, babe, I love you to the moon and back, but I’m not ready to commit suicide. Not yet, anyway. Let’s see what A’ Level results I get. If I fail, then I’ll be right there with you!’

‘You’re not going to fail. You’re a bloody genius, for goodness sake!’

‘Yeah, but I have barely done a moments studying or homework since the day you walked into that library three years ago.’

‘Oh, what a fateful day! And I can honestly say I’m like the proud parent at the playgroup. I changed you from an uber-geek to a grade-A super fly chic.’

‘I’m not a super fly chic,’ Bryony giggled.

‘Yes, Bryony, you are.’

She grinned from the inside out but said no more about it.

‘Come on then, tell me, what are we going to watch? I know you’re going to insist we watch the TV show first.’

‘Damn right I am. Right then, let me see.’

He began thinking about it as Bryony set the telly up and plugged the fan heater in.

‘Hmm. Nothing too morbid after our recent conversation. How about Dead to Me, or the Walking Dead, no Shaun of the Dead, no wait – After Life!’

They both began laughing so hard that neither of them could speak. Eventually, they managed to control themselves, and they got the Netflix menu up.

‘Jesus Christ! There’s so much choice!’

‘Babe, this is just on Netflix – we’ve got so much work to do.’

‘Well, if you start off with Suicide Squad, I will definitely take offence.’

At that, they both fell into hysterics all over again.

Chapter Six

Their routine formed very organically. Bryony went back to school the following week. At first, Isaac went with her, but it was too difficult to ignore him, so he agreed to entertain himself during school hours, doing goodness knows what until she returned. Then she would eat her dinner as fast as possible and run upstairs to where Isaac was waiting.

They would discuss whatever book Isaac had listened to the night before (ghosts don't need to sleep) before continuing binge-watching whatever series they were on.

She got used to wearing layers of clothing and doing her homework during lunchtime or a free period. She rarely spoke to her friends at school anymore, mainly because she didn't trust herself, not to mention Isaac in the present tense or in case she failed to look depressed enough to convince them she was still in mourning. They quickly learnt to leave her alone, believing she'd reverted to her old geeky ways, just working all the time. Her grades did not reflect this theory at all, and had these 'friends' bothered to look just a touch closer, they'd have noticed as much, but they didn't. Not that Bryony was bothered at all. She didn't care about her friends or her grades. She had given up her dream of going to Oxford University a long time ago. Her new dream, and all she cared about, was Isaac. Rushing home to Isaac. She felt they were closer than ever. They really, properly talked now. Argued about books, shows, films, characters, plot lines, and believability. If they disagreed, instead of storming off and not speaking to each other, they managed to talk it through and either compromise or agree to disagree amicably – usually. The occasional huff did not ruin the absolute perfection of everything.

On a particularly warm Wednesday afternoon in November, Bryony, following the usual routine, raced home to Isaac. She was a little bit miffed because this morning Isaac had told her he hadn't particularly enjoyed Wuthering Heights. Apparently, he had found the narrative dreary and *all* the characters annoying. Bryony had had to bite her tongue. She couldn't help but take it personally whenever Isaac didn't enjoy a book that she loved, and Wuthering Heights was one of her absolute favourites of all time. She had spent all day at school working through her counterarguments and had inwardly practised conveying them to Isaac in a calm, detached manner, knowing full well that if he disagreed, she'd be angry. So, on this particular afternoon, she was feeling a little bit anxious and moody and quietly determined not to enjoy the next episode of whatever they were planning to watch tonight.

They greeted each other in the usual way and were about to get into the inevitable argument about the book when there was a knock at her bedroom door, and her mother entered without waiting to be invited. Bryony was already changed into warm, thick layers and was sat huddled in her bed, under the duvet and wearing her winter dressing gown, hood up.

'Ooh, Bryony, it is freezing in here. Are you sure you haven't got a window open?

Her mother asked this every time she came in.

'What's up, Mum?' Bryony asked curtly, wanting her out.

'Maybe we should get someone in. The central heating must be broken in here,' Bryony could tell she was stalling and, quite frankly, was uninterested in anything she had to say.

'How are you, darling?' She asked, perching on the edge of her bed. It took all Bryony's self-control not to roll her eyes.

'I'm fine, thanks, Mum.'

'Really, Bryony, because we are very worried about you?'

'Why? I've been fine.'

‘Darling, all you do is sit up here in this ice box and watch telly. That’s not the Bryony we know. You barely talk to us. Even before Isaac died, you still spent some time with us.’

‘I’m sorry, Mum. I just don’t want to talk.’

‘Well darling, your dad and I really think that you need to talk to someone, so we have made an appointment for you with a private grief councillor.’

‘What?’

‘Your first visit is on Friday.’

Chapter Seven

Bryony was fuming.

'How dare she? How dare she!' she raged to Isaac when her mother left the room. 'For all she knows, I am in mourning for the love of my life. I am absolutely entitled to withdraw a little and be lethargic. You know what this is, don't you? What this is really about – She's just pissed because I am not a grade-A student anymore. She can't show off about me to her precious work pals about how *both* her children will be attending Oxford University.'

Isaac said nothing. In fact, he was so unusually quiet about the matter that it calmed Bryony down, and she finally stopped pacing the room and sat down on the bed next to him.

They sat quietly for a few moments.

'What will you tell him? About me, I mean?'

'Who, the counsellor? I don't know. Nothing, I suppose. I mean nothing about seeing you now. Probably lots about our relationship, though.'

'Won't he be able to tell that you're lying?'

'Well, I mean, they're counsellors, not mind readers. I guess they'll only know what I choose to tell them, and if I explain that you're dead and I'm in mourning for you, I imagine that he'll say, "Oh okay, well, you're acting perfectly normally for someone in your situation. Continue with your grieving process." If my parents want to pay out stupid amounts of money to a glorified agony aunt, then so be it. It's a complete waste of time.'

Isaac looked unconvinced.

'What do you suggest I do – tell him I can see the ghost of my dead boyfriend? That we are continuing our relationship, so I don't want to be a part of the rest of society now.'

‘No, of course not, but I just think that counsellors or psychiatrists or shrinks or whatever you wanna call them, they have ways of making you talk.’

They both burst out laughing. Having not long watched all three Godfather films, the wording sounded far more threatening than he had intended.

‘That’s obviously not what I mean. But I do think that they’re trained to get you to spill your deepest, darkest secrets without you even knowing that you’re doing it. I’m just worried, that’s all.’

‘Worried I’ll accidentally let something slip, and they’ll send me straight to the mental hospital?’

‘Exactly, and we haven’t even started on any of the Marvel films yet.’

Bryony chuckled. She ached to hold him and cuddle his fears away.

‘Seriously though, babe, without you, I’ve got nothing. You’re literally my whole world, so you have to be careful for me.’

‘How incredibly romantic and yet self-serving of you,’ Bryony grinned at him.

‘What can I say? I’m an excellent multi-tasker,’ he grinned back.

‘Listen, don’t worry about it. I genuinely believe the guy is going to think my behaviour is completely normal. He may just try to wrangle as much money out of my parents as he can, and that’s fine by me. I’ll change the subject if I get worried I’ll let something about you slip out. We can talk about my many mummy issues – we could talk for hours about them.’

They settled back down to continue watching their show, but Bryony could tell Isaac couldn’t forget about it.

When the day came for her first meeting, it was Isaac who suggested that he didn’t come with her.

‘I just think it would be best if you be 100% focussed on appearing normal,’ he said as she was getting ready. Bryony didn’t argue. They had both noticed the strange looks she had received when she inevitably reacted one way or another to something Isaac did when they were in public. She couldn’t help it, and it always looked weird.

‘I’ll be back in just over an hour,’ she promised before leaving him alone in her bedroom. She had told Alexa to begin reading aloud ‘The Lord of the Rings’ and hoped that very soon Isaac would be so absorbed in The Shire and the hobbits and Gandalf that he would forget to worry about this ridiculous meeting.

She joined her mother in the car, trying to ignore the hopeful expression on her mother’s face.

‘How are you feeling, darling? Nervous?’

‘No.’

‘It’s very important that you are as open and honest with the counsellor as possible. He can only help you if you allow yourself to be vulnerable with him.’

Bryony didn’t reply, and her mother wisely chose to remain silent for the rest of the car ride, opting to put the radio on instead.

She wasn’t sure what she was expecting of a counsellor’s office, but when they pulled up outside what appeared to be just someone’s house, she realised it wasn’t that. She looked at her mother questioningly.

‘Are you sure this is the right place?’

‘Yes. It’s a converted house. There are several counsellors and psychiatrists, and mental health professionals all together in there. They call it “holistic therapy,” I think. She said as she reached for her handbag and opened the car door.

‘What are you doing?’

‘What do you mean?’ her mother asked, confused.

‘Has the session already been paid for?’

‘Yes, of course, online. You’re meeting with a Dr…’

She rummaged through her handbag for her diary with all her scribbled notes and meetings and necessary papers.

‘Dr William Graeme,’ Bryony said, looking at her phone. ‘You forwarded the email confirmation to me. I have all the details. You can stay here, in the car.’

‘You don’t want me to come in with you?’

‘No, mother, I’m not twelve.’

She looked surprised, then disappointed.

As she climbed out of the car and collected her own bag, she heard her mother say, ‘I’ll wait here for you then.’

The tone of her voice, for some reason, infuriated Bryony though she didn’t really understand why. She slammed the car door shut and stormed off down the path. On the wall next to the door, there were some brass signs mounted onto wooden plaques. Each sign was dedicated to a different doctor with lots of letters after their name, so she realised that though it looked like a normal house, it clearly wasn’t someone’s home. She tried to push the front door open, and it swung inwards easily for her. The hallway was bright and airy but very quiet. She walked forward, and the first doorway she came to had no door on it. Instead, it gave a clear view into the room, which was the reception area. A woman was sitting behind a tall desk, and she greeted her warmly. Bryony walked in, and she asked for her name, then typed something into her computer.

‘Ah yes, you’ve an appointment with Will. His room is on the top floor. You’re a little early, though, he’s currently in session, so just take a seat on the third-floor landing, and he’ll call you when he’s ready.

Bryony nodded and began the climb to the third floor. The décor was decidedly classy. Crisp, clean whites with accents of sage green, gold framed abstract paintings hung on the walls in the hallways, and every now and then, there were occasional tables with either fresh flowers or glossy magazines on them. On the second-floor landing, there were five doors, each of them closed. One of them was clearly marked as a bathroom, and three others had brass plaques on the wall next to them, similar to the ones outside. However, it was the door without any signage that was the noisiest one. From behind it came the sound of many people attempting to make a similar sound, but the overall effect made the noise indistinctive. Whatever it was, it sounded like group work. Bryony shuddered at the idea of group work. Just the thought of the initial awkwardness of it all was enough to make her cheeks flush, and she rushed past the room, up the final flight of stairs to the third-floor landing.

Here there were only three doors, but again, they were all shut. One of the doors was marked as a toilet, and one had a sign saying Doctor William Graeme, MFPH, FRPsych. The other said Dr Elizabeth Sanders, FRCOT, AMHP. Between the two doctors' doors was a dresser laden with a coffee machine, kettle, tiny fridge, and a vast array of drink supplies. In the far corner was a water dispenser, and opposite the offices were two large, high-backed armchairs on either side of a small coffee table, upon which were more glossy magazines. The wall above the kettle had a clock so stylish and abstract it took Bryony a moment to work out how to read it, but when she did, she realised she was about fifteen minutes early. She sat down in the chair closest to Dr Will's door but immediately got up again and went to use the bathroom.

When she returned, there was another person occupying one of the seats. At first, all she could see were long, skinny, jean-covered legs sprawling endlessly out so casually, as though he'd been there a hundred times before. She had to walk past him to get to the other chair, but his legs took up most of the width of the hallway, and she had to step over him.

He made no attempt to move them as he watched her struggle to step over him without touching him. However, he did sit up straighter and stare at her unashamedly as she walked by.

Her first thought was how rude he was, but when she finally bought her gaze to his face and met his confident, lazy smile, she couldn't help but think there was something disturbingly attractive about him, despite or maybe because of his arrogance.

'Why hello,' he said, his voice deep and smooth, sounding like an old-fashioned gentleman. Bryony couldn't tell if that was his real voice or if he was putting it on. From nowhere, the instinct to either play along or play up this guy felt very appealing, so she sat herself down and crossed her legs as provocatively as she could angling her body towards him.

'Hello yourself,' she replied, attempting to make her voice low, rich, and husky.

The boy's grin grew wider.

'My guess is that you're here because you've been a very naughty girl,' he said, making it sound quite perverted. She was beginning to regret this move. She wondered if she could style it out until Dr Will rescued her, which hopefully would be very soon.

'Me?' She asked innocently, 'Absolutely not. No, I'm simply misunderstood. You, on the other hand, you look like trouble.'

'Nah, I'm not trouble. I'm like you, misunderstood.'

'Oh really? And what is it that people don't understand about you, Mr…?'

'Call me Jax.'

'Okay, in what way are you misunderstood, Jax?'

'Well, it's like this,' he leaned forward over the little coffee table, closing the space between them. Bryony remained where she was and not so discreetly examined his slightly spotty skin and unkempt, long hair but also his undefinable eye colour and the dimple in just one of his cheeks. He couldn't have been much older than her, where the hell did that confidence come from? 'People try to label me as an arsonist,' he began very quietly, and Bryony couldn't tell if he was being serious or not. 'But the truth is, I have a compulsion that I cannot control. If they have to label me, they should call me a pyromaniac. It's more accurate. Still, at least I didn't have to do any community service or a stint in the Juvenile Correction Centre. Instead, they insist I come here twice a week and have a chat with Liz to help me understand and have better control over my urges.'

Bryony hid her surprise well. If he was lying, then he was excellent at it. However, it still felt too clichéd-bad-boy for it to be true. He probably just had commonplace anxiety or something much more mundane but was showing off for her. Either way, her poker face was superb, even if she did think so herself. She nodded at him sagely as if she met arsonists, no, sorry, pyromaniacs all the time.

'And is it helping? Or are you still a danger to society?'

She couldn't believe how flirty she was being with him. This was so out of character for her, but the way she saw it, it was completely harmless because she doubted she would ever see this boy again after today.

'I'm not dangerous as long as everyone is always nice to me,' he said, making his eyebrows dance. Isaac could do the same thing with his eyebrows, but it was a skill Bryony did not possess and coveted. She laughed at him.

'So what about you, Miss…?'

'Oh, I'm not a pyromaniac,' she answered quickly, purposefully ignoring his attempt to learn her name.

'Really, not even a little bit?'

'No, I'm afraid not. If anything, I'm more interested in water. I'm not sure if there's a medical term for it... erm... probably... aquamaniac.'

It was his turn to laugh.

'Well, they do say opposites attract,' he winked at her, and she smiled indulgently at his blatant forwardness.

'So what are you really in for?' He asked, inclining his head towards the door of Dr Will.

Bryony looked at him hard for a moment or two, wrestling internally with how to answer the question. She glanced at the clock. It was just a few seconds until her session was due to start. She leaned toward him, and he reciprocated the gesture, so they were almost nose-to-nose.

'I can see and talk to the ghost of my dead boyfriend,' she confessed, throwing caution to the wind. She doubted he would believe her in the same way she didn't believe him, and she could tell from the surprise on his face that it was the last thing he was expecting her to say. She knew Isaac would be furious with her, and yet it felt both wonderfully freeing and incredibly risky to say it out loud to an actual living person. For the past two months now, since Isaac's funeral, she hadn't told another living soul what she was doing, and she knew she never really could.

They were both quiet for a moment or two as Jax examined her face to see if she was telling the truth. Bryony tried to keep her expression as neutral as possible.

A door opened to their right, and an older, intelligent-looking woman half-stepped into the hallway.

'Jaxon, come on in,' she said stiffly.

Jaxon continued to stare at Bryony as he stood up.

'Good luck, mystery lady,' he said, picking up his bag.

‘Stay cool, Jaxon,’ she replied, winking at him. He full-on grinned at her before turning to his counsellor.

‘Liz, how are you?’

The older lady frowned, and rolled her eyes at him.

‘Jaxon, there is a myriad of derivations of my name, and you know that is the one I like the least. Are you having a difficult time?’

Bryony didn’t hear his response as they had gone into her office and shut the door.

Whilst waiting for Dr Will, She sat reflecting upon that whole exchange. She didn’t really talk to boys outside of her family at all. Not since being in a relationship with Isaac. She’d never really had cause to. Obviously, when they all used to hang out together, there were boys in the group, but she had next to nothing in common with them except Isaac. She did chat and have fun with Isaac’s brothers, but they clearly saw her as a sister type – there was never any flirting. And she had just had a really fun, flirty chat with a complete stranger, and it turns out she is really rather good at it.

Why was that?

She’d always thought she was shy, especially around boys, and the idea of flirting felt almost repellent to her before. But now she didn’t feel shy. She also knew she wasn’t at all interested in that flirting becoming anything more. Perhaps it was because she was in the extremely unique position of being free to chat and flirt with anyone she liked, knowing full well that for her, it had absolutely no possibility of leading to anything as she had, quite literally, the most devoted boyfriend waiting for her at home.

She couldn’t help but let a little giggle escape from her lips as she thought about how very lucky she was.

‘Miss Duglass?’

Dr Will had poked his head out of his office as silently as a ninja. She had no idea how long he'd been observing her for. She felt her face flush in embarrassment as she realised she'd been caught smiling and laughing to herself by a head shrink! Isaac really would be furious with her. She was supposed to be being careful.

'It's lovely to see someone smiling before a session. Let's see if I can wipe it off!' he said cheekily with a grin. Bryony felt slightly relieved. In fact, with his rather short, rotund figure, his glasses and rosy cheeks, and his white beard, he reminded her a little bit of Father Christmas on his day off. His eyes were kind, and his expression was open and welcoming, not mocking or judgemental. She relaxed a little.

'Please, come in,' he said, opening his door wide for her. 'Come and get settled, and then we'll begin.'

Chapter Eight

The final bell rang out, and the class automatically began packing up their things despite the fact that the teacher had not yet dismissed them. He called over the din of chatter and scraping chairs, reminding them their homework was due in next week, but they were free to go, like they needed to be told. Bryony packed her things away, deliberately trying to be as slow as possible so that everyone would leave before her. She pretended to do up her shoelaces as the last stragglers edged towards the door. When they had finally left, she took a deep breath, squared her shoulders, and walked up to the teacher's desk. Mr Greaves was poring over something on his laptop and didn't realise anyone was still in the room until she was just a few feet away.

'Bryony!' he exclaimed, clearly surprised.

'Hello, Sir,' she said nervously, fiddling with a strap on her bag as she hovered by his desk.

'How can I help you?'

'Actually, it's a couple of things, sir.'

'Go on.'

'Okay, well, firstly, about that stupid thing I did before... well... I... I should have said this much, much sooner, immediately afterwards, actually. I don't know why I didn't. Honestly, I don't know why I did it in the first place.'

'You're rambling, Bryony,' he said, not unkindly.

'I'm sorry, sir. That's what I'm trying to say. I'm sorry. I wish with all my might that I could take it back. You're a fantastic teacher, my favourite, actually, and I hate myself for having done that and ruining our relationship. I'm filled with shame every time I think about it. It was a stupid dare. I'm not excusing myself because it was a dare. I just want you to know it wasn't my idea. I would never think up anything like that. Anyway, I need you to know how sorry I truly am.'

She stopped talking, stopped fidgeting, stopped shifting her weight from foot to foot, and forced herself to meet his eyes.

He didn't reply straight away. He held her gaze for a moment, then stretched his arms up and interlaced his fingers behind his head.

'Did you know that the prefrontal cortex area of the brain is responsible for making rational choices and controlling judgement calls? When a kid hits puberty, that area of the brain goes through some crazy changes and doesn't become fully functioning until you hit your mid-twenties. Add to that the influx of competing hormones, and honestly, I'm always impressed that you guys just manage to turn up to class on time.

'What I am saying, Bryony, is all of us do stuff when we're in our teens that we wish we hadn't. For the most part, it's not really your fault – it's your underdeveloped prefrontal cortex. Therefore, as you have made such a succinct and concise apology, I am very willing not just to forgive you but also to try to actually forget it ever happened. As we both know, life is too short to hold grudges.'

The kindness and concern in his eyes almost moved her to tears. She sniffed loudly, and he smiled and handed her a tissue from the box that was always present on his desk. She guessed he was so damn likeable, everyone came blubbering to him, so it was best to be prepared.

'You said there were a couple of things you wanted to talk to me about?' He prompted after he'd given her a minute to gather herself.

Bryony dabbed her eyes and wiped her nose, then pulled a chair up beside his desk.

'Yes, Sir. So given all that's happened, Mum and Dad got me to see a grief counsellor earlier this week, and one of the things that have come from that is to refocus my attention on other things. So, I have decided to try and really focus on my studies like I used to. Now, I know I've hardly been the perfect student for the past year… or two. And I know I'll never get into Oxford Uni now, but I think, if I really apply myself, I could still get some pretty good A' Level results.'

'I love everything you just said. How can I help?'

'Okay, so actually, what I'd like to do is get a head start on my revision for all subjects before the Christmas holidays start. So I was wondering if you had any revision notes or past papers I could have a look at.'

'Yes, yes, and yes!' he said, getting up and going into his tiny storage cupboard.

Bryony smiled to herself. Mr Greaves had been the last teacher she had approached, for obvious reasons, and everyone else had been delighted she was being so proactive and had given her plenty of study materials. Mr Greaves gave her three past papers and a few printouts of powerpoint presentations, which basically broke down all the lessons they'd had so far. She thanked him profusely and then went to her locker to collect the rest of it. She was so pleased her mum was picking her up today rather than attempting to get the bus with her enormously overladen rucksack. She was excited to get started and just hoped Isaac would keep quiet long enough so she could really get stuck into it.

When she got home, her mother immediately informed her dad, very loudly and proudly, that Bryony had actively sought additional revision materials from all her teachers. Bryony rolled her eyes but also couldn't help smiling. She didn't race upstairs as she usually did. Instead, she listened as her father explained the new theories of effective revision, which included doing exercise to ensure the body was as active as the brain, and it could help you absorb information easier and for longer. They explored avenues where that could be logistically possible, and Bryony resolved to make revision voice notes and listen back to them whilst on a jog/fast walk.

When she finally went upstairs, Isaac sat on her bed with his arms folded and a face like thunder.

'You bought home extra homework?' He accused.

'Revision notes,' she corrected unnecessarily. 'Isaac, my mocks are just after the Christmas holidays, which start in just over three week's time. I have to start studying for them.'

'Was this something else your therapist suggested?' He demanded.

Bryony sighed in exasperation. Isaac had been obsessed ever since her first meeting with Dr Will and was becoming, in Bryony's view, a little bit paranoid about it.

'Don't sigh at me, Bryony. Ever since that meeting, you've changed. You can't deny it.'

'How have I changed, Isaac?'

'You're more distant. You don't want to spend as much time with me anymore. He told you to ignore me, didn't he?'

'Oh my God, Isaac! I've told you a million times already, the only way we discussed you was about your death. I promise you, I did not mention that I can still see you.'

'So why, all of a sudden, do you want to start studying.'

'It's not all of a sudden. It's been coming on since the moment I decided to do my A' Levels! And yes, maybe Dr Will did suggest it may help me to focus on my studies a bit more – to help me get over losing you, by the way – but also, my parents have been desperate for me to start studying properly again. The teachers at school have started to go on about how important it is – honestly, Isaac, the only person who doesn't seem to get it is you.'

‘Studying is so boring,’ he moaned petulantly.

‘Well, I think watching telly is boring,’ she confessed. She wasn’t lying. Bryony had very quickly grown bored of the stuff Isaac tried to get her to watch. She often felt no connection to the characters or felt the storylines were too predictable, too unrealistic, or too boring. She often lost interest halfway through a programme and started talking or fidgeting or playing on her phone or looking longingly at her to-be-read pile of books. Isaac had noticed and grown irritated with her.

‘You’re the only person I know who cannot binge-watch anything,’ he whined perpetually.

‘I’m sorry, babe. I just don’t understand why we can’t do separate things. I don’t mind at all if you want to watch your programmes whilst I study quietly in the corner.’

‘Because Bryony, I’ve seen all these shows. The whole point was that I share them with you.’

They sat silently for a few moments. They’d reached an impasse. Neither was willing to do what the other wanted, and they couldn’t see why the other thing was so important to them.

Someone knocked on her bedroom door. Her mother came in without waiting to be asked, and Bryony was relieved that they had stopped arguing in time.

‘Hi, honey. I’m sorry to disturb you, but I just popped into the shop and bought you some supplies.’ Her mother handed her a bag full of her favourite pens, pencils, highlighters, study note cards, and two large bags of strawberry bonbons – her favourite study snack.

‘Aww, thanks, Mum.’

‘Also, just so you know, your brother has called me. He wanted to bring a couple of friends home for the Christmas break, but I said, “No, absolutely not, not when you’re studying for your mocks.

They'd be too much of a distraction." So, fair warning, he'll be in a right mood when he comes home for Christmas break.'

Bryony knew how much this would have cost her mum. She loved to play host. Loved to cook for lots of people, especially at Christmas. She loved the noise and bustle of people in the house, and she loved the late-night chats they always seemed to have about any topic anyone dared have an opinion on.

'Mum, don't do that. Steven can bring his friends home, don't stop him. I promise I won't let anything distract me,' she looked pointedly at Isaac, who scowled at her. Her mother looked delighted.

'Are you sure, darling? I must admit, he did sound disappointed. If you're absolutely sure, I'll call him back right now.'

'I'm absolutely sure.'

Her mother hugged her like an excited toddler. They had planned to put the tree up as soon as Steven returned home from uni, and that would be a much happier affair if he wasn't in a mood.

She pulled her phone out of her pocket and called him, sitting on Bryony's bed.

'Steven honey, it's Mum.'

'I know, Mum, your name still shows up on my mobile.'

'Listen, I've just had a chat with Bryony, and she assures me she won't let your friends distract her from her studies. So, it will be absolutely fine for them to come and stay too. They must, however, be respectful of Bryony's needs. They mustn't be too raucous or distracting.'

'Yeah, yeah, they will be. I promise they'll be as dull as dishwater.'

Her mother giggled.

‘Oh Steven, you know that’s not what I meant. Now tell me, do any of them have any dietary requirements? None of them are vegetarian or vegan, are they? I know that’s very popular at the moment. If so, I’ll have to go shopping again.’

Bryony picked up one of her many books and pointedly sat at her desk so her mother would get the hint. She did. Whilst still on the phone, she gave Bryony a dorky thumbs up and backed out of her room, shutting the door after her.

Bryony and Isaac looked at each other. Eventually, he relented.

‘Fine, fine, you have to study. But what am I going to do?’

‘You could help?’ Bryony suggested, trying not to look too smug.

‘Ugh, Bry, I don’t have to study ever again, so I am absolutely going to take advantage of that.’

‘Well, maybe you could watch telly still. I wasn’t lying when I said that I don’t mind.’

‘No, it’s no fun without you.’

‘Okay then, well maybe you don’t have to stay with me. You could go exploring.’

‘Exploring?’

‘Yeah. You could go off somewhere, anywhere. Maybe you could find us a romantic spot where no one ever goes. I can’t study all the time, I have to have some downtime now and then. We could have a picnic or something.’

‘Babe, I don’t eat! Besides, what’s the point? It’s not like we can fool around or anything anymore.’

Bryony tried hard not to lose her patience with him, but he was beginning to annoy her.

‘Why don’t you go back to your house? Visit your family, see how everyone is getting on?’

'No. Everyone will be really sad and stuff, and there will be nothing I can do to help. It will just be too depressing.'

'Well, then, I don't know Isaac! I can't think of anything else. Why don't you try and think of something, and if you can't, then just go and annoy someone else for a bit.'

'Well, I would love to, Bryony, but in case you have forgotten, I can't!' he yelled at her. 'No one else can see me! No one else can hear me! I *only* have you, and clearly, you don't want me.'

Bryony felt instantly guilty.

'I'm sorry,' she said meekly. 'I know it must be hard for you. And it's not that I don't want to be with you, you know that. It's just that I have to go on living, and that means doing stuff you won't be interested in. I'm trying to think of things you could do but being undetectable makes it diffi… wait a minute. You're undetectable. You could be the ultimate spy. You could spy on your friends. You could spy on the teachers. You could do anything.'

The minute she said it, she regretted it. She had just pointed out to Isaac in a roundabout way how he could go and watch Monroe completely undetected. Her stomach jerked uncomfortably.

'I could go and spy on that shrink of yours,' he said thoughtfully.

Bryony laughed, surprised that his mind went there first.

'Yes, you could if it would make you feel better. Go and see him. He's not a bad person Isaac, he seems like he genuinely wants to help people.'

'I thought the whole point was that you don't need any help.'

She softened towards him and all of his heartfelt insecurities. Her poor baby.

'I don't need help with you, Babe. I love you. I love that you're here. But maybe I do need help with communicating more effectively, especially with my parents. Or help finding the motivation to do some much-needed studying. These are not bad things. But I do appreciate the knock-on effect it has on you, so we do need to find stuff you can do without me. If that includes stalking my poor therapist, then so be it!'

He looked appeased and thoughtful.

'I'm sorry too. I didn't mean to yell at you. And if you want to study, I'll leave you alone to get on with it. Maybe I will go and check on my mum and the family. I could see how the twins are doing. Maybe they'll be okay. They might even be excited for Christmas; you know how crazy we all go for Christmas in my family. Eamon might finally bring his hot girlfriend home to meet everyone – I'd love to get a glimpse of her – oh my God! I can spy on people in the shower!'

Chapter Nine

Christmas came and went in a blur. Bryony spent most of her holiday studying and genuinely enjoying it. She spent a couple of evenings chatting with her family and Steven's two mates, Amir and Ben. Isaac thought they were boring and unkindly called them ugly geeks. Whilst it was true that neither of them was especially good-looking, and they both attended Oxford university, so they clearly were intelligent, Bryony hated it when Isaac was unkind like this. She thought it made him unattractive, so she ignored him and felt more inclined to stay with her family. Besides, Bryony didn't find either of them boring. Quite the contrary, really. They had some very lively debates about politics, the environmental crisis and potential ways to fix it, as well as hotly debated music and literature topics. There had been one awkward moment when Ben had tried to hit on her when they were alone in the kitchen one time. She had to explain that she was still mourning her dead boyfriend and wasn't ready for any romantic attachments. She suspected that was one of the reasons Isaac didn't like them. That and he hadn't read a lot of the books they discussed or know the MP they were talking about and hated the music they listened to. The differences between him and her brother and his friends were so extreme that Bryony found it hard to balance the two. She also found it hard to tolerate when Isaac laughed out loud at the gifts she received for Christmas.

Admittedly, the luxury spa day vouchers for her and her mum to take later in the year were a bit cringe and not something she was especially looking forward to. However, the first edition of *To Kill A Mockingbird* had almost made her cry, and she thought the personalised journal plus creative accessories to help her organise or purge her thoughts were really thoughtful presents. Isaac didn't get it.

'Your parents have all that money, and all you get is a used book and a diary! No new clothes or shoes or computer games! You're a girl, for Christ's sake, where’s the make-up or the perfume or the jewellery? Your family is so weird!’

Bryony had been quite hurt by his comments and had purposefully spent the evening downstairs, away from him. It took her a while to appreciate that Isaac was probably hurting too. He hadn’t gone to visit his family as he said he would. In fact, Bryony didn’t know where he went when he disappeared, and she didn’t really want to know. Ignorance was bliss in this instance, she felt. After all, it wasn’t as though he could actually *do* anything, even if he was watching Monroe in the shower, as she guessed he was. However, if he had been to see his family, he would definitely have told her about it, so she knew he hadn’t. And she thought she knew why. Christmas had been much harder for Isaac than either of them had expected. It is a time for love and family and traditions, and though celebrating the same thing, each household will do it a bit differently, and Isaac really felt those differences. In truth, Bryony genuinely believed that Isaac was homesick. He wanted familiarity and belonging, and things simply weren’t the same at the Duglass’s house. Plus, he’s dead, and this seemed to bother him much more than normal.

So after an unexpectedly pleasant evening during the weird time in-between Christmas and New Year, Bryony climbed the stairs to her room to face a very moody Isaac. To appease him and try to lull him out of his slump, she promised she would go with him to visit his parents, although, she insisted, not until after the New Year.

For the past three New Year’s Eve nights, when she was seeing Isaac, Bryony had spent the night at the Spencers' house, along with about fifty other guests who ended up crashing there after another epically awesome party that would go on until three or four in the morning. That would not be happening this year. Bryony had received a generic ‘send-to-all’ text from Melanie explaining that this year the Spencers would be having a quiet night in with just the family; there would not be a party. She had also received another text, straight after this, from Melanie. This one was specifically just for her, and it said that she was the exception to the rule; she was always welcome. However, they were just ordering pizza and would probably all go to bed early, so she totally understood if she didn't want to come over.

Bryony had felt a huge pang of guilt and shame, not only for politely declining the offer but also for not telling Isaac about it. She knew if she did, he would somehow convince her to go, and she really didn't want to. Instead, as she knew Steven and his mates were going out to a party, she chose to stay at home with her parents. They played board and card games most of the evening, then watched the television as they broadcast the fireworks going off over the Thames in London at midnight with a glass of sparkling wine each.

Steven called at about 12:30, and they all called out 'Happy New Year' to each other. Later, when snooping for more leftovers, they ended up having a little kitchen disco. It was silly and childish, and she absolutely loved it. At 1:30, Bryony kissed her parents good night and surreptitiously watched for a few minutes from the hallway as they slow danced to their wedding song.

She could tell that Isaac thought the evening was lame and boring, and when he started to slate it, she announced curtly and pointedly how much fun she'd had, putting an end to his critique.

At 8 am on New Year's Day, Isaac shouted her name so often and so loudly she had no choice but to wake up.

'What the hell is wrong with you?' She demanded angrily.

'I'm bored, Bry. I want you to get up,' he moaned.

'Do you really think that by waking me up like that, I'm going to be in a good mood and be fun to talk to? Stop being selfish and leave me to sleep.'

He left, and she tried to go back to sleep, but it was no use. She was awake now. And grumpy. And hungry.

She went downstairs to the kitchen, wondering what to have for breakfast. It was now 8:30 am, and no one else was up yet, but she knew her parents would be up before 9 am. She decided to make the whole household a full English breakfast.

No sooner had she put the sausages under the grill than she heard the shower being turned on. Someone was awake, and she'd put her life savings on it being her dad. She knew her mum would shower after, and they'd both come down together in about twenty minutes. Perfect. By that time, everything would be just about cooked and still piping hot. She wondered whether Steven and the boys would want to be woken up or not. Sometimes with a hangover, he could eat them out of house and at home; other times, he couldn't stomach even looking at food. It would depend on how much he'd had to drink last night. She hadn't heard him come in, and he'd left the house at 8 pm, so probably not.

'BRYONY!' she jumped so much, she dropped the tongs.

'Jeez, Isaac, you nearly gave me a heart attack!'

'Sorry, but you've got to come. You've got to come now.'

'Go where? What's the matter?'

'It's my parents.'

'Oh my God, are they ok?'

'NO! They're getting a divorce.'

'What?'

'I went round there this morning, just to check on them before you come over, and only Mum and Dad were up. Everyone else was still in bed, and they were sat there, just talking about their upcoming divorce, like it was a perfectly normal topic. And who the kids were going to live with and Dad's new apartment and how often they'd go over there, and when they were going to tell them. It was awful. You have to come now.'

‘Where? To your parent’s house? Isaac, I’m not going over there now.’

‘What? You have to. You have to help me fix it.’

‘I can’t.’

‘Of course, you can. We can’t let them get divorced.’

‘Isaac, stop. Just stop and think for a minute. What possible excuse could I have for going over to your parents before 9 am on New Year’s day? And even if I could think of a plausible excuse, what could I say? “So I hear you’re getting a divorce, well you should know that your dead son does not approve of this decision.”’

‘Oh my God, Bryony, it doesn’t matter. It doesn’t matter that you can’t think up a good excuse or how you know things you shouldn’t. All that matters is that we get over there immediately and make them change their minds before they tell the boys. Can’t you see that?’

‘No, Isaac. I can’t, and I won’t. You’re too upset. You’re not thinking rationally. I think you should go upstairs and take a few minutes to calm down. I will be up soon, and we will work out a plan together. But go quickly now because my parents will be down any minute, and they’ll hear us talking.’

Isaac stared at her in disbelief.

‘That’s all that you care about? My whole family is falling apart, my parents are making the biggest mistake of their lives, and they’re about to break my brothers’ hearts even more than they already have been. But heaven be damned, before we let Bryony’s parents hear Bryony muttering to herself in the kitchen. What kind of a girlfriend are you? How can you be so incredibly selfish? This is all about you. Everything is all about you these days. You are the worst.’

He stormed off out of the kitchen and away, probably back to his parent’s house, leaving Bryony gobsmacked and heartbroken all over again. Only when the smoke alarm went off did she realise she’d burnt the toast and the sausages were on fire.

Isaac did not return all day. Bryony spent a miserable first day of the New Year cooped up in her bedroom, waiting for his return. She was unable to settle enough to study or to read or to do anything really, except wait for him. She went to bed early, feeling exhausted and emotional.

She woke up freezing at 6 am the next morning. Isaac was back, but instead of shouting her awake, he just sat really close to her so she'd feel cold enough to wake. She didn't reprimand him this morning.

'Hi. How are you?' She ventured, sitting up and pulling the duvet tighter around her shivering shoulders.

His stony expression continued to stare at the wall, and he didn't reply.

'How was it yesterday? I presume you went home? Did they tell the boys? How did they take it?'

'I don't want to talk about it,' he whispered angrily.

'Isaac, come on. Talk to me. What are we gonna do, just sit here in silence?' She cajoled gently.

'I'm still angry with you,' he blurted out, louder this time. 'You weren't there for me when I needed you to be. You didn't care when I needed you to. You put your needs and wants ahead of mine. You always do. Even if I was overreacting or being unreasonable, a good girlfriend would have realised I just needed someone to help me, to calm me, to be with me.'

'Hey! Come on now, that's not fair. Isaac, you have to see that's not how it was. Of course, I care. I love them almost as much as I love you. But I couldn't go around there uninvited really early in the morning and discuss their private business with them. You have to see I couldn't do that. There are social rules one has to follow.'

‘Ooh, “There are social rules one has to follow.”’ Isaac mocked her scathingly. ‘You sound just like your mother. You two get more alike every day,’ he snarled as nastily as he could.

Bryony bit back a cruel retort and a sob in the same instance. She took a moment to calm herself and keep her voice steady.

‘Isaac, please understand. I still have a life to live…’

‘Wow! That’s real nice, Bryony.’

‘No, I just mean that...’

‘I know what you mean. You mean that your life is more important than mine, don’t you?’

‘Well, actually, I guess to me, it is.’

‘Wow! You are something else, do you know that?’

‘I don’t mean that in a bad way.’

‘Oh, you mean that in a loving, selfless way, do you?’

‘Isaac, please.’

‘Well, at least I know where I stand.’

‘Oh, come on, Babe, stop!’

‘Always in second place.’

‘I’m going to go and talk to your parents,’ she half shouted. It shut him up, she just hoped she hadn’t woken up anyone else in the house. ‘I am,’ she continued, quieter. ‘I promised you I would, so I’m going to.’

‘When?’

‘Today.’

‘Today?’ He said, standing up eagerly.

‘I was thinking at about eleven... ten o’clock.’

‘Ten o’clock? Four hours from now. Jesus Christ!’ He stood up and paced around the room. ‘Look, you carry on and let the social rules dictate your life. In the meantime, I am going to go and watch my family fall apart and be utterly helpless while doing so.’

He disappeared again, and Bryony lay back down in her bed and cried.

She showed up at the Spencer’s house at 9:30 am.

She left a little after 10:00 am.

The whole thing had been a disaster. The boys had all left to go and play football at a pitch they’d booked, and her arrival had clearly interrupted Melanie’s plans. Still, ever the gracious host, Melanie made her tea, and they sat together in the living room. They exchanged pleasantries, and the whole time, Isaac kept talking over Melanie, demanding Bryony ask about the divorce or suggesting inappropriate questions to ask, or making rude or stupid comments. This made her replies to Melanie stunted, forced, and, for the first time ever between them, awkward.

They managed to briefly discuss Christmas and plans for the New Year, how Bryony’s studies were going, and what she planned to do in the summer when her exams were over. Melanie told her how they’d met Eamon’s girlfriend, that Owen was now in a band, and how well Anthony was doing at school. By this time, Bryony had decided this wasn’t working, and she needed to get out of there. She burnt the inside of her mouth and throat by gulping down her tea, which was still too hot, but she didn’t care, and neither did Melanie.

She got out of there as fast as it was politely possible to do so, and she didn’t look back. She could tell from the look on Isaac’s face that he was furious with her, but quite frankly, she didn’t care. She was furious with him for putting her through that and angrier with herself for allowing herself to ignore her instincts.

Chapter Ten

Isaac didn't mention his family again for a while, and Bryony didn't broach the subject, aware he often needed time to process things. She did, however, amend her gruelling study schedule and incorporated more downtime, which meant she could spend more time doing what Isaac wanted to do. It was probably for the best, as she had massively overworked herself with her initial timetable.

They began to fall into a more sensible routine that suited them both, and everything was going well until she had a meeting with the careers advice teacher at school.

'Mrs Jenkins said I need to add more stuff to my CV if I want to get into a good uni,' she moaned, slinging her heavy bag off her shoulder and throwing herself dramatically onto her bed.

'Why? You're a massive nerd. You're a university's wet dream!' Isaac reasoned.

'Apparently, academic achievements are not enough to interest the big universities. They want to see a "more rounded persona,"' she quoted.

'What does that even mean?'

'It means I need to do other stuff that I can put on my personal statement that shows them that I'm not just a massive geek. I need to do volunteer work or a useful hobby or a team sport or, ideally, a job.'

'A job! But you already spend so much time studying! Surely university's are more interested in the fact that you're good at remembering stuff. Why would they care if you can get a job or not?'

'I don't know. Something about diverse interests and skill sets, time management, and responsibilities. I can't stomach the idea of a team sport, I have no hobbies other than reading, not even watching TV, as you have witnessed, and I don't see the point of doing volunteer work, so I am going to try and get a job. The experience will be good for me, and the money will come in useful.'

'What kind of job?'

'I don't know. I genuinely don't even know where to start. I know I'm too old for a paper-round but not old enough to work in a pub. I have no qualifications, no experience, and only limited times I can work, namely weekends and evenings, so I guess that leaves retail, cleaning, hospitality, or waitressing.'

'Jeez, that all sounds like hell. Maybe you could get a job in a sports shop. That could be cool.'

'I know nothing about sports.'

'I could teach you.'

'That's a hard pass.'

'So what are you thinking?'

'I mean, ideally, a bookshop. Or a fast food restaurant maybe, if I get a good discount.'

'Man, I miss food... and eating. I miss fried chicken and doughnuts.'

'In reality, I guess the first thing I need to do is find out who's hiring. Beggars can't be choosers, as they say.'

'Ooh, burgers. I miss burgers,'

'Stop waffling on about food,'

'Mmm, waffles.'

Bryony laughed for what felt like the first time all day. When Isaac was in this silly, playful mood, she didn't think it was possible for anyone, anywhere, to love someone as much as she loved him.

She was so relieved they were back in their happy place again that she didn't mind watching a couple of episodes of a cartoon with him, although she didn't get the point of the show at all. It made no sense to her, but Isaac thought it was hysterical, so she pretended to enjoy it too.

At dinnertime, she spoke with her parents about her plan to get a job and why. Naturally, they both thought it was a fantastic idea and vowed to keep a lookout for any places advertising for help. Her father promised to help her write a CV, and her mum said she'd go over some basic interview questions. By the end of the week, she had sent out over twenty-five emails with her CV attached and had three interviews lined up.

The first was at a super cool, bespoke fashion shop. The moment she walked in, she felt uncomfortable and inferior. She knew that even if she got offered the job, she wouldn't take it; her self-esteem and body confidence levels couldn't handle it. The second was at a fast food place, and she was amongst four other people going for the same position. She could tell from the expression on the interviewer's face when she told them she had no experience whatsoever that she would lose out on that one too. The final one was further away. She would need to get two buses there and back, but as she had a bus pass, that wasn't really an issue, except for the time it would take. Still, she reasoned, she could use that time to re-read her revision notes. It was in a coffee shop, and the manager assured her that experience wasn't necessary as she could train her up, but what she was looking for was someone reliable. She'd been let down too many times by people who were perpetually late or just didn't show up for a shift without any warning. She had two other members of staff whom she'd had for a long time who were brilliant, and she just needed one more to make up the team so they could cover all the shifts and allow others to have time off. The manager was also the owner and she was unbelievably lovely. The interview lasted for over an hour and felt more like a chat between old friends. Her name was Vee, and she was a single mum to twin seven-year-old boys called Cameron and Jeremiah or Cam and Jem. When they weren't in trouble, and when school was out, they were often hanging around but were usually pretty well-behaved. The other employees were a full-time member called Mary, who was a bit of a stress head, a complete clean freak, and absolutely wonderful. The other was a student called Joe who, like Bryony, was sitting his A' Level exams this year, so she fully anticipated that the two of them would be super stressed and need time off to study beforehand. And, as long as they were willing to work extra in the summer holidays, so they could all go on their holidays, that would be fine. Bryony agreed that would all work out, although she, too, had a holiday booked. They compared dates and found they all complemented each other, and Vee offered her the job straight away. Bryony accepted, and she said she would come after college the next day to begin training.

When she arrived home, her parents were delighted at the news and insisted they go out for dinner to celebrate. When she went upstairs, the greeting was far chillier.

'You got the job then,' he said when she entered.

'I did,' she responded, suddenly less jubilant. 'Third time lucky, I guess. Aren't you pleased for me?'

'Happy for you? Why would I be happy for you? You already spend all your time either at school or at the shrinks or studying, and now you're going to add a job to the many things you do without me.'

'Isaac,' she began softly, but he flinched away from her even though she couldn't touch him.

'Don't. Don't bother. I know you have to continue living your life, you have made that very clear. I also know you're going out for dinner with your parents, so go on – go out with your parents and celebrate the wonderful news.'

Bryony put her bag down but didn't rush off as he suggested. She sat near him on the bed but not close enough to impose upon his personal space.

'I am going in a minute, and I will celebrate with my parents because this is good news for me. However, I know this is bad news for you. I know you get bored and lonely. I know you only have me to keep you company. All I can say is that this moment in my life, with all my many responsibilities and claims on my time, are just temporary. You, my darling Isaac, are forever. We will not be short on time together.'

'It's not just that, Bry,' he said quietly, unable to look at her. 'You getting a job, it's the first thing you've been able to do that I will never, ever be able to. I'll never get a job. I'll never make money or buy a house. I'll never go out clubbing or get served at a pub. There's so much of life that I'll never do. It's just hard. That's all.'

Bryony couldn't think of anything that could ease the pain of this realisation. She sat with him for a while, but he eventually turned to her.

'It's okay, Bry. I know it sucks a bit for me, but you're right. This is good news for you. Go on, go and have fun with your mum and dad – or at least as much fun as you can!'

He smiled bravely, and her heart broke a little bit for him, but she figured that he maybe needed some alone time, so she begrudgingly left.

Isaac rallied himself, though it was clearly an effort for him. He wished her good luck the next morning when he found out she would go straight from college to the coffee shop. She did not return until gone 10 pm, and though she'd managed to get a message to her mother letting her know she'd have dinner at the coffee shop and she'd be back late, she could not get a similar message to Isaac. She returned happy but exhausted. As promised, Vee had begun training her how to make the various coffees and use the till. She was kind and patient, and fun. She met the twins, who were as lovely as they were different. She also met Mary and was happy to report that she was an angel. As hardworking as she was naturally cheerful, she constantly reassured her that they all make mistakes and not to worry about it all. The shop was not busy, just the regulars whom everyone knew by first name as well as their usual orders, plus a few commuters warming their fingers with a hot drink whilst they waited at the bus stop on that cold, dark February evening.

Mary spent most of her time chatting and laughing with Vee's two boys whilst Vee showed her the basics. They arranged her regular hours, she signed her contract, and Vee took her bank details. She would meet Joe at the weekend, but they both assured her she would love him, everyone did.

When she finally got home, Isaac wanted to chat but not about her day, he wanted to talk about people and things he knew, not stuff he didn't. She explained how tired she was and that she just wanted to have a shower and crawl into bed. When he scowled at her, she agreed to watch a couple of episodes of one of his shows, but when she put it on and sat on the bed next to him, she fell asleep almost instantly.

Bryony decided to do some Isaac damage control the next day after college. She raced home, made herself a quick sandwich, and ran up to him in her bedroom. She dropped her bag on the floor and, not taking her coat off, beckoned for Isaac to follow her. She had decided that part of their problem at the moment was that they spent all of their time cooped up in her bedroom and, as today was a beautiful, albeit cold, day, they should be out enjoying the world. She led them to a small wooded area that was infrequently visited by anyone. They sat upon an overturned tree and stared up at the blue sky, watching Bryony's breath rise up in clouds. They chatted amiably, mostly reminiscing about their relationship highlights. Bryony gossiped about a few of their friends, the bits she'd overheard through chance rather than experiencing it as part of the group.

They returned home well after dark, by which time Bryony was so cold she could barely move. Her mother fussed over her, trying to warm her up with hot soup, blankets, and a hot water bottle. She couldn't adequately explain why she had been out for so long, so she mumbled something about clearing her head and then went upstairs as quickly as possible. After a hot shower, she jumped into bed, and they giggled stupidly at a ridiculous teen drama they found on Netflix.

By putting him first occasionally, Bryony bought herself brownie points with Isaac, and she was able to study, go to school, the therapist, and her new job without unsettling him too much.

The first Saturday morning at work was something of a shock to the system compared to the gentle training evening she'd spent here. Saturdays saw the queue to be served go out of the door, all the tables needed clearing or cleaning, and there was a dangerously low number of clean glasses and cups available on the shelf. Vee was making the drinks, and Mary was busy taking the next customer's orders. Bryony didn't need to be told; she could see what needed to be done. She put her bag in the staff room at the back, put on her apron, washed her hands, and headed to the dishwasher. She unloaded that, then went to clear and clean up some tables and reload the dishwasher. Vee and Mary were delighted with her, and though she worked her socks off, she was surprised by how much fun she had. Vee was not one to get stressed under pressure, and her gentle guidance and good humour helped Bryony get everything done that she needed to. Mary clearly did feel the stress, but she was efficient and super clean and tidy, so it never felt chaotic, and Vee managed to keep her stress levels down as much as possible. They were both quick to tell her how well she had done and how happy they were with her work.

The next day was Mary's day off, and Bryony met Joe for the first time. He was a six-foot frame of skin and bone with terrible hair but a kind face. He had obviously been with them for a long time as he knew the regulars well enough to banter with them, and he was efficient and well-trained. He greeted Bryony with a wide smile that lit up his whole face.

The day wasn't as busy as the day before, and occasionally, Vee would go and do some paperwork in her tiny office for an hour or so. Joe turned out to be really friendly with a dry sense of humour, and she could tell they would get on well working together. When they weren't serving people, they discussed their A' Level choices and their horrendous workloads. They talked about universities and how they intended to celebrate once they'd finished their exams. It turned out they were both planning holidays to Spain or thereabouts. Admittedly though, they were having very different holidays. Bryony was going to Tenerife with her family, whereas Joe was going to Ibiza with five of his best mates for "the ultimate lads' holiday." Bryony learned that most of his mates he had been friends with since primary school, but one of them they met at senior school and one through gaming online, and when they first went to meet him, they all went together in case he turned out to be a 45-year-old weirdo! She also found out that he had a girlfriend called Kirsty and that they'd been dating for a little over a year now and that, whilst it was Joe who was in a band, Kirsty was actually the musically gifted one.

Bryony was pleased when she found out he had a girlfriend. It instantly relieved a lot of tension knowing he was in a relationship and therefore was unlikely to be flirty with her at all. And to ensure that it stayed that way, she lied to him. When he started asking her about her friends and boyfriend status, she realised she had absolutely nothing to say. She didn't really have any friends, and her boyfriend was a ghost, so what else could she say? So, she pretended that Isaac was still very much alive and spoke about him freely. She also pretended to still be a part of his clique of friends, though she tried not to mention them too much.

Having established that they were both in a loving relationship, they both relaxed more and fell into an easy comradery. He introduced her to some of the regulars, and they quickly developed a sibing-esque rivalry regarding anything competitive they could find. Who could bottle flip the fastest? Joe. Who could create the highest cardboard coaster tower? Bryony. Who could pour the fastest latte, Joe– for now, she warned him.

When she got home that night, having managed to read and learn much more of her revision notes due to the rubbish Sunday service of the buses, she told Isaac all about Joe and how she hadn't told Joe that Isaac was dead. Initially, Isaac had been surprised and annoyed that Joe was a boy and not a girl like he'd assumed; however, as Bryony told him about his long-term girlfriend and how he was a computer geek, Isaac calmed down. When he asked what he looked like, Bryony was prepared. She'd taken a sneaky photo of Joe ready to show Isaac when he inevitably asked. He wasn't kind about Joe's appearance, and Bryony had to stop herself from getting defensive on her new friend's behalf. Still, it seemed to assuage Isaac's insecurities, for now at least.

Chapter Eleven

'Hello, Bryony, come on in,' Dr Will greeted her with his usual warmth.

Bryony smiled her goodbye at Jax, who was still waiting for Liz.

'Goodbye, Bryony,' Jax smiled knowingly. He had finally learned her name and seemed intent on using it as much as possible. She rolled her eyes, but her smile remained intact.

'I'm sure Dr Sanders won't be long, Mr Ramsworth,' Dr Will assured him.

'Goodbye, Mr Ramsworth,' Bryony said, delighted with the new information about his surname. Dr Will smiled at her indulgently as if they had planned this exchange. Jax scowled as they closed the door on him.

Dr Will took his usual seat in the armchair.

'What will you play with today, I wonder?' He said aloud as Bryony took her usual seat at the far end of the sofa next to the box of assorted toys, sensory items, and fidget spinners. She rifled through the box, discarding items she'd already played with, and found a box at the bottom. Inside it were smaller boxes of coloured playdo along with tools and guidance sheets.

'Can I play with this?' She asked, lifting it out.

'Of course, pull the table across so you have something to lean on.' She did, and Dr Will removed the plant that was on the table.

He left her to play unbothered for a while.

'Last week, we began talking about your friends at school or lack thereof.'

'Oh yes, what a fun topic,' Bryony said without looking up.

’We don’t have to talk about that,’ he said.

‘No, no. Don’t worry. I don’t mind,’ she said, and when he said no more, Bryony proceeded to tell him all about Isaac’s friends and how she started hanging out with them when she started going out with Isaac, foregoing her other friendships even though she never felt like she belonged in the group. In fact, she hadn’t had a female friend or companion since she started seeing Isaac. She reflected on how she grew close to Isaac’s mum and that she was really the only woman she had had a positive relationship with for years.

‘Had your relationship with your own mother deteriorated before or after you started dating Isaac?’ He asked, not in a judgemental tone, just a curious one, as ever, but it gave Bryony reason to pause.

‘I suppose we grew apart after I started seeing Isaac. She didn’t really approve of him, you see. In fact, if we’re being honest here, she hated that I had a life with him, that I didn’t just stay in my room and study all the time like I did before. I think she hated that I wasn’t getting good grades anymore. She thought I was wasting my time and that Isaac was dragging me down.’

‘Dragging you down. In what way?’

‘Well, up until meeting Isaac, I was always getting straight A’s and was on track to go to Oxford University. My older brother Steven goes there too. Obviously, it’s a really prestigious uni, renowned throughout the world as being first-class. By being with Isaac, I wasn’t studying enough to go there; ergo, he was bringing me down. In my mother’s eyes.’

‘Did she say all of this to you? Can you recall instances where she expressed these opinions, or are these opinions you have supposed through other means?’

‘She really didn’t like Isaac. I really think she was a little bit glad he was dead. She just wished I wasn’t so sad about it. But in answer to your question, no, I don’t think she ever specifically said those words. She didn’t really need to; you could just tell by looking at her. Besides, we sort of stopped talking to each other as much. It got harder and harder for us to communicate civilly. We argued all the time. I know she blamed Isaac for that.'

'You know this how? Because she said so?'

'She implied that he was a bad influence on me,'

'Do you think he was a bad influence on you?'

Bryony didn't answer straight away. She tried to be as honest with Dr Will as possible, knowing she was already doing a big lie about Isaac's ghost and therefore wanting everything else to be as genuine as possible.

'I think that before Isaac, I was imbalanced. I had no life experience at all. Literally, all I would do was study and read novels. That's not healthy. It may get you on the fast track to Oxford, but it doesn't make you a very rounded person. So, when he came along, he balanced me out. He injected fun and spontaneity. He made me socialise and experience more of what the world had to offer, possibly, maybe a bit too much. There was maybe a bit too much partying or just hanging out together, which inevitably led to poorer grades, but I believe that eventually, we found a balance, our equilibrium. Mum just didn't see it that way.'

'She said that?'

'Not in so many words, no. But my grades were getting worse, and I did next to no studying, so…'

'How much of this disapproval you felt actually came from your mother, and how much was from you?'

'What? I didn't disapprove of myself.'

'Didn't you?'

Bryony stopped creating the playdo rose and looked at him. She had never considered this before and couldn't entirely dismiss it.

'Going back to the time before you met Isaac, you said you felt your life was imbalanced. You did nothing but study and had no fun at all?'

'Well, no, not no fun. I used to do stuff, other stuff that I enjoyed, like cinema and theatre and stuff like that. And if I'm being really completely honest, I did actually enjoy studying. I quite like learning stuff, sad as that is.'

'Why is that sad?'

'Not sad as in boohoo, just sad as in what a dork!'

'Is it a problem for you, being thought of as a dork?'

'No, it never used to be, but now I guess, or at least with Isaac, it did.'

They let that hang in the air for a moment.

'Just to go back once more to the activities you enjoyed before Isaac, you said cinema and theatre. Who did you go to these with? The friends you stopped hanging out with when you started seeing Isaac?'

'Erm, no, actually, not much. Usually, I did stuff with Mum.'

She dropped the fact like a clanger, and it felt heavy and uncomfortable, polluting the atmosphere. Dr Will continued in this vein, making her question everything she had assumed about both her relationship with Isaac, her mum, and almost everyone else until the session was up and her head was spinning.

'Take some time to yourself to process some of what we have talked about in today's session Bryony. You've got a lot to consider. We've covered a lot of ground. Remember to be gentle with yourself and be sure to drink plenty of water.'

Bryony grinned at him. He was always going on about staying hydrated, claiming it was a really simple solution to most of life's problems, and it had become a standing joke between them.

When she left, she stopped to do up her shoelace, and Jax exited his session as she did.

'Hi, hot stuff. How was your session?' She grinned at him whilst desperately trying to remember his surname. Their flirty little exchanges had become part of the session for Bryony, and she needed some comic relief to ease the ache in her brain.

'Oh, you know, fire is bad, don't play with matches, that sort of thing. How was yours?'

'Oh, you know, I've just got to question every exchange with everyone I've ever spoken to, that sort of thing!'

They grinned as they went down the stairs together, exchanging little quips the whole way down. When they left the house, they casually said goodbye and parted ways, Jax walking down the street and Bryony toward her mother's car.

'Who was that?' She asked, nodding at Jax as he ambled down the road; he'd glanced back a couple of times at Bryony.

'That's Jax. He sees a different doctor from me, but we're on the same floor at the same time, so we run into each other every now and then. He's serious trouble but quite fun to pass the time of day with,' she confessed.

'Okay, is there anything romantic between you?' She probed.

'Mum!'

'What? I can ask, can't I?'

'I have a boyfriend! I mean, you know… you know what I mean.'

'I know honey, I know. If ever you want to talk to me about moving on or not moving on or anything at all, you know you always can. I know you've got Dr Will to talk to, but I'm here too.'

‘I know, and maybe one day I’ll take you up on that, but I need to sort through everything in my own head before I talk to anyone else.’

‘Whatever suits you, darling,’

‘Thanks, Mum.’

‘I am just a little bit worried that you’re under an awful lot of pressure at the moment, what with your exams and whatever you're discussing with Dr Will. I don’t want there to be too much going on in that big, beautiful brain of yours.’

‘Yeah, I know what you’re saying, but I’m all good at the moment. I’m compartmentalising what I need to, and I’m not too stressed.’

‘Okay, that’s good. But you must know that if it does get too much, just tell me. We’ll drop everything to help you.’

‘Thanks, Mum,’ she muttered, suddenly feeling overwhelmed with emotion. She looked out of the window and surreptitiously wiped her tears away as her mother drove off.

Her first conversation with Isaac when she got home was not as warm.

‘I followed you,’ he opened with. She looked at him non-plussed.

‘I followed you to your therapy session,’ he clarified.

‘Okay,’ Bryony began slowly, casting her mind back over her meeting with Dr Will today, trying to figure out why she was getting such a frosty reception from Isaac.

‘We talked mainly about Mum today. You know all my issues with her, so I don’t see why you’re getting so worked up.’

‘Yeah, we’ll come onto the fact that your mum thinks I’m a complete loser later. First, let’s talk about Mr “Hotstuff,” who you walked out with. No wonder you've never wanted me to come along to a session before. You're too busy flirting your slaggy arse off.'

'Oh my God, Isaac, it's not like that. I literally only know Jax from the waiting area outside the therapy room. We've never exchanged numbers, never met up, or even talked to each other outside of that place. I know it may seem a little flirty, but it's just some stupid, harmless banter that helped to calm my nerves when I first went. I called him "hotstuff" 'cos he's a pyromaniac – he's obsessed with fire. It was a joke!'

'Well, you two certainly seemed very cosy as you came down the stairs together. You were practically arm-in-arm. It certainly didn't seem like harmless banter.'

'How do you know that? Where were you? You must have been close, but I didn't see you anywhere.'

'I was close enough to see the goo-goo eyes you were making at him. And, of course, you didn't see me. I was invisible, a new skill I have learned that you'd know about if you spent any time at all with your old dead boyfriend, but you're too busy hanging out with newer models, ones with a heartbeat and pulse,' he spat.

'Isaac, you're being ridiculous!'

'No, you're being ridiculous!' he began. If he had any blood left in his body, he'd have angry red cheeks by now; Bryony knew it. 'You literally had no time for me over the last few weeks, and yet I'm supposedly the absolute love of your life. Why the hell have I come back if not because of the adoration of my "heartbroken" girlfriend?' He demanded.

'Isaac, of course, I adore you. You know that. I don't know what more to tell you other than he means absolutely nothing to me. I really couldn't care less if I never saw Jax again. What I am interested in, though, is that you can make yourself invisible to me. When did you learn that? How did you learn it? Is this the first time you've spied on me?'

'Don't try and turn this around on me, Bryony. I am not the bad guy here. You're the one flirting with other guys and not spending any time with me.'

Bryony sat down heavily on her bed and put her head in her hands. She didn't have the energy to have this argument again.

'What do you want from me, Isaac 'cos honestly, I don't think I have anything left to give,' she said wearily.

'What do I want? I want to be able to have conversations with other people, so I don't have to rely so heavily on you all the time. I want to have something, anything else to do other than hanging around waiting for you to have some time for me, so I am not so completely and utterly bored all day and all night. I want to stop feeling so angry all the damned time. I want to not be dead! But most of all, I want to be more of a priority for you because you are my only priority, and I know you're moving on with your life. You're leaving me behind, and you're going to stop loving me.'

His final words were choked out thickly. Bryony didn't know if ghosts could cry, but she knew they could feel the depth of pain that makes the living do it. She felt her own eyes moisten, and once again, she felt the injustice of not being able to touch, to hold, to comfort, and reassure her poor, depressed boyfriend.

'Isaac, your very being here is a testament to how much I love you. You must never ever question that. It is a fact, immovable and solid. I love you. I will love you for the rest of my life and undoubtedly beyond. However, love doesn't mean we have to spend every minute of every day together. And I think that this moment in our lives is like a test. We both know that if you were alive, you and I would not be in each other's pockets the way we are now. You would have your family, hanging out with the boys, football and fishing – all that sort of stuff that you used to do without me. I also think that even without you being dead, this time would be a bit of a strain on our relationship because of the pressure of the exams. You know what a stress head I am. What I am saying is that you need to have more patience with me. Let me have some time to do the stuff I need to do, like studying and therapy. I will, in return, ensure to make you more of a priority from now on. And I promise that come the summer, nothing will be able to keep us apart.'

Isaac said nothing for a while. She could tell from the way his shoulders relaxed that whilst he was still mad and still sad, he had softened a little bit.

'I don't ever want you to talk to that kid at therapy again,' he said as a final clause. Bryony was surprised. Isaac had never been jealous before, but then, he'd never had cause to, so reluctantly, she agreed.

Chapter Twelve

During the Easter holidays, her mother insisted that she take a break from her relentless studies, and they both used the vouchers they received at Christmas to go on a spa day.

'We could make an evening of it,' she suggested, trying a little too hard to sound nonchalant. 'We could do the spa day on the Tuesday, say, stay overnight in a hotel, then go for lunch and do some shopping on the Wednesday, if you want.'

She dared to glance a Bryony to judge her reaction. Bryony carefully kept her expression as neutral as possible. She had really wanted to spend as much time with Isaac during this much-needed break as possible. She had agreed to work a couple more shifts at the coffee shop to cover Mary's holiday, as well as trying to fit in a fairly gruelling study schedule.

'I thought we were saving that until the summer,' she said carefully.

'Well, we could, but we've got our trip to Tenerife then. I have some annual leave to use up before April, and I really think you could use a break. Not to mention some new clothes, it will be lovely to see you out of those big jumpers for a change.'

'Oh, Mum, you know I feel the cold much more than everyone else, and I still have to work at the coffee shop,' she argued, attempting to put her off.

'Well, if you're that concerned about it, then we can just go for the spa day, then dinner. We will be home the same night, so you just need to book one day into your calendar.'

She clearly wasn't going to take no for an answer. Bryony agreed and went upstairs to tell Isaac the news.

'Oh my god, that's going to be really awkward, isn't it?'

'Awkward? I wouldn't say awkward, just boring. But I can't get out of it, so we'll just have to deal with it.'

'Hahahaha, you and your mum getting hers and hers massages. It is definitely going to get awkward.'

'Shut up, no, it won't. Besides, you're going to be there too.'

'Erm, what now? I don't think so. You're on your own with this one, babe. I may have to live for eternity, so I cannot have the image of your mum naked going around in my head!'

'Eww, gross! Stop perv. Why would you see my mum naked? If we get massages, we just lay down on our front. You won't see anything. Plus, I know her, I know what she's like. She'll relax and go to sleep for most of the afternoon! We could spend some time together walking around some beautiful gardens. And, as my contingency plan against looking mental, I can wear a Bluetooth earpiece, so it looks like I'm just on my phone.

'Err, Bryony, I don't know. It sounds kinda creepy hanging around in a spa!'

'Hang on a minute, Mister. You're the one always going on about us spending time together, and here I am offering you a bona fide two to three hours of my undivided attention, and you're not sure?

'What else are you doing? And who, other than me, will know that you're being a perv? I already know that you're a perv, so it really makes no odds to me.'

This time Isaac laughed, and Bryony's heart sang. She loved him so much when he was chilled and playful.

'Okay, fine, but I will demand some sort of compensation if my eyeballs are burned out by the sight of old lady bodies.'

***

The spa her mother booked turned out to be approximately two hours drive from home. It was a beautiful day. Her mother played the chill-out playlist they had made years ago, and they sang along to Adele, Sarah Mclachlan, and Otis Redding with the windows down. Isaac was on his best behaviour, sitting silently in the back of the car.

The spa hotel was super swanky, and Bryony instantly regretted refusing to stay over. After a hard day's spa, a hot bubble bath with their luxury oils and potions sounded very tempting. They checked in and changed into their complimentary robes and slippers. Her mother was surprisingly un-annoying, and Bryony found herself enjoying herself.

They decided to go for a swim before their massages, both of them reflecting on how long it had been since they'd been swimming together. They used to go every week, and a pang of guilt rippled through Bryony, though her mother didn't seem to notice it.

After their swim and an intolerable five minutes in both the sauna and the steam room, they met their massage therapists. Her mother had opted for the Indian head massage, hot stone back massage, and pedicure. Bryony went with the Indian head massage, Swedish back massage, and manicure.

Isaac informed Bryony that he didn't think he could handle watching the two of them get their treatments and that he would go and explore the grounds and meet her after. She vaguely nodded in his general area, secretly relieved as she knew she was really going to enjoy this and could relax even more if he wasn't loitering.

She was correct. Neither of them spoke most of the afternoon as their treatments were carried out, allowing the music, the smells, and the massages to completely remove their stresses.

When they finally emerged into the relaxation room with their herbal teas and fruit juices, they both felt like they were floating. They sat side by side in their loungers by the pool in companionable silence, Bryony admiring the taupe nail colour she'd chosen. Her mother lay back and suddenly looked so serene and content Bryony felt a rush of warmth toward her.

'Thank you for this, Mum,' she whispered to her as her mother's eyes grew heavy. 'You were right; it was exactly what I needed. If you want to have a little doze here, I'll go and explore the grounds for a while.'

'Are you sure you'll be okay on your own, darling? I could really use just an hour's nap.' Bryony knew if she said no, her mum would drag herself up, ignore her tiredness and keep Bryony company. With renewed affection, she covered her mum with a fleece blanket she found in a nearby box of blankets, kissed her forehead, and whispered, 'I'll be fine, Mum, you sleep.'

It was a lot chillier outside than it looked, and Bryony was pleased she'd had the foresight to put her socks in her pocket and to bring a fleece draped across her shoulders like an overgrown shawl.

She had no idea where Isaac was and decided the best thing to do was walk right to the edge of the grounds and circle the perimeter. She placed the Bluetooth buds in her ears and googled the building she was at. The spa was set on 5.2 acres of land! God, she hoped he'd stayed nearby and would join her soon. Otherwise, this would turn into an exercise workout rather than a relaxing stroll.

She wandered through a little wooded area and found herself in a tiny, deserted paradise complete with a pond, benches, and, looking breathtakingly handsome in the bright April sun, Isaac.

'Hey,' he said, walking over to meet her with a huge smile on his face. 'Guess what, this place has its own golf course and guess who I saw practising there – Rory McIlroy! Can you believe it?'

Bryony shook her head in disbelief, though, if she was being honest, she had no idea who that was.

‘Yeah, I spied on him for a bit, but they were heading off through the course. I couldn’t watch for long ‘cos I didn’t know how long you’d be. How was your massage?’ He asked as they began walking.

‘Incredible, I felt like jelly when it finished,’ she confessed, noticing the clumps of bluebells spreading across the floor.

‘Neither of you accidentally dropped a fart whilst it happened, then?’ He enquired wickedly.

‘Nothing audible, at least,’ Bryony grinned.

They walked unperturbed by strangers for an hour and a half. They talked about Isaac’s new invisibility skill and what other things he may be able to learn, given time, both of them hoping it would be the ability to touch and feel each other again. They discussed the possibility of other ghosts being out there and where, how, and if Isaac should go looking for them. At Isaac’s insistence, they went to spy on the famous golfer when they realised he was close by and, though Bryony didn’t recognise him, even after Isaac had pointed him out, she still felt a tiny thrill about being near someone famous and Isaac’s excitement was palpable. They watched him take a few shots, and then both agreed that golf was not a sport that interested either of them, even when played by professionals, and besides, Bryony was too cold to stand there anymore.

The sun had gone down by the time they neared the building, and Bryony’s teeth were chattering despite the blanket. She received a text from her mum the moment she stepped inside.

Mum - Hi darling, I’m awake. Where are you?

Bryony - Just in reception. R U still in relaxation room? Meet there?

Mum - No meet me by the lockers. We should get changed for dinner – I’m starving!

Bryony – On way

When she got there, her mother was deep in conversation with a staff member. They stopped talking as Bryony approached.

'Darling, I have been chatting with Grace here, and she's just informed me about an excellent deal they're doing. We could stay overnight here in this hotel and have a three-course meal in their Michelin-starred restaurant and get breakfast thrown in, in the morning, all for a very reasonable price. What do you think? Can you stay, and we'll head home in the morning?'

Bryony grinned from ear to ear.

'That sounds brilliant, Mum, thanks.'

Her mother reciprocated the grin and passed her credit card over to the eager Grace, who disappeared to organise their stay.

'Aww, thanks for this, Mum. I'm really having a great time. Are you sure it's not too expensive?'

'No darling, It's absolutely extortionate, but sometimes you just have to say, "Sod it, I bloody deserve this." And we do.'

Right on cue, Grace returned with a very butch man to help carry their not-very-heavy hold-alls up to their room. The room turned out to be a suite and a very luxurious one at that. Her mother asked Grace to ensure there were plenty of bathroom smellies so Bryony could enjoy a soak later, and Bryony looked through the little catalogue she was given to pick out pyjamas for them both. Trying not to visibly balk at the pricelist, she chose the cheapest set for both of them and attempted to hand the order form to Grace, but her mother checked it over first and made some alterations.

Grace assured them they'd have all they needed for the evening before they returned from their dinner and let them know they had a reservation at the restaurant in twenty-five minutes.

When Grace and the butch man had left, Bryony and her mother giggled like school girls and raced around to explore every inch of the suite. Her mother called her father whilst Bryony got dressed for dinner, then she too made herself presentable and insisted they pose for a few selfies before heading downstairs, even though they were already ten minutes late.

At first, Bryony felt self-conscious in the incredibly posh restaurant, aware she was in some fairly old clothes and that her hair was still greasy from the massage oils earlier. When her mother visited the ladies room, she asked Isaac, as surreptitiously as possible, if she looked okay. He grinned at her.

'Babe, you look stunning,' he said without hesitation.

'I don't want you to just say what you think I want to hear, babe. I genuinely need to know if there's anything I can do to make myself look better,' she attempted to say all this without moving her lips.

'And I am telling you, babe, that you are positively glowing. Look,' he pointed out her reflection in the mirror by the bar. She was surprised to admit that he was right. Her hair actually seemed to fall rather sexily around her face, which was clear and fresh, looking after both the massage and the walk in the cold air. She looked relaxed, natural, and radiating health. She couldn't help but smile. Her mother returned.

'What are you smiling at?' She asked.

'Oh, just… actually, I was smiling at my own reflection,' she confessed a little bashfully. 'I just thought I looked quite pretty in this light.'

'In this light! Oh, darling, you look beautiful in any light. I know you won't believe me because you think I'm just biased, and yes, admittedly, I am, but that doesn't make me wrong. I really and truly believe you are the full package. I love showing off about you, you know I do, and please, please believe me, it's not just because you are so clever and kind and thoughtful and funny. You really have no idea how totally gorgeous you are, do you? Huh, well, maybe that just adds to the overall charm that it is you, I suppose. Still, I wish you could see yourself the way I do and stop selling yourself short all the time.'

'Selling myself short? How do I do that?'

'Oh, you know, lots of ways,' she said vaguely. Bryony immediately knew she was being coy.

'Do you think I was selling myself short by dating Isaac?' She asked before she could stop herself. She glanced nervously at Isaac, who was suddenly concentrating wholly on her mother. There were so many things she had assumed about her mother, especially where Isaac was concerned, and since her meeting with Dr Will, she wanted her mother's point of view. She just wished she'd asked for it when Isaac wasn't around to hear it.

Her mother considered the question carefully, nibbling on a breadstick to stall.

'As your mum, I was never going to think anyone was good enough for you,' she admitted. She looked as though she was going to say more when the waiter came over to take their order. Bryony bit back her frustration, ordering quickly. She worried her mother would change the subject, but she didn't. She looked Bryony straight in the eye.

'I don't think it's a secret that I wasn't Isaac's biggest fan,' she said frankly.

'I don't understand why, though. He loves me. Loved me. He was good to me. Kind and gentle and so much fun. Is it because of the studying thing?'

'The studying thing?'

'Yeah, 'cos, you know, I stopped studying as much, and my grades got worse, so I wouldn't get into Oxford Uni.'

'Bryony, Oxford was your dream, not mine. I distinctly remember when Steven decided he wanted to go to Oxford

University because he thought it was the best, you were about ten at the time, and you looked at me and said, "I'm going to go there too, Mummy." Your little face was so serious and determined. I told you what a prestigious school it was and how it would be very hard to get into it, and you assured me that you didn't care how hard it was. It was your "biggest ever wish." Do you remember that at all? Your father and I giggled about it, and we did not expect for one moment that you would be as steadfast and tenacious as you were in chasing that "wish." We knew Steven would, he's always been headstrong and ambitious, but you really surprised us. In a lovely way, obviously.

'So when Isaac came along, and your grades inevitably began dropping, it was disappointing but not altogether that surprising. You'd found a new priority, a new "wish," that's all.'

Their starters came out, and they effused over the food for a while. Bryony was ravenous, and whilst she tried to eat daintily and in a lady-like fashion, she was too hungry, and the starter was too good. Her prawns disappeared within a few mouthfuls.

Unaffected by the food, the smell, the warmth of the room, or the cosiness of the chair, Isaac urged Bryony to continue questioning her mum.

'So, if it wasn't my grades that bothered you, what was your issue with Isaac?' She pressed, non-too-subtly.

Her mother had a sip of wine and assessed her for a moment.

'Bryony, you adored Isaac, I know you did, and you're finally starting to get back to being and feeling normal again. Plus, you and I are just starting to get on again. The last thing I want to do is to jeopardise that by trash-talking your beloved dead boyfriend. I wasn't his biggest fan, but I know you were, and I can respect that, so can't we just leave it as it is?'

'No!' Isaac exclaimed loudly. Bryony forced herself not to acknowledge him.

'Dr Will suggested that the reason our relationship has suffered so much over the past few years is that I was projecting my disappointment with my own decisions onto you. That way, I didn't have to take the blame or admit it was me who was annoyed at myself. I think that he was pretty much right about that one. I just think it would help me if I could understand where you were coming from over the whole Isaac thing 'cos maybe I have massively misconstrued it.'

The main meal arrived before her mother could answer, but she smiled at her thoughtfully. Bryony had ordered a decadent, rich, and creamy pasta that smelled so incredible that she had difficulty controlling herself. Her mother's seafood stew had sounded disgusting, but now it was here, it looked and smelled amazing. How can stew look so pretty?

For a few minutes they both barely spoke, instead revelling in the most delicious food they had every had. Finally they began a rather staccato conversation as they spoke between mouthfuls.

'How are you getting with Dr Will?'

'Yeah, really well, actually. He's really nice. He just makes me reassess everything I'd taken for granted.'

'Oh really, like what?'

'All sorts of things. Like if my friendship with Dana, Ash, and Jorgia is as irreparable as I originally thought or, you know if I'm as big a disappointment to you as I think I am.'

Her mother's fork clattered noisily as she dropped it on her plate. She stopped eating to stare horrified at Bryony.

'A disappointment!' She exclaimed a little too loudly. She lowered her voice and continued earnestly. 'Bryony, you could never, ever be a disappointment to me. You may make mistakes or do things I don't necessarily agree with, but that doesn't make you a disappointment. You're a teenager. These are your formative years. You are naturally going to get things wrong and mess things up, and that's all part of the learning curve, but you can never, never disappoint me. Do you understand?'

Bryony nodded, taken aback by the intensity of her mother's reaction. When she was satisfied Bryony got it, her mother returned to her food and, a moment or so later, so did Bryony.

'This really is the most incredible thing I have ever eaten, but please do not tell your father I said so. He still believes his shepherd's pie is celebrity chef level.'

'Oh God, I know. I mean, it's good and all, but it's just…'

'Shepherd's pie.' Her mother finished, and they both laughed. They finished their last bites, feeling delectably satisfied. The chef was clever enough not to fall into the trap of putting too much on the plate. They must have known that whoever ate those meals would have to finish every last bit, so they took care not to overstuff their clients. Bryony would have been completely satisfied if Isaac wasn't staring at her meaningfully. She sat forward in her chair.

'So, sorry, going back to what we were talking about earlier, I guess my question is then, why did you disapprove so much of Isaac?'

'Because Bryony,' her mother said, a little exasperated, 'He changed you, and you broke my heart.'

'Was everything okay with your meals?' The waiter asked expectantly.

'Yes, everything was delicious, thank you. Please pass our sincerest compliments to your chef.'

The waiter nodded a little smugly as if he had been expecting such a response. He turned to Bryony.

'Yes, it was incredible,' she confirmed. He walked away to go and interrupt another group whilst they were in the middle of a very deep conversation. She looked anxiously at her mother, who sighed and sat up, so they were very near each other.

'We were so close, darling. Do you remember? We did everything together. Maybe I was naïve to think we were going to Gilmore Girls our way through adolescence, but I thought our relationship would weather any storm.

'When Isaac came along, you dropped me like a sack of spuds, and that was okay. He was your first love; of course, you were going to be obsessed. I mean, I had hoped that maybe you'd be able to find a little bit of time to hang out with your mum, but no. So that was one thing. But then you began acting like I was your enemy or something—some archetypal bad guy who always ruined your fun and made you do boring stuff. You began treating me differently. Disrespecting me and acting like I was some fuddy-duddy old loser who didn't know you at all, and that broke my heart too. You would never hang out at home, you'd always go over to his house, and you'd talk about Melanie as if she was some sort of maternal superhero that you'd been missing all your life. Now that's always a difficult pill for a loving mother to swallow – that you've been outmothered by a younger, cooler model.' She smiled at Bryony, trying to make light of it, but she could see the pain still in her mother's eyes. 'But again, I could take that. What I couldn't stand, and my real problem with Isaac, was that he could make you doubt yourself.

'We raised you to be an independent, confident, self-assured young woman. You were headstrong and unique. You had your opinions, and you were confident enough to voice them, but somehow, amazingly, you were also happy to reassess them and say you were wrong if someone pointed out something you maybe hadn't considered before, and I was so incredibly proud of you for that. You were so enigmatic and gracious. But with Isaac, you seemed to lose all that. You seemed to lose you. You did what he wanted to do. You hung out with who he wanted to and where he wanted to. You know yourself how you let your other friendships fall away, and again, that happens. But your opinions became his opinions, and they were fixed and rigid. Then you began to see yourself the way Isaac saw you. I've no doubt you were beautiful to him as long as it was presented in a certain way. You wore the same clothes the girls in his group wore, the same makeup, the same hairstyles. You even started talking like them. You lost all that wonderful individuality that made you, you. You became diluted. A carbon copy of Monroe and the like, just to fit in and please Isaac, so you wouldn't be labelled a geek or a whats-the-word… a Try-hard. That is what my problem was with Isaac. He changed you in the worst possible way, and from where I'm standing, he didn't add anything except his continued presence.'

She sighed heavily and took a sip of wine. From the corner of her eye, Bryony watched Isaac storm off.

'I'm sorry, darling. That must feel horrible to hear. I know you loved him, but you never shared that part of your life with me. You shut me out, so I don't know how he rocked your world from your point of view. I'm willing to listen. I'd love to hear about it if you're ready to talk about it.'

Bryony suddenly felt exhausted. She wished Isaac had stayed to hear more, but she wanted to be honest with her mum.

'I guess I never felt special the way you saw me until Isaac saw me. He really did make me feel special, Mum, and I really do love him, did love him… whatever. But ultimately, I think you're right. You're one of the many people I treated appallingly because I was so obsessed with him. And maybe I did change, and Isaac was undoubtedly a factor in that, but don't you think you're placing too much blame on him? It was me who changed. Me who hurt and disrespected you. Me who chose Isaac over everything else. I think most of your issues are with me, not him.'

'Of course. If he had changed another girl who was not my daughter, I wouldn't have minded one bit. It's just it's hard to lay all the blame on you when it only happened when he came along. Still, maybe you are right. Everyone knows teenagers are meant to hate their parents and go through crazy hormonal episodes. And similarly, I am probably partly to blame, too, for not embracing him as much as I could have and not making him feel as welcome as I should have.'

The waiter hovered nearby. Her mum made eye contact with him.

'Would you like to order dessert, Madam?'

Victoria looked at her daughter.

'Yes, we would, but we would like to have them sent to our room,'

'Of course, Madam.'

Bryony's eyes lit up delightedly. It would be sacrilegious not to order a pudding after the starter and mains were so delicious, but the idea of eating them in the comfort of their own rooms, in comfy clothes, was perfection. They both ordered something, Bryony something chocolatey and her mum something creamy, then left the restaurant and caught the lift to their room.

As promised, the staff had delivered their pyjamas, a super soft jersey for Bryony, and a cotton set for her mum, and the bathroom was stocked with gorgeous little bottles of perfumed bubble bath, oils, bombs, and soaps. Bryony had a bath first, her mother decided to have another glass of wine and wait for the room service to arrive. The water was so hot and filled with a luxurious scent that she couldn't place. Probably the smell of money, she thought cynically.

Her brain felt overloaded with her mother's confession and memories of how she and Isaac had used to ridicule her mother and kept rearing their ugly heads, filling her with shame and remorse. No amount of expensive toiletries could clean her ugly soul, she thought, and she shed a few tears of deep regret and self-loathing for ever, treating her wonderful mum so badly. She vowed never to do it again and made herself cheer up before getting out, getting dry and dressed in her new PJs, and going to see her mum.

'Shall I run the bath for you?' She asked, stepping into the bedroom area, but her mum was already in bed, confessing she was too sleepy. Ignoring her decadent and very tempting dessert, she crawled into bed next to her mum and, after just a moment of hesitation, she sidled up close and wrapped her arms around her, pressing her head against her mum's back.

'I love you, Mum. I'm so sorry I changed. I'm so sorry I hurt you and broke your heart,' she whispered over the lump in her throat. Her mum turned over and pulled Bryony in close, holding her tight and stroking her damp hair.

'All children break their parent's hearts. It's sort of inevitable. A good parent will always forgive and forget. Don't you feel too badly about this, my darling girl,'

Bryony fell asleep wrapped up in the heat of her mum's arms like a child, and she slept so soundly.

Chapter Thirteen

Isaac didn't show up again until she returned home from her shift at the coffee shop two days later. When he did, their greeting was awkward and strained.

'Hi. Where have you been?' Bryony asked him.

'Trying to find famous people,' he said. 'I went to the football stadium and stalked a few players for a while. Their houses are incredible, by the way,' they both smiled, but it didn't last long.

'Look, about the other night,'

'Listen, what my mum was saying,'

They both began and stopped at the same time.

The awkwardness grew intolerable.

'My mum didn't mean what she said the other night. Well, she meant it, but after you left, she pointed out how she realised her view was one-sided, and we talked about your good points too.'

'Oh okay. But I've been thinking about that too, and I think she's actually maybe right. I'm a spoilt brat, Bry. I always have been, you know that. I remember when we first started going out, and I would bug you to come and hang out with us rather than stay in and study. I teased you about the girls you used to hang out with, and we always did do what I wanted. If we didn't, I'd be a real jerk about it and just moan – remember that film you asked me to watch with you – I can't remember what it was even called now, but I know I pretty much ruined it for you with my moaning. I also remember thinking to myself, "Okay, next time we'll do whatever Bryony wants to do," but then I either just forgot or chose not to or whatever. Anyways, I'm really sorry, Bry.'

'Oh, Isaac, it wasn't just you. I can't let you take all the blame. I should have kicked up more of a fuss if I was that bothered about doing something else. I chose to tag along or do what everyone else was doing. It was as much me as it was you. More me, probably.'

'Err… No. Probably not. And anyway, since I've been dead, you've stopped hanging out with all our friends. Don't deny it; I know you have. You have a look of panic every time I mention them. So, if you stop hanging out with them when I'm not around, and you want to study more and do more good girl stuff with your mum and whatever now I'm sort of gone, then it has to be because of me, doesn't it?'

'Isaac, I've stopped hanging out with those guys because they were your friends. I didn't fit in with them, I fit in with you. You were the glue that kept us together. Without you, we just don't mesh. That doesn't mean that you're the reason I changed so much. I changed because I found something, someone who bought so much joy to my life; I wanted to be with him more than I wanted anything else I'd had before. And just because I am studying more now doesn't mean I'm reverting back to the person I was before; it just means that I'm an A' level student. I would probably have started studying even if you hadn't died.'

Her second point was less convincing than the first. Neither of them believed she would have studied much if Isaac was still alive, and certainly not to the extent that she was now. Her conviction wavering made it hard to continue arguing with him.

'Anyway,' he began, now she'd run out of steam. 'My point is, neither of us can do anything about how we were before, and I guess it doesn't matter who was or wasn't to blame; it's done now. We need to learn from it and move on. Therefore, I have decided that I am going to be less selfish and give you some time. I'm not going to completely leave you alone, I'll keep popping back, but for the most part, I'll be out of your hair so you can study and work and whatever else you need to do,' he said with a flourish and a smile.

'What do you mean? Where will you be? Where are you going?' Bryony asked, feeling instantly needy and panicky.

'I've got myself a mission, one that will take up most of my time, I think.'

'What mission? How much time?'

'So, I've been thinking about what we were talking about at the spa, as well as about what your mum said. I think you're right. I think there must be other ghosts out there, and I'm going to try and find one,'

'Find a ghost? How? Where?'

'Well, I'm not entirely sure, but they definitely won't be in your bedroom, so I'm going to go off and explore all sorts of places. Actually, when I was following one of those footballers I told you about, he gave me a really good idea. He went to an old people's home to visit his Grandad, and I thought that would be the perfect place to start looking.'

'Why an old people's home?'

'Because everyone's old there, so loads of them die. There has to be at least one ghost hanging out there. Or maybe not at that particular one cos, to be fair, they all looked in pretty good shape, but I could go around loads of them. Increase my chances of finding one.'

'Don't you think there is more likely to be a ghost somewhere like a hospital or a morgue or a cemetery?'

'Yeah, I thought about that too, but cemeteries are too spooky, and hospitals would freak me out too much. I mean, what if I met like a ghost baby or something? I can't handle that kind of responsibility. Or what if someone was really disgusting looking from like burning to death or something like that? I'd be all freaked out and stuff, so, nah, I'll say a hospital is my backup plan. At least I know that at an old people's home, they'll all definitely be older than me and probably look pretty normal.'

Bryony laughed, but she was quite impressed with his plan. It seemed very well thought out, which was unusual for him.

'How long will you go for? Will you come back every night so we can talk and I'll know you're still here?'

'Well yeah, of course, at first. But if ghosts are as rare as we think they are, there may not be one living locally to us. I may have to look pretty far and wide to find one. If I have to start going far away to search, then I can't come back every night; I won't have time. I might only be able to come back every week or so.'

'But what about if you can't see them? What about if you're as undetectable to other ghosts as you are to other humans and vice versa? Won't this whole endeavour be completely pointless?'

'Yeah, but what about if there are other ghosts out there and I don't find them 'cos the only place I go is your bedroom? Look, if I don't find anyone by the time you finish your exams, we have to assume that they're either undetectable or they simply don't exist, and I'm the only one.'

'That's kind of a scary thought.'

'What is – being the only ghost in the world or finding another ghost?'

'Both, I suppose. Aren't you a bit scared to meet another ghost?'

'Errm… No, not really. I guess they'll just be a bit like me but old.'

'Besides, I mean, what could they do to you? You're already dead,'

'Exactly.'

'So when are you going to put this plan in motion?'

'As soon as you want me to get out of your hair so you can get down to studying, I suppose.'

Bryony suddenly seemed to forget why she had thought studying so much was important.

'Are you okay, Bry? You look a bit worried.'

'I am worried, actually,' she said, looking up at him. 'If we are right and you came back as a ghost because we love each other so much, then what's going to happen if we don't spend as much time together? I mean, is your being here a proximity thing? What will happen if you're not around people who can see you? Will you still exist if we're not together as much? Plus, I'm kind of scared that I'm going to miss you too much like I did when I thought you were gone. I mean, I know you won't be gone, like forever gone, or at least hopefully not, but last time I didn't have you nearby, I was a complete wreck. And now that you are here,' she paused and looked him straight in the eyes. 'Look, I know we drive each other crazy sometimes, but that doesn't change how I feel about you. I still need you with me so I can function as a normal human being, even if I'm as mad as hell at you.'

'So what are you saying? You want me to stay here with you all the time?'

'No, no. That's selfish of me. Plus, we'll probably kill each other. I just think I'm going to miss you, that's all, and I'm scared you'll go away for good if you go too far away.'

'Okay then,' he said softly, stepping really close to her. 'How about I only stay real local until you finish your exams? If I don't find anything by then, we can explore further out together. Until then, I'll do my thing during the day so you can do your studying undisturbed. But every night, I will come right back to you, right back here, so you don't get a chance to miss me. How does that sound?'

His voice had gotten real deep, and Bryony knew if he could have, he would have very gently swept her hair behind her ear the way he had always done, as he knew it made her knees weak. She felt the coldness of the air on her cheek, and she could have cried. She wanted to touch and be touched by him so very, very badly. She swallowed hard before speaking again.

'That sounds great, but I think, once my exams are out of the way, we need to prioritise finding a way to make you be able to touch and feel again. I think all our efforts should go into that.'

'Oh really,' he said, grinning.

'Mmm. I think so.'

'I really do miss being able to kiss this neck,' he admitted lowering his head to her collarbone. She felt the icy thrill and ached for more. Isaac stepped back, a look of frustration marring his beautiful features. 'I think you're right, babe. This not touching thing is seriously beginning to suck. Maybe if I can find another ghost, they might know some tricks or whatever.'

'Yeah, maybe,' she didn't sound too convincing.

'What's up? Why did you say it like that?'

'I don't know. It's just… not everyone is friendly, and ghosts sort of have a reputation for being, well, you know… scary. I guess I just don't want you to get your hopes up that you're going to meet Casper when in reality you could meet, I don't know, Bloody Mary.'

Isaac laughed. 'Bloody Mary! Bloody hell Bry!'

'Well, I don't know! What other famous ghosts are there? In all seriousness though, you will be careful, won't you, babe?'

'Yes, babe, I'll be careful and be on the look out for Bloody Mary.'

'You know what I mean. Promise me.'

'I promise.'

'I love you.'

‘Love you too.’

And with that, Bryony was alone in her room. It felt like a huge weight had been lifted off her shoulders. She got straight down to studying. When she took a break for tea time, she realised she hadn’t thought about Isaac once in all that time. And more importantly, she didn’t feel guilty about that.

When he returned later that night, she’d had a successful and productive day, as well as studying, she’d managed to spend some quality time with her parents at dinner time. She’d also showered and dried her hair. On the other hand, Isaac finally had something new to talk to her about, and whilst he hadn’t been successful in his search for other ghosts, he made her laugh with some of his observations of the people who lived and worked in these places.

By the time Bryony broke up from school entirely in May, she was so comfortable with her schedule, she agreed to take on an extra shift at the coffee shop and was feeling uncharacteristically unstressed about her life. Of course, that all came crashing down one Thursday morning.

The day started off normally enough. Isaac was gone by the time her alarm went off at 7:30, so she went downstairs and made herself some breakfast and a coffee, a new addiction thanks to her job. Then she showered, dressed, and studied until about 11:00, when she would snack and stretch for ten minutes, then get back to it. However, on that particular Thursday, her studies were interrupted by Isaac.

‘I’ve found something,’ he announced, floating into her bedroom through the wall, nearly giving her a heart attack.

‘Jeez Louise!‘ She gasped, clutching her chest. It wasn’t like him these days to interrupt her day, but the look on his face suggested it was important.

‘What was it? Another ghost?’

‘I don’t know,’ he said cryptically. He couldn’t look pale, but from the confused, scared look on his features, she knew he was really shaken up.

‘Are you okay?’ She ventured.

‘I don’t know if it was a ghost or not, but it could see me, Bry, and – it could hit me!’

‘Hit you? What do you mean?’

He shook his head, and Bryony gave him a minute or two to gather himself. She couldn’t remember ever seeing him like this before.

What could possibly hit a ghost? She pondered. When he looked a little bit calmer, she began questioning him again, gently.

‘Start from the beginning. Where did you go this morning?’

‘I went back to the old people’s home I was telling you about last night, you know, the one with Dawn and Lawrence and Giovanni.’ Last night Isaac had told Bryony about a conversation he’d overheard between some of the residents at an old people’s home. It must have been hilarious because the three of them were talking, but not one of them was about the same thing. ‘It’s called Ivy Bush House, and I just got this feeling about the place. I was sure I’d find something there.

‘Anyway, this morning, I was watching some of them have breakfast when someone asked about some fancy plates they wanted to use for their annual summer party. They hadn’t seen them for a couple of years, and did anyone know where they had got to? Well, Giovanni said they must be in the old cow barn at the end of the property. Kelsey, the manager, hadn’t even heard of the cow barn. Apparently, she’s only been working there for eighteen months, so she wouldn’t know anything about it. Anyway, they all began arguing and talking over each other for like five minutes or something, but eventually, Dawn said that the cow barn is haunted and no one ever goes in there anymore, but she'd bet her last shilling that the fancy plates were in there along with all the rest of the stuff that goes missing in that place. Either that, she said, or someone there was a pulferer? Pilferer? I don't know what the word was, but maybe she meant like a poltergeist or something.'

'No, she meant pilferer. A pilferer is a thief.'

'Oh, right. Why didn't she just say that then?'

Bryony shrugged. No need to preach about the niceties of broadening one's vocabulary now.

'Anyway, Kelsey decided she was going down there to check it out, and naturally, I'm going to go with her, especially if there are rumours that it's haunted and I thought there was a poltergeist in there.

'But holy hell, Bryony – it is! The minute you walked in there, you could feel it, like you were trespassing on a psychopath's land or something. I know Kelsey felt it too 'cos she was all cocky and saying how ridiculous they all were as we were walking down, but she went real quiet and pale when we got in there.'

'Did you actually see anything, or was it just a feeling?'

'Hang on, I'm getting to that. So Kelsey goes in, and it's all dark and cold even though it's bright daylight and a hot summer's day outside, and she even says it's freezing in there, right.'

'Okay, and were you stood next to her when she said that?' Bryony interrupted. Isaac thought for a moment before looking a little disappointed.

'Well, yeah, I was at first, but not all the time, and she was cold the whole time,' he justified. Bryony nodded and tried to hide her doubts. 'Anyway, she's got a flashlight, and she started looking through stacks of boxes of stuff. Honestly, it's like a hoarder's paradise in there, but I wasn't looking at that stuff. I was on high alert 'cos Bry, I swear, my spidey sense was tingling. And after like three or four minutes, this thing, this real ugly, scary thing, comes rushing at us, and at first, I didn't think it was a ghost because it was so scary looking, but it was really charging at us, and Kelsey didn't know. I swear down, she looked freaked but had no idea this thing was there.

'So then, as it got closer, I, like, waved at it to see if it could see me, and that's when I realised, not only could it definitely see me, but it was charging at me! It didn't care about Kelsey at all. When it got closer, I could see its face, and man, it was so freaky! It was all snarling and angry, and its eyes were like black black, like darker than just a normal black, and it was so furious – like it was really, really mad that I was there. Then I didn't know what to do, so I just stood there right, 'cos I figured, like you said before, what could it do to me, but Bry it came straight up to me, and it punched me so hard, I clean lifted off my feet and fell on my back on the floor. Kelsey must have sensed something then, though, 'cos that's when she got out of there real quick. She hadn't even found the plates! I went straight out with her. I wasn't going to stay in there on my own with it, especially as it can actually hit me. What the hell is that about?'

'Oh my God, did it hurt?'

'Being hit? Yeah. Well, actually, now I come to think about it, no, not really, but still, you know, it freaked me out. And honest to God, you should have seen the look on its face. It was so so angry.'

'And it really made physical contact with you?'

'Bry, it knocked me off my feet.'

'I mean, did you feel it? Are you absolutely sure you didn't just fall over something because you were a bit… um… freaked out?'

'No, I'll swear on anything you want me to, it hit me, and I fell. It wasn't me falling over.'

'Wow.'

‘I know.’

‘You have to go back. Go and talk to him… er… it, they…’

‘Wait, what? Bry, I’m not going back there.’

‘Isaac, you have to. You have to talk to this thing. It’s a ghost of some sort that knows how to touch people. That was your mission. It’s the skill you have been desperate to learn.’

‘Bryony, he was furious! He’s not going to talk to me. He’ll just try to hit me again.’

‘So. What can he do? Kill you? You said yourself it doesn’t actually hurt; it just *seems* like it should.’

‘So what, I should go back there and let him beat the crap out of me?’

‘If it helps him calm down, then yeah, absolutely. Why wouldn’t you?’

He was stumped. Torn. He clearly did not want to return to that place, but Bryony’s argument was valid.

‘Come with me?’ He asked her finally.

‘Isaac, come on. I can’t go with you. What excuse would I have for visiting an old people’s home, let alone their haunted cow barn?’

‘It’s right on the edge of the property, and you wouldn’t have to come through the house; you could climb over a fence at the back.’

‘That’s trespassing and then breaking and entering.’

‘Bryony, please. I don’t want to go back there on my own.’

She melted. He looked so scared and vulnerable she couldn’t not. However, she had assumed they’d go under cover of darkness to help prevent her from getting caught. Isaac had other ideas.

‘Oh no, no, no. We go in the day.’

‘Isaac, I could be seen.’

‘Bryony, that thing is scary enough in the bright sunshine. I would literally poo my pants if I had to go at night time.’

‘Isaac, you’re a ghost. You can’t poo your pants.’

‘Yeah, well, I could have a heart attack and die for real.’

She argued with him over and over till she was practically blue in the face, but on this point, he would not budge. The experience had really shaken him, and at first, he wanted to go straight away to get the whole ordeal over with, but Bryony convinced him to wait till tomorrow. She figured he needed time to calm down, and she needed a contingency plan. Plus, they were running out of daylight anyway, so it was probably best to wait one day.

All evening Bryony kept talking to him about the possibility of them being able to touch each other. The things they could do that they had both missed so much. Her plan worked well because, by the next day, Isaac was itching to go back and get started on the learning. His fear was apparently forgotten, or rather, less important now there were other emotions to fuel his actions. Bryony didn’t tell her parents of her plans to ditch studying that day, and whilst she herself was a little bit worried about a whole day of revision to make up on, it was not enough to put her off. She had to admit, ignoring the practicalities of the whole endeavour; she was a bit excited herself. This day could change their whole lives.

The nursing home turned out to be on the other side of town, three buses away. By the time they got there, it was nearly lunchtime. Isaac showed her how to get around the back, but the fence turned out to be much higher than either of them had anticipated. There was no way she would get over it without something to step on. They began searching the area when they heard a voice from the other side of the fence.

‘We’ve been waiting for you to come back. We knew you wouldn’t be able to leave the cow barn alone,’ it said loudly.

They both froze as though they'd been caught doing something naughty, but it couldn't be addressing them – Isaac was a ghost, and they didn't know Bryony was there. She kept statue still and silent for a long moment.

'I know you're there,' the voice called again. She sounded like quite an old lady, so there was a chance she was just crazy. 'And I know one of you, the boy, is a ghost, and the other is a young woman. My grandma is a ghost, too, and she can see you both. Show yourself, Grandma.'

Bryony and Isaac stared at each other, neither of them knowing what to do. They heard a slight cough from behind them, and they spun around.

It took a few long seconds, but sure enough, the figure of a middle-aged lady appeared, just materialized out of nowhere, and both of them could see her. Bryony couldn't help but cry out in shock, and the voice from behind the fence called out.

'I told you so. Why don't you two come in through the front, and we will have a little chat? Tell Chloe at the reception that you're here to see Veronica Wainswright. You can have some lunch with me in the summer room as it's such a nice day. Oh, and tell them you're my niece or something like that. They're funny buggers about visitors unless they think you're related.'

The ghost lady walked through the fence back to the voice. Bryony and Isaac stared at one another for a moment, but then they shrugged, and Isaac led her back to the front door. They didn't really feel they had any choice in the matter.

Chapter Fourteen

Bryony was given a very strange look when she announced to Chloe at the reception desk who she'd like to visit.

'Is that okay?' She asked, suddenly doubtful.

'Are you a relative?'

'Yes, she's my Mum's aunt.'

'You've never visited before.'

'No, well, Mum and Aunt Veronica never really got on. I'd like to hear her side of the story,' Bryony lied smoothly, surprising herself.

This seemed to placate the young, cynical receptionist, and she showed her through to the summer room, where several old people were sitting at tables waiting for lunch, many of them alone. Bryony had no idea which one was Veronica, and she suddenly realised Veronica wouldn't know her either. She could feel the panic sweat forming on her back, her hairline, and her palms. Isaac was behind her, so she couldn't get any help from him either.

'Veronica,' Chloe called out loudly, and a white-haired, painfully thin woman looked up. Well, actually, everyone looked up, but Bryony was able to tell which person it was she was addressing. She had harsh, sharp features with old-fashioned, thick pointy glasses that gave her the appearance of a very strict, retired teacher. 'You've got a visitor,' Chloe announced to the room with relish.

Bryony noticed the collective surprise in the audible gasps, the sudden interest in her, along with the rise in chatter.

'You lot all stop your gawping, you nosy buggers,' Veronica instructed, but nobody listened to her. Bryony tried to ignore the open stares, the mutterings, and even the outright questions of "What's your name?" and "Are you a relative?" She focussed on

Veronica, who, she only just now noticed, was in a wheelchair. Veronica tutted loudly at the room, then as Bryony approached, she said, 'You'll have to roll me out into the grounds. We won't be able to talk in here with this nosy lot.'

'Ronnie, we're serving lunch in a minute,' protested someone nearby in a uniform.

'We'll be back in for lunch,' Veronica assured her.

'Well, it's cold outside. At least have this blanket over your knees,' she said kindly, starting to tuck an orange, knitted blanket down the sides of her chair.

'Will you stop fussing, woman?' Veronica screeched, tearing the blanket off her and launching it across the room. 'I may be in this wretched contraption, but you will not treat me like an old lady. Besides, I've been sat out there all morning. It's not bloody cold.'

Horrified, Bryony smiled apologetically at the poor carer; her name badge said she was called Sharon. She simply shrugged off Veronica's bad manners with good humour.

'Good luck,' she half whispered as Bryony tried to manoeuvre the wheelchair between all the tables. She smiled gratefully at the woman.

'I heard that.'

'I meant you to.'

Outside was quite cold, in Bryony's opinion. The summer had taken a sudden turn, and the grey skies bought with them a strong wind that was far from the beautiful warm days they'd been experiencing up until yesterday. She wished the old lady had kept the blanket. Even if she hadn't wanted it, Bryony would have used it.

Under the strict directions of Veronica, Bryony wheeled her over to a table with a bench on the other side, and she sat down opposite her, unsure of what to say.

'Your boy ghost, is he your brother?' She began, not bothering to lower her voice. Bryony looked around, there were people milling about everywhere, but no one appeared to be listening to them.

'No, he's my boyfriend. Was my boyfriend, I mean.'

'I know what you mean,' she snapped. She seemed very angry for some reason.

'And you say your ghost is your grandmother.'

'Yes, I've been talking to her for over eighty-five years.'

'Wow.'

'Yes, wow, and I got locked away in a loony bin for the pleasure of it.'

'Oh no, because no one else could see her?'

'Exactly. They medicated me for years.'

'That's awful.'

'It's a learning curve. You have to learn not to acknowledge them in public.'

'Yeah, I learned that too.'

'Well, you're much older than I was,' she snapped. 'A four-year-old who can see her dead Grandma as clear as day doesn't know you're not meant to tell people. Doesn't know you have to lie all the time.'

'No, of course not,' Bryony agreed meekly. 'Is she here now, your Grandma?' She asked, looking around her to see if she would materialise again.

'She's always here,' Veronica said sadly. 'Still, she won't be for much longer. It will be time for her to move on soon. To cross over. That's why I wanted to meet you.'

'To cross over, you mean to go to heaven?'

'Well, if you believe in that sort of thing,' she shrugged.

'What does that mean?' Isaac demanded, his face suddenly tight with worry. It took a moment for Bryony to remember she didn't have to ignore him in this company.

'Not everyone believes in a Heaven, Isaac,' she said gently to him but looked at Veronica to confirm her meaning.

'Heaven is a concept made up by scared, simple-minded people who can't own the bad things they've done,' she announced like it was a fact. 'Tell your boy to show himself. I'm curious as to what he looks like.'

'I… erm, he hasn't learned that particular skill yet.' Bryony confessed on Isaac's behalf. She was beginning to regret agreeing to speak to this woman and wondered how soon she could leave without being rude.

'Not learned it yet! How long has he been dead?'

'Over eight months now,' Bryony answered whilst Isaac tried to work it out.

Veronica laughed a really throaty, dusty laugh.

'Why his body hasn't even decomposed yet!' she guffawed. Bryony frowned. She was liking the woman less and less each moment she spent in her company.

'And there you are, attempting to bother old Abediah. He'd have eaten you for breakfast, boy,' she added, looking vaguely in Isaac's direction.

'Ask her who…'

‘So Abediah is the thing Isaac saw in the cow barn?’

‘Yes, he’s a ghoul.’

‘Isaac tells me that this Abediah, the ghoul, was rather frightening looking, and it, he could hit him. I mean, he could see Isaac and physically knock him to the floor.’

‘Yep. That sounds like Abediah,’

‘Well, who is he, and how is it he can do that?’

‘I already told you, he’s a ghoul.’

‘And ghouls are different from ghosts?’

The sandpaper laugh again, but this time she started having a coughing fit that lasted five minutes and made her face turn bright red.

Bryony grew anxious and was relieved when Sharon, the staff member she’d been rude to earlier came over to check on her. She insisted they go inside now. They could take tea in Veronica’s bedroom if she was so concerned about eavesdroppers, but it was too cold for her to be out of doors now.

Bryony was relieved, between the cool breeze that occasionally whipped around them and the close proximity of Isaac, not to mention the Granny ghost she couldn’t see, she was dithering, so Veronica must have been freezing.

She followed them in at a slight distance so she could speak surreptitiously to Isaac.

‘You need to find out what a ghoul is and if they’re the only ones who can touch things or if we ghosts can learn to do it too,’ he whispered to her. ‘Also, see if you can find out how the granny ghost was able to make herself visible to other people, that would be awesome too. You did see her, didn’t you, when we were on the other side of the fence?’

Bryony nodded.

'Can you see her now? The granny ghost?' She asked, trying not to move her lips or speak above a whisper.

'No, she's not visible to me now.'

'Okay, I'll see what I can find out,' Bryony promised.

'Bry,' Isaac added just before she stepped into Veronica's bedroom, and she and the nurse were busy getting her settled, 'You don't believe all that stuff she said about heaven, do you? I mean, heaven has to exist, doesn't it? Otherwise, where will I go when I cross over?'

'Don't stress about that, Babe. She's clearly quite a weird, mean old lady. She probably only said all that stuff 'cos she knew you were listening. Or maybe she really does believe that, but who cares what she believes? It's not like she knows any more than anyone else. She can't change your mind about what you believe, so it really doesn't matter what she thinks, does it?'

'No, I suppose not,' he conceded, still sounding worried.

'And besides, she's such a horror, it's unlikely she'll be let in when it's her turn anyway,' Bryony added, which made Isaac grin.

'Are you coming in?' The nurse asked Bryony. She had managed to hoist Veronica into a comfortable armchair and placed a blanket over her knees, which, this time, the feisty old woman had not thrown off. Bryony stepped into the small but clean room, which was littered with all sorts of random bric-a-brac. There was a small two-seater sofa behind the door, which, whilst old, looked very cosy. Bryony placed herself on that, feeling the heat from this tiny bedroom envelop her. When Isaac chose to sit next to her, she was quite pleased. The heat in this room had warmed off the chill from outside and was already becoming a little stifling.

'Your lunch will be with you soon enough,' the nurse said before retreating from the room and closing the door behind her.

'Thank you Sharon.' Bryony said pointedly. 'So, you were saying,' she prompted when Veronica didn't start any conversation, 'About Abediah, the ghoul.'

'No,' Veronica said, jutting her chin out stubbornly.

'Excuse me. What do you mean "no"?'

'I mean, you want something from me. You want all the information I've got stored up here in my head. Information you won't be able to get anywhere else, missy, let me tell you. Well, you can't have it, not unless you do something for me in return.'

'I… erm.' Bryony looked at Isaac. He seemed as clueless as she was. 'What do you want?' She ventured, already getting anxious about it.

'Company.'

'Company? Erm, haven't you got your Grandma?'

'My Grandmother and I have spent every single moment together since I was four years old. There is nothing we don't know about each other. I want to spend time with someone else.'

'Well, there are plenty of people here. The nurses seem lovely, and there are other residents here closer to your age.'

'The nurses are all pilferers! They'll rob you while you sleep and show off their wares in the staff room. And the residents, those nosy old tarts! Absolutely not. I want someone new. Someone who knows what it's like to see a ghost.'

'How much time are we talking about?'

'I think twice a week will do it. That should give me a chance to say all I have to and find out all I want to know about you and your boyfriend.'

‘Okay. Well, I guess I could start coming over twice a week at the end of June up until about October time, but then I’m going to university, so I won’t be able to come at all.’

‘No, no, no, no. You don’t understand, silly girl. I am dying. I only have a few weeks left if the doctors are to be believed. You’ll have to start coming straight away.’

Bryony couldn’t hide the look of horror on her face. Veronica spotted it, and instantly her face morphed into a scowling witch-type creature – her whole expression suddenly angry and cruel.

‘Well, fine then. Don’t come,’ she snarled. ‘How dare you deny an old woman her dying wish, you evil, cold-hearted girl. Do you suppose your own time is so precious, so much more important, that you can’t spare just a couple of hours to keep me company? Well, that’s just fine, then. But you rest assured, I’ll never tell you a damn thing, and you and your stupid boyfriend can rot in hell for all I care.’

Bryony was so flabbergasted she couldn’t speak for a moment. She wanted to explain to this woman that it wasn’t that she didn’t want to spend time with her; it was just that she physically couldn’t fit her into her already tight schedule. She wanted to say that if she had more time, she would love to spend it listening and learning from her. However, the truth was, even if she had all the time in the world, she wouldn’t want to spend it here with this horrible, nasty woman who was rude, arrogant, and obnoxious. She didn’t like her sense of humour, her mannerisms, or the way that she presented her opinions as fact. She was a stubborn old lady with a vile temper.

‘We’re not going to get another chance like this any time soon, Bry. You’re just gonna have to suck it up and do it,’ Isaac leaned over and whispered in her ear.

Bryony glared at him, and he held his hands up in surrender.

She said nothing for a long time, trying to keep her temper in check and trying to work out how best to handle the situation.

Having finished her rant, Veronica sat staring out of the window. Bryony knew if she didn't say anything soon, she'd probably be kicked out.

The nurse returned and placed their lunch things on the coffee table, apparently completely oblivious to the tension in the room. Veronica muttered something that sounded like "about time," but everyone ignored her.

'I am very sorry to hear that you are dying,' Bryony finally said softly when the nurse left, taking the older woman by surprise.

'Sorry? I'm not sorry. I'm eighty-nine years old. It's about bloody time I died.'

'Have you any other family, other than your Grandma?'

'I had an older sister, but she died three years ago this October,'

'Oh, that's a shame. Were you very close, the two of you?'

'No,'

'Oh. Well, do you have any friends outside of the nursing home?'

'Listen up, Missy. Stop trying to palm me off just so you can get what you want without having to earn it. That's the problem with your generation. You all just think you're entitled to everything, well, not this. I already told you I was a freak. Freaks don't have friends. Even their own sisters don't believe 'em when they insist their granny is still around and talking to 'em. So no, I don't have no family, and I don't have no friends. If you want to know all about Abediah and how he can do what he does. If you want to know all the tricks we've learnt about handling ghosts, 'cos God knows you need to handle 'em, and if you wanna know how to cross over because believe you me, your darling beau is going to have to do it someday too, unless he wants to turn into a ghoul like Abediah himself. If you want all of my knowledge, then you'd better agree to my terms,' she pointed her finger in Bryony's face aggressively as she spoke. Bryony fought the urge to slap it away. She tried to remain calm.

'No.'

For a moment, there was absolutely no movement in the room at all. Isaac and Veronica both stared at Bryony like she was insane, and Bryony simply looked back calmly at Veronica. The moment the older lady looked like she was going to speak again, Bryony continued.

'No, now it's your turn to listen, please, Veronica,' Bryony said, her voice cold and steady. 'We didn't come here looking for your help; you are simply, to me and Isaac, a happy accident. You are the one who is supposedly dying, not me. This could all be some sort of play on your behalf, a trick. A con to try and get someone to spend some time with you. You don't have any friends because you are rude and mean to other people, not because you are a freak. Lots of people are weird, but they still manage to be civil enough to people to make friends. I won't stand for that sort of behaviour. I have no guarantee that you have any information whatsoever that will be useful for me or Isaac. As far as I know, you could just be making it all up. The only thing I am sure of is that we both are able to see the ghosts of people we love. That makes us pretty unique, as far as I am aware.

'Now, unfortunately, my time is regrettably limited due to the very pressing matter of exams, which will dictate my future. Therefore, I am prepared to come and see you once a week; however, I have some conditions of my own. The first is, if I feel you have not given me any useful information by the end of our hour together, yes I said one hour, don't interrupt me to complain, that's all I'm willing to give at the moment until you prove yourself useful and better company. Anyway, the minute I feel that you're not useful, I'll stop coming. STOP INTERRUPTING. The second condition is your behaviour. When I am here, you will be civil, not just to me but to the carers and nurses and everyone else you interact with. If I feel you are being rude or mean, I will give you one warning, and then I'll leave. If you lose your temper with me again, I won't even give you a warning, I will just go. Do you understand and accept these terms, Veronica?'

It was Veronica's turn to be gobsmacked.

Bryony fought to keep her expression neutral as Isaac exclaimed, 'I am so turned on by you right now. I don't even think it's wrong that I'm in a nursing home.' Bryony drank some tea to hide her smirk. Veronica poured herself a cup and then spoke up.

'Fine, I'll agree to your terms,' she said quietly, moodily.

They arranged to meet again on Thursday at lunchtime for one hour as long as Veronica kept up her end of the bargain.

'As a show of good faith on your part, ' Bryony began, the spark of an idea occurring to her as she thought of ways to fill the awkward silence, 'Will you, please, ask your Grandma how she is able to show herself to other people? I think Isaac would love to learn that skill.'

Veronica scowled, but after a pointed look from Bryony, she stopped. She looked over into the corner of the room. Without a word, after a few moments, her grandmother materialised.

Bryony was still caught off guard. She nearly dropped her sandwich.

'It requires focus, determination, and a lot of energy,' her grandmother, who actually looked much younger than Veronica, told them. 'You have to focus your mind on every part of your body and try to forcefully project yourself. It takes more than just practise. It takes strength of mind and the strongest, most fervent desire to be seen. It could take years.'

Isaac nodded hungrily. 'I'll do it. I'll practise every day.'

The grandmother faded away.

‘Don’t get your hopes up. There are no guarantees,’ Veronica said with some sandwich in her mouth. ‘It will probably never happen for you. And besides, even if you did learn to do it, you can’t just show yourself to people willy-nilly. You’ll give someone a heart attack,’ she paused as if listening and then shoo-shooed what could only be her grandmother's ghost away. ‘Yes, yes, I know that. Fine. The other thing you should know is that you can only be seen by another if they are open to the idea that ghosts are real. Okay?’ She said to the corner of the room.

Bryony hid a smile and helped herself to another sandwich. The food here was really rather good. Either that or she was starving. She was beginning to think, with Veronica on a tight leash and with the help of her grandmother, this might not be as bad as she had first thought.

‘Wait,’ she began, another thought suddenly occurring to her. ‘How is it that your Grandma can see Isaac whenever she wants, but he can’t see her unless she shows herself?’

Veronica opened her mouth to answer but thought the better of it. She looked at Bryony with a very sly smile.

‘Maybe that can be one of the useful pieces of information I offer to you on your next visit,’ she said, tapping the side of her nose.

Bryony rolled her eyes.

‘Fine. I’d better be going anyway. I’ve stayed far longer than an hour for this, our first meeting. Don’t be expecting it again.’

‘Wait, don’t go. I don’t know anything about you yet.’

‘Don’t worry. Make a list of things you want to know, and I’ll answer them next time. I promise I won’t hold anything back unless you ask me something too personal.’

As she stood up to leave, she had to promise Veronica vehemently that she would definitely return, and the desperation in the old dear's tone strengthened Bryony's resolve to keep that promise.

'Well, that was progress, I guess,' Isaac said whilst they waited for the first bus to come. 'God, that woman is a nightmare. The cheek of exchanging information for company. It's no wonder she hasn't got any friends.'

'Yeah, well, you should know, my Thursday afternoons with Veronica are coming out of my scheduled time with you,' she informed him.

'What! That's not fair.'

'Of course, it is. My schedule cannot fit any extra time in it, something had to give somewhere, and if you had come here on your own as I'd suggested, none of this would have happened.'

By the time the bus arrived, Isaac wasn't talking to her. That suited Bryony perfectly; she had a lot of revision to catch up on.

Chapter Fifteen

Bryony was as good as her word. Every Thursday, she took the three buses across town to visit Veronica. The first time was just as painful as their initial meeting, and Bryony had to lay the law down again to ensure that Veronica knew she would leave if she was rude or didn't offer her any of the information she needed. After that, though, Veronica softened. She began using her manners with the staff, needing only occasional reminders. She also began talking about some of her life experiences, some sad, some funny, some bittersweet. Bryony began to enjoy the ritual of visiting the old lady, not least because after the first one, Isaac decided not to join her anymore, claiming it was too boring for him to even listen to. Admittedly it wasn't exactly fun, but in Bryony's opinion, Veronica was never boring, and she grew evermore interested in the lady whom the world assumed was crazy in a time when mental health was a dirty topic. She was fascinated by the methods they used on her and the ways she would try and fit in, some more successfully than others. Bryony once described Veronica to Isaac as a character in a TV series that you grew more and more invested in until they were one of your favourites.

In turn, Bryony began talking a little about her life. Her relationship with Isaac obviously and how she navigated appearing normal whilst having a supernatural boyfriend. She also started speaking about school and why she had no friends there, her family and the strengthening bond with her mum and the coffee shop, and some of the characters she met there. She found the old lady could be very insightful and wise, albeit brutally honest.

With a little coaxing, Veronica began to explain more about ghouls. The first thing Bryony learned was that ghouls were once just ordinary ghosts who didn't cross over when they should have. They don't turn immediately into ghouls; they roam around the earth all alone for about one hundred years or so. The loneliness is what tips them over. They grow bitter, angry, and vengeful. Wandering around, observing all the things they'll never do, never have, never feel. It drives them crazy, and it builds and builds until it erases any humanity that ties them to the world. They become so rage-filled that they are able to cause damage, and eventually, their whole, ghostly self dissolves into the horribly disfigured ghoul appearance that Isaac saw.

Bryony shivered after hearing it, not from the cold as it was quite a warm May afternoon, and yet Veronica still had her little fan heater on full blast.

'Is there no hope for the ghoul once it becomes one?'

Veronica took her time to answer. This was arguably the most annoying thing for Bryony, who naturally moved at a fast pace with everything she did. She would bite her lips and the inside of her cheeks to prevent herself from trying to hurry the old lady on.

'They can't stay around forever. Otherwise, there'd be hundreds of them all roaming around and destroying stuff so we'd hear more about them,' she said, and Bryony had to concede that it made sense. 'However, I don't know of anyone, ghost or living, who would be able to get close enough to find out. Even if they could get close enough to ask the question, I don't think a ghoul would be able to think logically; they're just too angry.'

'So what happens to them then? Do they just disappear? Explode in a cloud of rage dust?'

'I don't know. Maybe they run out of steam or fade away, but where to God only knows.'

They sat quietly as they both thought about this and its implications for their loved ones. Bryony had been visiting for a few weeks now, and these silences happened regularly but were rarely uncomfortable.

'This is why we have to make sure they cross over,' Veronica said sadly, her gaze distant and bleak.

'And how do we do that?' Bryony probed gently.

Veronica's eyes snapped back to her, narrowing shrewdly.

'I've told you enough information for this visit,' she said haughtily, 'I'll save that little gem for another occasion.'

Bryony shrugged nonchalantly. It had become a game of theirs; she would always push her luck with Veronica, and in turn, Veronica would always know when she'd given enough and never let her get away with it.

She drained her cup of tea and began to gather her things together. Veronica recognised the signs.

'You can't leave because of that. That's not fair! I've given you plenty of other information this visit.'

'Yes, I know you have, and I'm very grateful, but I have to go now anyway. It's getting late.'

'What? No, it isn't. We've only just had lunch.'

'Ronnie, we had lunch two hours ago. It takes me a long time to get home from here, so yes, I am leaving now.'

Veronica folded her bony arms across her non-existent chest and pouted like a child, as she always did. Bryony did up her coat, then crossed the room to hug her unresponsive host and kiss her cheek. Bryony didn't really have any grandparents. Her mother's parents had both died, one before Steven was born and the other not long after she arrived. There was a picture of her maternal grandmother holding her as a newborn in the hallway, but obviously, she didn't remember her. Her father's parents had emigrated to Australia before Steven was born. They occasionally skyped, although it always felt awkward and stunted. They had met up a few times over the years, sometimes in Australia, sometimes here, and they were very nice people, but she didn't really have a relationship with them as such. Veronica could not be described as nice exactly. Nevertheless, Bryony was forming a bond with her. She genuinely liked the eccentric, mean old lady who was actually just insecure and clingy. Once you managed to see past the mean and the rude aspects of her personality, it was surprising to see she was actually quite funny, intelligent, and interesting. Bryony just wished she would let other people see those parts of her too.

Isaac refused to believe that she was anything other than the cranky old woman they met on the first day. He also refused to return to the old people's home, claiming he would rather do literally anything else, and yet he always insisted Bryony ask if there was anything else Veronica's Grandma was not telling him about being able to materialise. This was becoming his new obsession. He practised all the time, night and day, to try to make himself visible. According to Rose, Veronica's Grandma, you will know if you have mastered it when you can see your reflection in a mirror. She had also suggested he focus just on his hand or his head to start with. He spent hours in front of the mirror, grunting with effort and then screaming with frustration as absolutely nothing happened. Veronica warned Bryony, who passed the message on to Isaac that it was highly unlikely he would master this particular skill in this millennium, a decade if he was dedicated but in the next week or so, he had to be joking.

He didn't take the news well. His mood recently was becoming more and more depressed, which showed itself in a number of new and alarming ways for Bryony's liking. He would sometimes disappear for days on end, which was fast becoming her favourite of his coping mechanisms, although the reassurance he needed about how much she had worried about him whilst he was gone was time-consuming and draining. Her least favourite depressed mode was when he followed her literally everywhere, including the bathroom even. He was completely oblivious to her discomfort or her need to focus when other people were around. The other sign of his depression stages was complete apathy, where he would lie on her bed all day, sighing audibly every three or four minutes as she tried to study. Bryony was convinced that this was a form of torture in some cultures. His need for attention throughout these stages was the thing that bothered Bryony the most. Depending on his mood, he was unhappy or frustrated, but either way, he needed something from her all the time. He grew more and more vexed with her "relentless studying" and jealously coveted any other time she spent with family or at work. And though she explained to him, almost daily, her needs, her anxiety regarding her exams, her need to sleep, eat, shower, and have quiet times, he seemed unable to take them on board. She began craving the few times she was alone, which were getting rarer and rarer. The trip to and from visiting Veronica every week was becoming sacred. She even, occasionally, intentionally missed one of her buses to eke out a few more minutes to herself. Most of the time, she studied or read over her extensive notes, but every now and then, she took just a few minutes to sit back, relax, look up and out at the world she inhabited, and just breathe. She didn't care that her seat was hard and undoubtedly riddled with disgusting germs. She didn't care that her scenery was rundown council estates and graffiti-marked industrial areas. She didn't care that her companions were loud and rude or that the air she inhaled was often full of the scents of stale urine or marijuana. In those few precious minutes, the world, her world, stopped feeling like it was spinning out of control, and it settled down.

Reset.

Calm.

Quiet.

Eventually, her whole week began revolving around those few minutes of sanctuary.

She always returned home on a Thursday just before her father. Her parents still didn't know that she visited Veronica, and she had no valid reason to tell them why she was visiting an old lady who was of no relation to them or had any other prior knowledge of, past a few weeks ago, on the other side of town, every week. So she kept them in the dark about such things. On this particular Thursday, though, she almost got caught out as her father walked through the front door just a few minutes after she did. If it was her mother, she'd have noticed Bryony walking down the drive, but fortunately, her father was quite oblivious to most things, so he had no idea she had just walked in before him, which is why she was in the kitchen getting a drink.

'Hey Bry, how was your day?' He asked as he washed his hands in the sink.

'Yeah, it was good, thanks. How about you?'

'Same old, same old.'

'Yep, same here.'

'How's the studying going? What are you looking at today?'

'I'm going over some poems I have to learn.'

'Anything I can help you with?'

'No, not really. I've just got to learn it. Are you starting dinner now?'

'Yeah. Lucky you, it's my famous shepherd's pie, but you can still stay in here if you want. I won't disturb you. Or if you want a break, we can have a little catch-up if you like. Better yet, you can help me with dinner, just like you used to when you were little, remember? I mean, if you want to,' he added, almost shyly.

On a whim and a desire to defer going up to her bedroom with Isaac's incessant rants, she agreed.

Her father put his favourite playlist on, which included many of Bryony's own favourites from the Beatles, Queen, Elton John, and the Rolling Stones, plus some more contemporary numbers from the Foo Fighters and Imagine Dragons. They set to work preparing dinner whilst their amiable chat was punctuated by the occasional line of the song they were listening to, sung loudly and badly by both of them.

Bryony didn't return to her room until it was almost past her usual bedtime. She was a little bit stressed about missing out on some of that study time, but ultimately she'd had an unexpectedly lovely evening with her parents.

Isaac was in a foul mood.

Her gentle happiness evaporated almost immediately. She muttered a general apology, but he barely heard it over his own ravings. She didn't say anything else. She didn't need to; Isaac went on and on about her selfishness and his ongoing turmoil. At one point, Bryony was so convinced that she was unneeded to his endless monologue that she pulled out her study notes.

That was a mistake.

His tirade continued well into the night, and though she was exhausted, she valiantly tried to hide her yawns. Still, there is only so much a reasonable individual can take, and eventually, through tiredness and boredom, her patience disappeared.

'Enough, Isaac,' she interrupted, feeling her temper rise. 'I get it, you're frustrated and lonely, but how often can we have this argument? I cannot and will not devote all my time to you. You don't own me. And yes, I know it sucks for you some of the time, but the fact of the matter is, I am still alive, and as such, there are things I have to do that simply do not involve you. One of them is sleeping, which I need to do right now. So if you don't mind, just eff off and leave me alone.'

He was shocked into silence. Bryony rarely lost her temper, least of all with him. For a moment, she thought she'd gone too far, but when he zoomed off out of her window, she was so grateful for the peace and quiet that she didn't really care. She settled down into her bed, knowing full well she would have to deal with the aftermath of her snapping in the morning, but by then, she'd have slept, so she would be in a better mood to be sympathetic.

At 1:15, when she was in the deepest of sleeps, Isaac returned.

He began by yelling, not singing, one of his favourite songs. Bryony woke with a start. After rubbing the sleep out of her eyes, she asked him what he was doing, but it soon became evident he was ignoring her and completely intent on making as much noise as possible. She tried reasoning with him, and she tried pleading with him. At one point, she demanded, in as loud a voice as she dared use in the middle of the night, that he stop this nonsense immediately. He drowned her out with the next few bars of his nightmarish serenade. Bryony attempted to ignore him and lay down with a pillow over her ears, but no pillow could keep out that noise. Two hours later, he had not stopped, and she was at the end of her tether. Nothing she said or did would stop him; he was oblivious to her words, her tears, and her actions. All he seemed to care about was keeping her awake. She eventually left her room and attempted to hide from him downstairs. He found her almost immediately and continued his torment. He was relentless.

The sun had come up, and Bryony had cried for hours before Isaac finally stopped. The silence that followed was deafening. She looked up from where she had hid her face in a blanket, and he was so close she almost screamed.

'If you ever try to ignore me or purposefully avoid me again, I will do this every night until you die of exhaustion. Don't you ever tell me to "eff off" again.' He threatened, sounding so cruel, so cold, so heartless. Bryony was genuinely scared. From the look on his face, she didn't doubt he was capable of it. In that moment, he seemed to truly hate her. After that, he disappeared. She cried a few more tears before she fell asleep, sitting up on the sofa.

Her mother woke her a few hours later, her expression so full of concern and worry Bryony cried again. She told her she'd just had an awful nightmare and not to worry about her. After accompanying her to her room, her mother insisted she took a look at her study schedule. Having decided, due to the facts she had been given, that Bryony's trauma was due to her excessive workload, Victoria made some adjustments, then assured her that neither of her parents had any expectations of her academic success. They didn't care if she failed every subject; none of it was worth putting herself under that much stress.

With a burning ache to confess the truth to her wonderfully understanding mother, Bryony settled for a cuddle and then immediately fell asleep again.

Isaac didn't show up again that day, and her mother didn't go to work. Instead, she worked from home, and when Bryony woke up, she made her eat a full brunch, have a hot shower then go on an invigorating walk with her around the block before settling down to do some studying with regular breaks and snacks.

By the end of the day, the events of last night seemed almost like a bad dream. Almost. She felt a flurry of anxiety before she opened her bedroom door that evening, then a rush of relief when Isaac wasn't there.

He didn't return until after she had been to visit Veronica again. And he didn't just show up or pop into her bedroom unannounced, either. She was walking home from the bus stop when she saw him leaning against the garden wall, waiting for her to come home, just like he had used to when he was alive and had football practise on Thursday afternoons so she would go and study late at the library. The memory seemed to lodge in her throat rather than fill her heart as if it was now tarnished.

When he saw her approaching, he didn't grin inanely and rush over to her as he used to. Instead, he hung his head in shame, barely able to meet her eyes. Bryony swallowed her own anxiety and held her head high, aloof and untouchable. When she got close enough, she stood in front of him, her arms crossed. For a while, neither of them said anything, but Bryony refused to back down first.

‘I’m sorry, Bry,’ he mumbled finally.

‘Excuse me?’

He lifted his head and looked her straight in the eyes.

‘I’m really, really and truly sorry,’ he said.

‘I don’t think that’s going to cut it.’

‘I don’t know what else I can say or do.’

‘No. Nor do I. But you threatened me, Isaac. You tortured me relentlessly all night. I was genuinely frightened of you.’

‘Oh God, Bry. I’m sorry, I don’t know why I did that, but the only thing that keeps going through my head is that I think I am turning bad.’

‘What?’

‘I think I’m already becoming one of those things, those ghouls.’

‘Don’t be ridiculous. That process takes hundreds of years.’

‘I know, but I am so angry all the time, and the other night, honestly, I couldn’t control myself. I knew what I was doing was wrong, but I couldn’t stop. I didn’t want to stop until you had suffered. I’ve never done that before. That’s not me. I would never do anything to hurt you. So what else could possibly explain it?’

Mr Gordon, her next-door neighbour who was doing some gardening, started surreptitiously staring at her. She put her hand to her ear and pretended to be talking on the phone.

‘Let’s go inside,’ she quietly said to Isaac.

Once in private, she rounded on him furiously.

‘How dare you! You are a self-centred, scapegoat-using, responsibility-avoiding jerk!’ She puffed, her face becoming red as she got angrier and angrier. ‘You’re not “turning bad.” Don’t you dare try to use the concept of a ghoul as an excuse for you just being a horrible rat! Why would you want to hurt me so much? Is this all just because you're not getting enough attention from me? Are you really such a complete and utter spoiled brat?'

'Wow. Go ahead and say what you really think, then, Bry. Don't let my feelings hold you back. I'm joking!' He added, throwing his hands up in surrender at her expression. 'In all seriousness though, do you really think I might not be turning into a ghoul because I really don't wanna get all ugly and deformed and stuff.'

Bryony stamped her feet and screamed into the hallway.

'Isaac! Get it through your thick head that this is about me and not about you. About what you did to me and how completely out of order that was. I have the right to a good night's sleep and the right to live without fear of interrupted sleep. I have the right to spend time with my parents or to study or to just not be with you all of the time. Don't you dare interrupt me – now is not the time for your stupid jokes. I know you feel like I don't spend enough time with you, God knows you go on about it enough, but I have told you a million times, so this time, you need to really listen and understand me. This is a temporary situation. Once I have got my exams out of the way, we can spend plenty of time together, but by God, I swear, if you ever behave so abominably towards me again, I will ignore you until the day I die. Do you understand me?'

He looked up at her like a chastened child. At first, he refused to say anything, but when he saw her expression reflect her rising temper, he quickly spoke up.

'Yeah. Yes. I understand. I get it. Good plan. Exams first, then quality time together.'

'Don't you have anything else you want to say to me?'

'Umm, you… er… look real pretty?'

'An apology, Isaac.'

'What? I've already apologised,' he began protesting. 'But you are right. I will continue to beg your forgiveness until the day you see fit to forgive me,' he added, seeing the look of pure outrage on her face.

She stared at him sternly for as long as possible until eventually, somewhat mollified, she relented and softened her demeanour towards him.

'So, what you been doing without me?' He asked, twisting his upper body in a cutesy, aren't-we-besties, sort of way.

'Researching how to get rid of poltergeists?' She replied, only half joking.

'Oooh, someone get me some ice, 'cos I just got burned.'

And now she was smiling. God damn him.

'Babe, I know you're still mad at me, and you probably will be for a long time, and rightly so, but you have to know, in a really weird way, I only did all that stuff because of how much I love you.'

'No. I'm not listening to that sort of talk because it's the sort of thing a serial abuser would say.'

'Oh, my God! Is it?'

'Yes, so all I want from you is to regularly apologise 'cos I'm never going to let you forget it and to never do anything like that again. If you do, I will speak with Veronica and have you crossing over the very next day.'

'Whoa, Jesus, you realise that that sounds like murder.'

'How can it be murder when you're already a ghost?'

'Yeah, but that sounds like you want to get rid of me properly,'

'I'm not saying that I want to do that, but I am saying that there have to be consequences for your actions, even for the dead. Or the undead. Whatever you are.'

‘Wow! At least I know where I stand!’ He said, but his tone was light and teasing. ‘Anyway, how are you getting on with the old bat? Learned anything new?’

They made their way up to her bedroom, and she got settled on her bed. ‘Actually, Veronica has been very helpful. I personally think she has told me everything she knows about ghosts and the whole crossing-over process. She hasn’t told me anything new for a couple of weeks, just the same stuff told in a different way.’

‘Oh wicked! You can stop going to see her now. That should free up some of your time.’

‘Yeah, I’m actually going to keep going to see her.’

‘What? Why?’

‘She really is dying. She wasn’t lying about that. She has bone cancer. The nurse said she only has a few weeks left to live and that the only time she really smiles or is happy is when I go and see her. Besides, like I keep telling you, once you get to know her, she’s, well, she’s not nice, but, well, I just like her.’

‘You like her? She’s a horror.’

‘No, she’s not. You haven’t seen her for ages. She’s actually really mellowed.’

Isaac was about to protest further but rightfully changed his mind.

‘So, what do we know so far, then?’

Bryony told him all that she had learned, and Isaac listened with interest. After they had talked, Bryony told him she had studying to do and, like a good, repentant boyfriend, he sat quietly watching telly whilst she studied, and all felt right with the world.

Chapter Sixteen

Everything was not alright with the world. As her first exam grew closer, Bryony's stress levels rose to astronomic heights. She snapped at everyone but especially Isaac, who, because he no longer had to sit exams, could not understand what all the fuss was about. Foolishly, he voiced these thoughts aloud to Bryony, who screamed her head off at him and forbade him from speaking for the rest of the evening. The only time she wasn't cranky was when she was visiting Veronica, who she had become extremely fond of and who usually helped her to step back and put things in perspective. She also managed to act more civilly at work. In fact, the coffee shop had become her other safe haven. No matter who she was working with, they all managed to calm her soul and restore her back to factory settings before her shift was over, each in their own unique way. Vee was able to regale her with the extraordinary foolishness and mischief that her boys got into, though they looked like butter wouldn't melt in their mouths, and Bryony refused to believe a bad word their mother said about them. Mary became a mother hen around Bryony. She sympathised with her about her impossible workload and got excited with her about the prospect of a new adventure when she went to university, whichever one she got into. She told Bryony how her two children had never gone to university, but her eldest grandchild was hopefully going this year, but they lived over in America, so she couldn't really get excited with him, so Bryony and Joe became her surrogates. As for Joe, well, he just made her laugh. He, too, was struggling with his workload as he was also in a heavy metal band, playing bass and occasionally doing gigs but more often, attending band practise and trying to fit his studies around that and work.

Bryony had met his bandmates, their girlfriends, and Joe's girlfriend, whom, she was relieved to say, she liked very much. She had begun to cherish Joe as a friend and would have been gutted if he was dating someone she couldn't get along with, her thoughts immediately conjuring an image of a Monroe type of girl. However, Kirsty, his girlfriend, was nothing like that. She was a curvy girl with dyed bright red, long hair, multiple piercings, and a tattoo on her thigh which she only saw a part of when she wore some ripped denim shorts. She oozed confidence but in a very different way from Monroe. She wasn't conceited or self-centred. She didn't monopolise the conversation or talk over people. She was self-assured, and when she made a mistake, like when she thought Chile was pronounced Chyle, she just owned it, laughed, and moved on. In truth, Bryony was becoming a bit obsessed with the girl herself and regularly had to remind herself not to stare at her.

She had met them all because they all started coming to the coffee shop on a Sunday afternoon, where they would monopolise the whole back wall and have a study session. When the coffee shop closed, Vee would allow them all to stay behind and continue their session until whenever they needed to, as long as they kept a tally of what they ate and drank (and paid the bill), cleared up after themselves and Joe made sure he had locked up properly.

Naturally, Joe invited Bryony to join them, but she declined at first, having always believed that study groups were more about chatting with mates rather than actually studying. However, after watching them a few times and then being asked by Kirsty to join them, Bryony agreed to give it a go, and she was amazed by how useful it was. Obviously, everyone was studying different things and of different levels of intelligence, and it was quickly ascertained that Bryony was the brightest of the bunch. However, she found that when she was explaining something to someone that they were struggling to understand, she was able to retain that information easier than if she'd just re-read her many notecards. Pretty soon, the session became more about Bryony giving lectures about the subjects or the areas they were struggling with most, and it became a win-win for everyone concerned.

That was, of course, until Isaac found out about it. Now, Bryony recognised and accepted that she had been very moody, bordering on hostile towards Isaac recently, especially since the "no sleep incident." However, she also felt this was because he antagonised her when she was feeling her worst. When he wasn't belittling the importance of her exams, he was criticising the way she studied or getting bored and purposefully doing things to annoy her, like randomly singing along with adverts. These annoying little ditties would then get stuck in her head, so it would be all that she could think about instead of learning the information on her notecard, and Isaac would think that was funny and laugh hysterically, which also wound her up incessantly.

He also still complained about her lack of free time, no matter how often she reminded him of how temporary it was and that in four weeks' time, the exams would all be over, and she would be all his, something she wasn't necessarily looking forward to as much as she once had.

So, in an effort to bowl her over with romance and support, Isaac made his way to the coffee shop just in time for her shift to end so they could spend some quality time together on the bus ride home. Admittedly, as romantic gestures went, this was fairly lame, but he was limited with what he could do as he had no… anything.

He arrived to find that not only was the coffee shop closed and, according to the sign, closed over an hour ago, so she had been lying about what time her shift ended. But that also his girlfriend, who was too busy these days to even spend an hour with him a night, who was grumpy all the time and who claimed she didn't want or need any other friends as she had him, was in the middle of a large group of people laughing and chatting. If he had blood in his body, it would have boiled at that moment.

Bryony was sitting with her back to the door, so she hadn't noticed him when he came in. Plus, there was so much chatter that she didn't hear him call her name several times, either. His rage grew.

She turned, like everyone else, though, when the jar of biscotti on the counter smashed on the floor. Unlike everyone else, she didn't wonder aloud how the hell that had fallen off the side or attempted to explain it away with "it must have been left too close to the edge" or "maybe there's a breeze coming in from somewhere."

She stared disbelievingly at Isaac and the absolute fury on his face.

'Are you alright, Bry? You've gone super pale,' Arthur, the band's lead singer, remarked. He'd been paying special attention to Bryony since they met as he was the only single one in the group, and no one, as yet, had met this "Isaac" she spoke of.

'You look like you've seen a ghost,' Kirsty agreed, and everyone but Bryony laughed at the notion.

'That's it! It was a ghost.'

'Wooo – the coffee shop is haunted.'

'A ghost knocked over the biscotti jar. It sounds like an awful lyric. I'm going to write that down,' Paul, the classically trained pianist, songwriter, and drummer, added.

Bryony continued to stare at Isaac.

Isaac glared back.

Joe and Kirsty went over to clean up the mess. Bryony was vaguely aware of Joe, wondering aloud how the hell they were going to explain this to Vee.

'Don't stress, love. There's no such thing as ghosts. We're only pulling your leg,' Arthur assured her gently, wrapping his arm around her shoulders. Bryony had been kindly but firmly rejecting Arthur's advances since he first started making them. At this moment, she wished she'd been a little less kind and a little more assertive as she once again shrugged herself free of his touch. By the time she turned back to look at Isaac, he was gone.

She debated inwardly whether she should follow him or not. A good girlfriend would. A good girlfriend should. But he was so angry right now, there was no way he would listen to reason. He was so angry he could move things. Actually, violently push things. How the hell could he do that already? Maybe he had been right before; maybe he was turning bad, turning into a ghoul already. The thought made her whole body run cold, and she shivered.

She snapped out of it and pretended to help with the clear-up and packing away their things; all of them had decided they ought to call it a night anyway. She escaped to the toilet for some thinking time. If she went home now, she was sure that Isaac would be too angry to deal with her and might do something awful, something they'll both regret. No, she decided; Isaac needed some cooling off time. She would face him tomorrow. Maybe. If she was being really honest with herself, she was scared. Scared of Isaac. Scared, he might hurt her either physically, now that he could, or mentally like he did last time he got angry and wouldn't let her sleep.

She came up with a plan. She would convince Joe to let her have the keys to lock up. She'd either tell everyone she was going to the toilet as they were all leaving, or she'd leave with them and then just double back and come back here. She could do a few more hours of study and then just sleep along one of the back booth benches. She could then get up really early in the morning and lock up so no one would know the difference.

She called her mum and told her that the study session was going to run late, so she was going to stay over at her friend Kirsty's tonight and get the bus home tomorrow morning. Her mother sounded surprised but equally relieved that she was making new friends. She hung up, put her phone in her bag and exited the cubicle.

Kirsty was standing, leaning against the washbasin, having clearly heard every word.

Bryony blushed to the deepest beetroot red colour. Her reflection in the mirror showed her how ugly her embarrassment made her, and she blushed even further.

'So, what's going on?' Kirsty said, picking the yellow nail varnish off her fingernails.

'I... erm...' she floundered, hoping something, some excuse, some explanation that sounded halfway normal, would pop into her head. It didn't.

'I'm so sorry. Obviously, I'm not staying at yours. I just had to tell my mum that because... well... I can't go home.'

'Yeah, I thought it was something like that. Did your boyfriend walk past the window or something? I could tell from the look of horror on your face. Vee is not the type to instil that level of terror. He's the controlling type, is he? Not told him about our little study sessions, I'm guessing. I've known dudes like him. I'd say you're probably best getting rid, but I literally know nothing about it, so I'll keep my nose out. So, if you're not planning on stopping at mine and you're not going home, where are you planning to sleep tonight then?'

'Um. Here, I guess,' she mumbled, still burning with shame and amazed at Kirsty's insight. Proper Sherlock Holmes, that one.

'Nah, I don't think so. You can stay at mine. It's no biggie.'

'No, no, Kirsty, it's fine, honestly.' Except, of course, it wasn't.

'Look, relax. I'm not a gossip. I won't bug you for details of whatever you're going through, but if you want to talk, I'll obviously listen. However, I draw the line at letting you sleep here. There's not even a bed or a duvet, or a cushion. How would I sleep knowing I'd left you here, when there's room at my house? I wouldn't, so don't argue. It's not about you, it's about me and my ability to get a good night's sleep.'

‘Please, Kirsty, you really don’t have to do this. I feel as if I’ve sort of forced you into it, and I…’

‘I’m not offering you the Ritz here, Bry. I’m offering to share my bed, or if you prefer, you can sleep on the sofa, which is soft and has cushions and throws. But you’re not stopping here. I won’t allow it. You’ve just taught me how to make sense of Shakespeare’s sonnets in, like, half an hour or something. My English teacher has been trying and failing for, like, two years. The least you deserve is somewhere comfortable to sleep, for goodness sake. Besides, you’ve already told your mum. We don’t want to make you a liar now, do we?’ She winked naughtily and left the bathroom. Bryony smiled gratefully but felt the warmth spread over her cheeks again. She was really going to spend some time alone with Kirsty!

Bryony still hadn’t worked out what to say about Isaac when they went to Kirsty’s after their study session, so she said nothing, and as promised, Kirsty didn’t pry. Instead, they discussed and listened to music. Fortunately, Kirsty had an eclectic taste and didn’t subject Bryony to heavy metal music that the boys in the band were all into. She had the coolest bedroom Bryony had ever seen. It turned out Kirsty was very creative but couldn’t decide which outlet for her creativity to focus on, so she dabbled in everything. She had painted a beautiful seascape mural on one of her bedroom walls. She had made her own personalised patchwork quilt and knitted toys and cushions, which littered the room. Various hand-crafted ornaments were dotted about her small bedroom along with, to Bryony’s delight, stacks and stacks and overflowing bookcases of books. Plus, one whole half of her bedroom was full of a variety of musical instruments.

Bryony discovered a lot about Kirsty, as she was unwilling to discuss much about herself. Things such as her passion for writing and playing music, DJ’ing, painting, and clearly reading, although she was more into non-fiction books than the novels Bryony devoured. Still, their interests did cross over here and there.

They talked until late into the night, and Bryony even talked Kirsty into playing and singing some of her songs. She had the most surprisingly sweet and clear voice; it almost moved Bryony to tears. She reminded her of vintage Norah Jones or Eva Cassidy, and when she told Kirsty as much, she laughed as though she were joking.

When they went to bed, it felt perfectly natural to lie next to each other in her small double bed, but when the lights went out, and the warmth of Kirsty's soft curves lay next to her, Bryony found herself suddenly not tired at all, and her thoughts were uncontrollable and inappropriate.

Untroubled, Kirsty fell asleep almost instantly, and she turned in her sleep to face Bryony, her breathing gentle and rhythmic, her minty breath mingling with her own. Overcome with the desire to stroke her hair or touch her face, Bryony forced herself out of bed, gathered up the beautiful handmade quilted throw, and slept on the sofa downstairs, enveloped in the heady scent of Kirsty.

She rose before anyone else in the house. She folded the throw neatly and placed it in the bedroom where she'd found it, then left a note thanking her for her company last night and assuring her she'd slept well. Then she left as quietly as she could, secretly hoping they wouldn't see each other much again. It was simply too confusing.

It took her an hour and a half to get back to her house from Kirsty's, and when she got there, she realised she still wasn't ready to face Isaac, so she turned and went back to the bus stop. It was rush hour now, everyone trying to get to work, and at first, Bryony had no idea where to go until she realised her subconscious had already worked that much out for her, and she was halfway to seeing Veronica already.

When she arrived, she immediately realised she'd made a mistake. She visited Veronica every Thursday from about 11 to 3, and every week, Veronica would be waiting for her. Her hair would be done, she would be clean and dressed, and even wear a little make-up to make herself presentable for her only visitor.

It was 9:40 on a Monday morning, and Veronica had not been expecting her. As such, Bryony found her in her little room with her nightdress still on, her hair a mess, and her complexion wan and pale.

It wasn't that she was unkempt or undressed that bothered Bryony; it was how very frail and ill she looked. She was so thin, her bones seemed to protrude, something which had clearly been kept covered up whenever Bryony had visited before.

She looked every bit like an 89-year-old lady in the late stages of bone cancer, only Bryony had never seen it before, and it blew her away. She felt like she'd been kicked in the stomach, and she decided it would be best for everyone if she just waited in the sunroom whilst the carers helped to clean and dress Veronica.

When Veronica was wheeled in a few minutes later, her expression was stony and distant.

'Why are you here today and not Thursday?' She demanded by way of greeting.

'I... I'm sorry. I guess I just wanted to see you,' Bryony stammered.

'You will not feel sorry for me,' she half yelled. 'You will not look at me with pity in your eyes. You will not concern yourself or me with my health. If we are to continue to see one another, we must continue as equals, as we have before you rudely interrupted me today. Do you understand?'

'Ronnie, I cannot unsee what I just saw,' Bryony began, but as Veronica attempted to manoeuvre her wheelchair out of the sunroom, she added hastily, 'But I don't see why it should change our relationship.' Veronica stopped and turned back cautiously. 'You, yourself, told me you were dying. I guess over the last few months, I sort of forgot. I have come to cherish our friendship Ronnie, so I'm just sad, that's all.'

‘Well, stop being sad,’ Veronica insisted.

And though she knew it was impossible, she nodded her agreement and attempted a smile for her friend. Veronica eyed her more shrewdly than usual, then demanded some breakfast from a passing carer. Bryony raised an eyebrow, and Ronnie begrudgingly added a “please”.

When breakfast arrived for both of them, Bryony devoured hers heartily, realising she was starving, whilst Ronnie picked at her piece of toast like she was a small bird.

‘So, without meaning to sound rude, why are you here? You can’t tell me you were just passing. I know you live miles away, and you cannot tell me you had nothing to do because I know you have your big exams coming up, and you’re always revising. Too much, in my opinion, not that you’d ever ask for that. So, why are you here with me?’

Bryony considered making something up, but having seen Veronica in all her vulnerability, she felt it was only fair to be as vulnerable with her. So, she told her everything, how Isaac had kept her awake all night once before, his new rage issues, and being able to move things now. She even spoke about her confusing feelings for Kirsty and how she just hoped everything would calm down once she’d done her exams. Veronica listened intently, without interruption, until she had finished.

‘And so, as I was halfway here anyway, I thought I would just come and see you,’ she concluded. ‘I’m sorry. I didn’t mean to lay all my problems on you.’

‘I asked you to, didn’t I?’ Veronica snapped. Then she sat thoughtfully for a few quiet minutes. Bryony refilled their teacups. She was used to these moments of quiet reflection. Ronnie often thought things through before speaking unless it was an order or retort, in which case she had no filter. Bryony sipped her hot tea as she waited anxiously for Ronnie’s harsh tongue to pass judgement.

‘Well now, this is interesting,’ she finally said, indicating Bryony could now speak again.

‘What is? The Isaac thing? Has your grandmother ever gotten cross with you? Have you any ideas how to deal with an angry ghost?’

‘What? Oh yes, Isaac. That’s easy, you can just banish him. Serve the little scamp right for being such an impertinent little toe rag. I’m more interested in your feelings for the girl. Are you a lesbian now?’

‘Oh, erm, I don’t know. I’ve never fancied a girl before. It’s just her, so I don’t think so.’

‘Maybe you’re one of them who likes everyone. A bisexual, is it? There’s so many different names for them all now. I can’t remember all the words. In my day, you used to call someone queer, but you can’t say that these days, can you? Or is that the one you can say? Is it lesbian you can’t say? Doreen says it all the time about her daughter.’

‘Right. Okay,’ Bryony said cautiously.

‘I thought I was a lesbian once. Turns out it was just a bit of bad chicken. Or maybe it was all the drugs I was on. For a long time, I thought I was an albino parrot.’

Unsure how to answer that, Bryony tried not to laugh and kept quiet.

‘So.’

‘So what?’

‘Are you a lesbian or not?’

‘Jeez, Ronnie! I don’t know. I’m not even sure if I really do have feelings for her or if I’m just confused about Isaac. Maybe we don’t need to put any kind of label on this just now, okay.’

‘But I want a lesbian friend.’ She moaned petulantly.

'Ronnie!'

'It would be so exciting and exotic. Mabel's grandson has come out as gay, and she doesn't bloody well shut up about him. Doreen's daughter is a married lesbian with two children! How does that work? I don't bloody know, but I'd love to tell them all that my friend is a lesbian. Wipe their smug smiles off them. Their gays don't even visit. My lesbian friend visits me every week,' she grinned naughtily.

'Ronnie! That's enough now. You ought to be grateful you still have a friend who visits you at all after comments like that,' Bryony chided.

'I'm going to tell her you are anyway. And if you see her, don't you dare contradict me. It's my dying wish,' she looked up coyly at Bryony, whose shocked expression made her grin slyly.

'You manipulative monster,' Bryony stated. Ronnie cackled wickedly.

'Tell me more about how you banish ghosts. That I'm very interested in.'

'Oh, it's easy. All you have to do is say out loud that you banish them.'

'That's it?'

'Well, you must say their full name, and you really have to mean it. You can't half-arse it. But if you really, really mean it, they'll just disappear.'

'How long for?'

Veronica shrugged.

'It depends. I once banished my grandmother for a whole year. I guess they come back when you're ready to see them again.'

'And where do they go?'

'I've no idea. Grandma never spoke about it.'

'Do you think I should be worried that he can move things now?'

'I think that boy of yours is destined to break the record for the fastest transition from ghost to ghoul. The sooner he crosses over, the better for both of you. Then you can concentrate on that girl of yours.'

Bryony half smiled, but she couldn't deny she was worried. An hour later and she felt much better about life in general, but Veronica was beginning to show signs of fatigue, so she left, promising to return on Thursday as usual. During her long trip home she considered all that Ronnie had said about Isaac crossing over before it was too late and his speedy transition to a ghoul. She had no idea if, when she returned, Isaac would be calm or still raging, possibly angrier than ever. The last time he had lost his temper, it was because he'd felt she had ignored him. Goodness knows what he had taken from what he saw last night. She cursed Arthur for his unwanted advances. Maybe she should have just followed him home last night. Dealt with it all head-on. But then she wouldn't have had last night with Kirsty.

She called her mum to let her know she was on her way home and to surreptitiously find out if, by any chance, anyone was at home. Sometimes one or both of her parents worked from home but not today. Her mother confirmed that the house was nice and quiet so she could study in peace. She reminded Bryony to have regular breaks before hanging up.

With great trepidation and a deep, resolved sigh, she walked inside the house. Everything was normal. There were no noises, nothing out of place. She tentatively called out a "hello" to the house at large. There was no answer, and a tiny spark of hope that Isaac might not be there flared within her chest. She grabbed a drink and an apple and toyed with the idea of studying downstairs, she had all her books in her bag from last night, but she knew she couldn't put off the inevitable forever. She climbed the stairs to her bedroom, keeping the fact that she could banish him if she needed to at the forefront of her mind. She listened at the bedroom door for a few seconds, but it was quiet, so she went inside.

Isaac was not in the room. However, Bryony still stood in horror for a full minute. Her usually perfectly ordered and tidy bedroom was a complete mess. Her books, her bedding, the telly, her clothes, and her trinkets. Everything was everywhere. Isaac had definitely honed his skills at moving things. He had completely annihilated her bedroom. And what was scarier for Bryony was that she knew her mother would have popped into her bedroom last night to make sure the window was shut, and she never mentioned a mess or hearing any strange noises last night. Therefore, Isaac must have caused all of this mess, all this destruction, this morning after they left for work.

Feeling weirdly emotional and violated, she began to pick some random things up, though she hardly knew where to start.

She had barely picked up three books when she felt the familiar chill and looked up, expecting to see her so-called boyfriend, but he wasn't there. Or, at least, he wasn't visible.

She shivered and knew he must be close by.

'I know you're here,' she said aloud, trying to sound confident and annoyed, not scared and upset. 'How dare you do this to me, Isaac?' She said to the empty room.

Then she felt fingers so cold around her throat that they felt like they were burning her.

She gasped in surprise, then in fear as the fingers tightened, but she couldn't touch him back and had no way to fight him off. He managed to lift her clean off the floor, just gripping her neck, and then he showed himself. Bryony flailed in the air, entirely unable to fight back, and the look on his face when he appeared was so murderous, so full of utter hatred, all she could think was that he was definitely going to kill her. She was so scared she became still, limp in his grasp. Unable to move, unable to talk, barely able to breathe.

Then he threw her. He launched her over the bed as though she were a toy doll. Bryony gasped for air but otherwise didn't hesitate. She scrambled to her feet, and though her voice was croaky and weak, her feeling was strong and powerful.

'I banish you, Isaac Thomas Spencer.'

He disappeared mid-stride.

Chapter Seventeen

Once she'd had a good cry and cleaned up her room, Bryony spent little to no time thinking about Isaac. She did not regret or feel guilty about what she did to him, and though he had left no mark on her neck, she did have a very sore throat for a few days, and she had to assure her mother she wasn't overdoing it with the studying, she wasn't getting ill or anything, it was just a sore throat.

Besides, the next two weeks were taken up with exams. Every hour of her waking days were filled with last-minute revision or mulling over answers she had given and analysing where she may have possibly gone wrong. The exams themselves rarely lasted more than three hours, and only once or twice did she have to sit more than two a day. When they were all over, her parents took her out for a meal at a restaurant of her choosing, and then she slept for fifteen hours straight.

After a few days of much deserved chilling, she decided to go shopping. She had been working at the coffee shop for nearly six months now, and she'd barely spent a penny of what she'd earned. However, the family were going on holiday the next day, and having recently gone through all the clothes in her wardrobe, she decided it was desperately lacking, so she was going to treat herself to some new ones.

She'd barely browsed through two shops in town when she saw Billie and India from school. Her instinct was to avoid them both and, well, not hide exactly, just avoid being seen by them, but it was too late; they'd seen her and seen her notice them. They had to acknowledge each other.

The two girls whispered to each other before Billie waved her hand in a cautious greeting. Trying to keep the disappointment out of her expression, Bryony smiled back, and they walked towards each other. They exchanged pleasantries and discussed the exams and how just awful they were. Then they discussed shopping and what they were looking for. Bryony explained she was going on holiday with her parents, so she was treating herself, and the girls told her of their holiday plans for the summer. It was all wrapping up nicely, and both parties were pleasantly surprised with how painless the experience had been when Billie ruined it.

'We're having a party tonight. You should come,' she said. Both the other girls looked at her in a mixture of disbelief and horror for a split second until social decorum took over.

'Yes, definitely,' India added, smiling half-heartedly.

Bryony floundered. She desperately tried to think up an excuse, but her brain, having worked so hard for the past two weeks, decided to go on strike. Billie proceeded to give her the low-down on the party details whilst Bryony continued to be awkwardly silent. To cap it all off, Billie asked her to promise she'd come, and in unbelievable stupidity, Bryony said she would. As they walked away, Bryony was sure India would demand an explanation of Billie's stupidity and then wondered if the promise she'd made was actually one she had to keep. Surely, neither of them and no one in the whole wide world would expect her to go. She continued with her shopping trip, and the rest of the day was very enjoyable. She found some lovely new bikinis, some bargain denim shorts and a nice pair of sandals. She treated herself to lunch and spent a good hour people-watching before going on to buy two new tops and some new make-up, including a rather daring shade of lipstick that reminded her of Kirsty, which led her thoughts onto what it would be like to kiss Kirsty. She'd only ever kissed a boy before. One boy. Isaac.

Isaac!

This was the first time she'd even thought about him in over two weeks. Two weeks! She couldn't even blame her exams, she'd finished them a couple of days ago, and in all that downtime, she hadn't once spared a thought for her exiled boyfriend. She wondered where he was, what he was doing or if he was even conscious in this exile. If he was, she wondered if he was still mad. A shiver ran through her as she remembered his ice-cold fingers around her neck, and her guilt disappeared instantly. He'd fully deserved to be exiled and ignored. His temper needed controlling, and this appeared to be the perfect solution. Now she knew that she could do it, she didn't feel so frightened of him anymore, which she was begrudgingly willing to admit to herself, she had been. Still, things should be better now. She was no longer stressed out with exams and had no school whatsoever to take up her time. In fact, the only other responsibility she had now was her job. Oh, and the family holiday for two weeks. And visiting Veronica. But that was it, those were the only other things that required her time and attention, although her to-be-read pile was becoming out of hand, but Isaac was more important than some reading downtime, wasn't he? Of course, he was, she chastised herself.

She wondered what she had to do to get him back. She vaguely remembered Ronnie saying something about having to really want to see them again before he'd be able to reappear to her. She briefly worried if that was going to be an issue but quickly pushed the possibility out of her head and reminded herself that she had been a complete mess when she had believed he was really dead. Then she began to think practically. If she wanted to bring Isaac back then for their initial reunion, she would want privacy in case they started arguing again. So, if she went home now, she'd have a good hour and a half before her dad came home from work, and she shouldn't really put this off until after her holiday, should she? No, what if he was in some awful place? Ronnie really hadn't had a clue where they go when in exile, but it would worry her all holiday if she left him there, probably. Making her mind up, Bryony rushed home, only stopping to window shop once or twice.

When she got home, she had to mentally gear herself up for bringing Isaac back. She realised she'd have to really, really want him to come back. Her feeble thoughts, which were tinged with anxiety and dread, would not cut it. So, she sat remembering all the good times. Going through old text messages and photos to encourage her wavering heart.

As she was swiping through, something in the background of an image caught her attention, and she full-screened it. The photo was a rare one of just her and Emily. She was the one girl in Isaac's group of friends that she actually liked, and they'd been chatting at a party and decided to take a selfie. However, it was the background of that photo that really interested Bryony. She used her fingers to zoom in on it, and there it was, clear as daylight.

Isaac kissing Monroe.

Her face flushed, and she felt her fingers tremble as hurt, anger, embarrassment, shame, and betrayal ripped through her. She had known. Deep down, she'd known for ages. Monroe had wanted her to know. Of course, she had, but how many other people had known? If they were happy to snog in front of all their friends when she was in the same god-damned room, then she guessed they all did. And not one of them, not even Emily, had told her or even hinted or tried to warn her. A fresh wave of betrayal and embarrassment washed through her. No wonder she didn't miss or crave their kind of friendship. Still, one thing was for sure now. She really, really wanted to see Isaac again.

As soon as she thought about it, he appeared in her room.

He stumbled slightly and blinked as though coming from darkness. He took a few seconds to orientate himself and understand the situation he'd just somehow been plonked into. And then, with the memory of their last encounter burning freshly in both of their minds, there was a very awkward, very silent few minutes.

'Is there anything I could say here that could help you to forgive me?' He began, having the good grace to look devastated and heartily ashamed. This time it had no effect on her.

'No,' she answered flatly, unemotional.

He nodded and remained quiet.

'That doesn't mean you shouldn't at least try. You should still be on your knees, begging for my forgiveness, even though you know you don't deserve it because of the truly, unbelievably shitty thing you did to me.'

'Bry…'

'I mean, how lucky am I that I learned, just an hour or so earlier on that day, how to banish you? What would have happened if I hadn't? Would I be dead? Is that actually your endgame here? Is that what you ultimately want? Are you so unspeakably selfish that you would rather kill me so you'd have company rather than let me continue to live my life?' She demanded, her voice like a battering ram to his soul.

'No, of course…'

'Shut up. Just don't even talk about it. I don't want to hear any of your excuses or your apologies. All I want from you right now is the truth. Can you do that for me? I have a burning question I want an answer to, and I want to hear the absolute, God's honest truth from you now. Do you think you can do that?'

He nodded dumbly.

'When you were alive, did you ever kiss Monroe whilst you were going out with me?'

'What? Where is this coming from now? Has Monroe been making stuff up about us again?'

'Just answer the question, Isaac. Answer it truthfully, please. This is still unresolved for me. This is the argument we were having the night you died. This is the question that plagued my thoughts and my dreams all the time before your funeral. Hell, it plagued our relationship even before you died. So tell me, Isaac, once and for all, hand on your heart, pinky promise truth now. Did you or did you not snog Monroe when you were going out with me?'

He looked her dead in the eyes. He didn't blink, didn't splutter, didn't hesitate, or break eye contact.

'No, babe. Of course not.'

Bryony released a huge sigh she hadn't realised she'd been holding on to, then sat on the bed with her back to Isaac. He moved to sit by her, cooing gentle assurances of his innocence on this matter, his absolute love for her, their unbreakable bond, and the vicious rumours Monroe liked to spread to get attention. Bryony had heard them all before. Believed them all before. Without saying a word, she found the picture on her phone, zoomed in on the area of the image she needed to, and held it up for him to see. She watched him flounder for a moment, his mouth opening and closing slightly as his brain worked furiously to try and give her a reasonable explanation that would still bring him out on top.

'You're a liar, Isaac. I won't believe another word you say,' Bryony said quietly. She left him sitting on her bed and had a shower. There was no need for any drama. Now she knew the truth, she could move on with her life. When she returned, he was pacing around. This time though, he wasn't fuelled by scary anger, it was desperation. He repeatedly tried to engage her in conversation, but it was as though she had found a mute button for him. She completely tuned him out whilst she got ready.

Her mother knocked and entered.

'Hi honey, how was shopping?'

'Pretty successful, actually. I got a few things for holiday,'

'Excellent. Are you packing?'

'No. I'm going to do that tomorrow. Don't worry, I know exactly what I'm taking, so it won't take me long. I ran into Billie and India whilst I was out. They invited me to a party tonight. Actually, they sort of made me promise I would be there. It was sweet, really. So I thought I would pop in. Sort of a farewell to traditional schooling,'

'Oh, right. Well, that's unexpected. I thought you were done with that crowd?'

'Oh God, yeah, I definitely am. But from the sounds of it, the whole school will be there. It just feels like a sort of rite of passage or something. I probably won't stay long, just show my face. It might be good for me, you know, like closure or whatever.'

'Yes, of course, darling. Obviously, I'm going to ask you to be careful but also have fun.'

'Thanks, Mum.'

'Do you want a lift?'

'Yeah, actually, that would be great, thanks.'

'Okay, I'll let your father know. And just give us a call when you're ready to come home.'

'Will do, cheers.'

'And darling, if you do decide to have a drink, just remember that we're going on holiday tomorrow. You haven't packed yet, and you have a long flight, so be sensible.'

'Of course, Mum, like I said, I probably won't be long.'

'Oh, one more thing. I love that shade of lipstick on you.'

Bryony grinned.

'Thanks, Mum. I'm trying out something new.'

As soon as she left the room, Isaac began his tirade again, or maybe he'd been doing it all the time, she didn't know and didn't care. She tuned him out completely as she got herself dressed and ready.

Her dad was his usual taciturn self as he drove her to the address she'd been given. She tried to ignore the insecurity and paranoia that told her that the girls had been playing a cruel trick and there was no party, or they'd given her the wrong address, or just something horrible. It didn't help that the outfit she'd chosen was more revealing than anything she'd worn in public in England before, and she'd curled her hair into gentle waves, which was a new style for her. It is always unnerving releasing a new look on the general public, especially when it's your catty teenage peers.

Finally, Bryony recognised a few people going into a large house on the right, and she vaguely recognised the place as somewhere she had been before, maybe for Billie's birthday one year.

Her father reiterated her mother's earlier concerns but, as ever, in a far more concise way. He pointed to the house and the people milling around outside and simply said, 'Be careful.' Bryony chuckled and assured him she would be.

Isaac followed her out of the car, but he sensed her nerves, or she was still in control of his volume. Either way, he remained quiet. She realised her father would sit and wait until she got safely inside, so gathering her confidence together, she stepped into the party.

The noise seemed to physically hit her in the face. She knew she was a little late, it was almost nine, but the party was definitely in full swing. People were everywhere; dancing, chatting intensely, entertaining each other in small crowds, or snogging in dark corners. As she moved through the house, she realised the whole school year and more must be there, though she'd really only said that to reassure her mum, and she was a little peeved that her invitation had been a begrudgingly offered afterthought. It wasn't that long ago she was a shoo-in with this crowd. She knew she wasn't exactly Miss Popular these days, but still, she was part of the senior year.

A few people recognised her, and they gave her the once over appraisingly, though no one said hello or initiated a conversation with her, so she kept on walking. She was beginning to massively regret coming here. What had she been thinking? Had she thought that somehow she'd just miraculously fit in? This wasn't some movie, this was real life with real teenagers who hold grudges or are all just genuinely very awkward.

She pushed her way into the kitchen and, not knowing what else to do, she opened the wine she'd bought and poured herself a glass. She stood, squished against a cupboard for a while, watching people do shots, mix crazy cocktails and help themselves to snacks from the fridge. She caught snippets of conversations, but she'd been out of the loop for so long that she couldn't keep up with it. Bryony's mother had always insisted that parties begin and end in the kitchen, and that certainly seemed to be proving true. As Bryony minded her own business in the corner, exchanging her empty wine bottle for a can of lager, then for a gin and lemonade, then a couple of cocktail concoctions of her own making, she observed pretty much everyone else in the party as they came to refill their drinks. She watched plans being formed, mainly practical jokes, arguments taking place, reconciliations, selfies, groupies, kisses, spills, trips, and falls. Occassionally she would chit chat with people but once they had what they wanted from the kitchen, they wandered off again. And then SHE swanned in. She was wearing a blue halter neck crop top and some barely there denim shorts. She didn't notice Bryony. Of course, she didn't. She was too caught up in her own drama. Bryony had heard all about the new scandal surrounding Monroe already. Everyone at the party had been talking about it. She had supposedly snogged Jordan, who was the long-term on-again-off-again boyfriend of India, which maybe explained why she hadn't been with them on their shopping trip. Rumour had it, the couple were definitely on again when Monroe moved on him.

She sashayed her way around the kitchen island, ignoring the beers and heading straight for the spirits. Her groupies followed her. Emily spotted Bryony and waved. Bryony waved back but turned her attention back to Monroe like nearly everyone else in the kitchen, which had gone eerily quiet. Bryony stepped forward for the first time all evening. The alcohol she had consumed egging her on.

‘Hello, Monroe,’ she ventured, only slurring slightly.

‘Bryony!’ She exclaimed delightedly. ‘Well, don’t you look very… quaint.’ She looked her up and down. Bryony felt her blood boil and willed herself not to blush.

‘You don’t,’ she retorted. Monroe threw her head back and laughed.

‘You are hilarious!’ She announced, a little forced. ‘So how come you’re talking to us now? I thought you had no time for us little people without Zachie.’

‘Well, I think we both know neither of us has much in common. It seemed silly to continue to act like we were friends. Like we liked each other.’

‘Wow, the claws are out tonight, tiger. Maybe you wanna ease up on those drinky-poos, hun. You may say something you regret. Besides, that’s not true. I made sure you were included when you hung out with us. I always took the time to talk to you. I cannot be held responsible if your inferiority complex kept you from actually liking me, darling.’

This time Bryony threw her head back and laughed heartily, only vaguely aware of the large crowd gathering in around them.

‘I do not feel inferior to you, Monroe,’ her voice louder now, even though the kitchen was so silent. ‘I am appalled by you. Appalled by your lack of empathy, lack of loyalty, and lack of intelligence. Tell me do you consider India to be a friend? I only ask because you appear to be as much of a “friend” to her as you were to me.’

Monroe began to answer back, but Bryony was on a roll.

‘I knew you were a horrendous flirt. I knew that, despite your charade, we weren’t particularly close, but still, I thought you had a shred of common decency. Apparently, you also lack that.’

Bryony pulled the photo that she had blown up and printed out of her bra and launched it at Monroe. She caught and studied it for a moment. It took her a few seconds to find herself in the photo. A few people who were looking over her shoulder found her at the same time and let out gasps. It was passed around the kitchen quickly. Monroe looked defiantly at Bryony.

'Please. It's not my fault that you couldn't keep your man happy. You're so painfully dull and boring; it was inevitable he would look for someone more fun, someone more his calibre.'

'What is amazing to me is that you see this as a win for you. The fact that you and Isaac snogged, literally behind my back, does not reflect badly on me. It simply shows that you are a terrible friend, and Isaac was either drunk or angry with me. There is no other explanation. You didn't win Isaac. He would never want you to be his. You made an absolute fool of yourself the whole time we were together, flirting madly, desperately throwing yourself at him, and never once did our relationship flounder. He never even considered if he would rather be with you. Oh, he obviously snogged you, there's no denying that. He may even have done more with you, what guy wouldn't when it was offered so blatantly? But did he ever walk into a room with you on his arm? Did he ever take you home to meet his family? Has anyone, for that matter? No. And do you know why? It's because no one actually likes you. Fancy you - of course. Use you enough for a quick shag – sure. But actually have to spend time with you – absolutely not. You are a shallow, mean, vicious pair of tits. You're the dirty little secret that they all laugh about when it's just the boys chatting. You're worth little more than some light relief when the girls they really want are unable or unwilling to put out for them.

'So no, Monroe, I really don't feel inferior to you. I pity you. I laugh at your lack of self-respect. I wouldn't be you for all the money in the world.'

The elation at finally being able to let rip at Monroe after all this time was like a drug rush, she imagined. Silence fell upon the kitchen. Monroe said nothing, and Bryony thought she might have been battling tears.

Then someone started clapping.

Jax stepped forward from the crowd and gave her a little "whoop whoop." He was wearing dark jeans, a white t-shirt, and shades on top of his expertly ruffled hair. His skin looked clear, and his eyes were shining with laughter. He looked incredible, and Bryony knew the girls in the room agreed; she could practically smell the pheromones coming off him.

'Jax! What are you doing here?'

She felt another thrill run through her as people's (Monroe's) jaws actually dropped when they realised that Bryony knew this drop-dead gorgeous hunk.

'Oh, I came to see the catfight. Anyone got any mud, or maybe jelly?' He called to some general hollers.

Bryony couldn't help but grin as he stepped closer.

'Mind if I cut in?' He asked Monroe as he stepped between the two girls and bent his head to kiss Bryony in front of everyone. She was drunk on alcohol and revenge, so she threw caution to the wind and wrapped her fingers in Jax's lush hair, pulling him closer, deepening the kiss.

The kitchen suddenly erupted with cheers, whoops, laughs, and chatter.

Jax pulled away, looked down at her, and whispered, 'Wanna get out of here?'

Bryony didn't hesitate. She'd done all she wanted to do at this party and was now desperate to leave. She nodded and allowed Jax to lead her out of the kitchen. She didn't look back at either Monroe or Isaac, who was still standing in the corner of the kitchen, both watching her silently as she left.

The fresh air outside hit her like a sucker punch, and she immediately needed help to stand up. Jax laughed at her unsteadiness and wrapped an arm around her waist.

'I knew you must have had some sort of Dutch courage to talk the way you did in there,' he said, bringing them to a stop once they were off the driveway. He made sure Bryony was stable enough to lean against the garden wall without his support before he let her go, then rummaged through his many pockets until he located what he was looking for; cigarettes and a lighter. Of course, he was a smoker. His whole demeanour and attitude should have told her that. She watched him light up, take a quick drag, then play with the lighter, running his finger across the flame. She realised that smoking was secondary for Jax; it was just a reason to use the lighter that drew him to it. She watched as his fingers extinguished the flame and then re-lit it. She was surprised when he stopped suddenly, and she realised he was looking at her intently.

'I'm not boyfriend material,' he blurted out. 'Don't go getting all obsessed with me 'cos it's a one night only kinda deal.'

He looked so serious. Bryony burst out laughing. He was shocked, which made her laugh even more.

'I'll do my very best to resist you, Mr Ramsworth,' she finally managed to say. He grinned, then rightfully looked a bit embarrassed.

'I'm sorry. I didn't mean to sound big-headed or anything. I know we've been flirting for a while, but I'm not really someone you'd actually wanna be with. You seem like a one-man kinda girl, and I've had issues with girls like that in the past. Although I realise now that if you're not immediately falling in love with me, then that may have sounded rather…'

'Conceited? Arrogant? Egotistical?'

‘I was going to say presumptuous, but I guess all apply,’ his cigarette had burned down to the filter, although he had barely had two or three drags from it. He threw it away and moved to lean against the wall next to her. ‘I figured that after you’d said all of that in there, you’d want to leave pretty sharpish.’

‘That was very considerate of you.’

‘I actually thought you were going to slap me when I kissed you.’

They both chuckled.

‘Well, don’t worry. Despite your obvious charms, including your modesty, I think I’ll be able to resist falling in love with you after just one kiss. Actually, it would be better for me if we did think of this as just a one-night thing,’ she added, hoping not to offend. Boys were weird sometimes.

‘Awesome.’

‘So what are we doing here?’ Bryony asked. ‘I mean, I appreciate the exit strategy, but aren’t we supposed to like exit, as in further than the driveway?’

‘Well, I’m just waiting for my boys to come out. A couple of them are trying to chat up some of your classmates, but I doubt they’ll succeed, so they won’t be long now,’ he rustled around in his jacket pocket and found his phone. He quickly typed something and showed her the WhatsApp chat message he’d just posted.

‘Outside. We movin or wat?’

She nodded, acknowledging it but unwilling to admit the words swam around in front of her. Jax pulled a can of lager out of another pocket of his jacket. He opened it, took a long swig, and offered it to Bryony. She had no idea why she accepted it and took an equally long glug of it.

‘So who was that in there, then? With that girl?’

‘Ugh, I so do not want to talk about her,’ she said immediately. ‘I’m much more interested in what you guys are doing here. Do you know Billie?’

‘Nah, Milo’s cousin was invited. Do you know David Sanchez?’

Bryony nodded. He was one of the members of the football team. She knew of him rather than knowing him personally. He was always at parties but not necessarily part of Isaac’s group. In fact, she didn’t think she had ever exchanged any words with him at all.

‘Well, he told Milo about this party, so we thought we’d crash.’

‘I didn’t think that happened, people crashing other people’s house parties outside of American teen films.’

‘We do it all the time. We really need a better social life, but we’re too young to get served at a pub, so whatcha gonna do?’

‘So you just go to random people’s houses?’

‘We don’t cruise around looking for balloons and banners every night,’ he said, grinning at her. ‘Usually, someone knows someone who’s having a party, so we just invite ourselves.’

As he spoke, a small group of people exited the house and made their way over to them. There were two boys and two girls, one of whom Bryony recognised as Anna Bower from her history class. She had one of the boys' arms draped across her shoulders, and his fingers kept worrying her nipple over the top she was wearing, and she didn’t seem to mind at all.

Suddenly, Bryony didn’t want to be there. She didn’t like the energy these other people were bringing with them.

‘How’s it going?’ Jax greeted them as they joined.

‘Not bad,’ said the nipple feeler, grinning at Jax.

‘Are we ready to do one?’ Asked the other.

‘Yeah, you got some wheels?’

‘Not yet, but I can get some.’

‘Awesome,’ and with that, the guy ran off up the street.

‘What does that mean? Where will he get wheels from?’ Bryony demanded.

‘Probably best not to ask too many questions,’ Jax grinned at her. She felt really uncomfortable now. She didn’t want to continue her night with them, so she tried to think of an excuse not to go with them that didn’t sound completely pathetic.

‘Um… so…’ she began quietly, nervously watching the nipple feeler remove his arm from Anna’s shoulder and pull a roll-your-own cigarette out from a tiny food bag in his pocket.

‘I am starving,’ he announced, patting his pockets for his lighter, the cigarette held between his teeth. ‘Can we stop for some food before we go back to Marc’s?’

Jax lit his cigarette for him and nodded.

Bryony didn’t want to go for food or to Marc’s house. She pulled her phone out and tried five times to put her pin in it after it failed to recognise her fingerprint. She’d have to wait at least thirty seconds before she could call her dad. Sighing heavily, she put her phone away.

‘So I’m gonna…’ she began again.

‘Aye up, here he is,’ Jax interrupted, indicating with his head towards a navy blue ford Astra coming down the road. A moment later, Marc pulled over, and they all began to climb in. Anna perched on the nipple feelers lap, and whilst one hand held the cigarette out of the now open window, the other had disappeared up her top, and they began noisily sucking each other’s tongues.

Jax held the back door open for her on the other side of the car. Marc’s girlfriend begrudgingly got in the middle.

'Actually, I'm just gonna call my dad to come pick me up,' she said, trying once again to get into her phone.

'Bryony,' Jax said firmly. 'You are smashed out of your mind. There is no way I'm gonna leave you here on your own until your dad gets here.'

'Hmm, I don't want to go to Marc's house,' she told him in a rather loud whisper.

'That's fine. Look, just come with us to get some food and soak up some of that alcohol, then we'll get you home. I promise, okay.'

Bryony could tell he wouldn't take no for an answer, and he was probably right. She could barely stand up without support. She probably shouldn't be left alone, and she was hungry. She climbed very ungracefully into the car.

Immediately, her first thought was that the cigarette was not basic tobacco. It was weed. Of course, it was weed. The sweet, distinctive, heady smell permeated through the car, and she instantly felt sick. She made her window go all the way down and hung her head out of it like a dog. She glanced up at the house where the party was still in full swing. She could just make out Isaac standing at the front door, watching her. Her heart lurched, and a familiar yearning to be with him washed over her. Then she remembered the photo and Monroe and the choking and the all-night singing, and she stubbornly turned her gaze forward, refusing to acknowledge him.

The journey was not a pleasant one. The only time the couple on the other side of the car stopped kissing was to pass the spliff around. The girl sitting next to her took a deep drag before offering it to Bryony. She refused emphatically, and the girl shrugged and sent it forward to Jax and Marc, both of whom, Bryony noticed, had a drag.

From then on, Bryony white-knuckled it all the way to the fast food restaurant car park.

There was a big debate about whether to pull in or go to the drive-thru, but eventually, it was settled by the girl sitting in the middle. Her name turned out to be Laura, and whilst she barely said a word, when she did say something, Marc listened. Bryony heard Jax chuckle as Marc promptly veered out of the drive-thru lane and moved to the car park moments after Laura announced she wanted to go inside.

Bryony was grateful to get out of the car, but she was still so unsteady on her feet Jax had to help her walk straight.

'You need to eat something. Something carby to soak up all that booze,' he said.

'You're very bossy,' she remarked, but she had no objection to eating. 'Then you're taking me home, right?' She asked, but Jax, who was looking at his phone, didn't answer.

Inside the restaurant was bright. Really bright. It took her a while to get used to the harshness. Jax asked her what she wanted to eat. In fact, she thought he had asked her a few times, but she didn't know, and she couldn't focus on the menu.

'Chicken,' she finally answered. 'I'll just have some chicken.'

Jax moved her backwards and sat her on a hard, plastic chair.

She put her head in her hands and took some deep breaths, trying to stop the room from spinning and make the sick feeling go away. Suddenly Jax put a tray of food in front of her; a box of chicken strips and chips. She began eating and immediately felt better.

'Let me give you some money,' she said between mouthfuls. She noticed only Jax sat with her while the others were sitting in a nearby booth.

'We'll square up another time,' he said with a smile. 'So listen, our plans have sort of changed. We're gonna head out to this development place we know and do some skateboarding. Now, clearly, you are not up for this. I wouldn't be surprised if you and I actually have very little in common.'

He grinned at her, and Bryony smiled back, suddenly feeling so much better now the food was in her stomach, and she felt her head clearing a little.

'So what we're gonna do is call you a taxi and wait here until it comes for you, okay? Sorry, we can't take you home ourselves, but it's the other side of town.'

'Um, actually, I could just call my dad to come get me.'

'Yeah, okay. That's even better. Do that.'

She began searching her pockets for her phone. When she finally fished it out, she realised it was blank, the battery had died.

'Um, Bry, do you know that guy?' Jax asked her.

Bryony looked up. To her astonishment, Joe was waving to her from a nearby table. He was surrounded by people. People she knew. His study buddies were all there, and to her delight, so was Kirsty. She grinned happily.

'They're my friends from work,' she told Jax, waving dorkily back at them. She stood up, steadier on her feet now, and walked over to them. To her surprise, Jax joined her.

'Hi, Bry.' Joe greeted her warmly. A chorus of hellos followed from everyone else, including one from Kirsty, whose husky voice stood out to Bryony.

'Hi, guys. What are you all doing here?'

'A mixture of being starving and needing the loo. Not necessarily in that order,' Joe explained through a mouthful of burger.

'Joe's got a bladder the size of a frigging test tube,' Brandon, one of the non-band member friends, added.

'Don't we all know it,' Bryony agreed.

'What about you? What are you doing here? Is this your boyfriend? Arthur will be gutted,' Chloe asked.

'No, no. Not my boyfriend. This is Jax, he's just a friend,'

'Yeah, good friend,' Jax added, looking surprisingly menacing.

'It's okay, Jax. You guys can head off whenever you're ready. I'll stay here with my friends until my dad gets here.'

'You haven't even called him yet,' he pointed out.

'Oh yeah. My phone died,' she explained to the others. A few people groaned in sympathy.

'Do you know his number? You can use my phone if you like?' Kirsty offered.

'Oh no. I can't remember it off the top of my head.'

'No worries, Bry. A few of us are driving. We just spent the day at the beach, and we're dropping people off as we go, so there's definitely a space in my car since we dropped Arthur off. You can get in with us. I'll drop you home.'

'Aww. Are you sure, Joe? I don't wanna put you guys out.'

'No, don't be silly. Carys lives over your way, so we were going that way anyway.'

'Bryony, can I talk to you for a second?' Jax asked, then gently guided her out of earshot.

'Are you sure about this? I mean, how well do you really know these guys?'

'What? Yeah, it's fine, Jax, honestly.'

'Look, all I'm saying is you're quite drunk, and your judgement is kind of off. You kissed me earlier, for Christ's sake.'

'Erm, for the record, you kissed me first.'

'Whatever. I just don't wanna wake up tomorrow and read about you in the newspaper 'cos you got kidnapped or worse, okay.'

'Jax, you're so sweet, but seriously don't worry. These guys are my study buddies. We're all total nerds!'

Jax stared at them, then at her for a moment before his face erupted into a huge grin. Bryony could understand why girls would massively fall for him.

He nodded and guided her back to Joe's table.

'Just make sure she gets home safe, okay? If not, I'll hold you personally responsible,' he said without any humour.

'Be careful, Jax, or people might start thinking you're actually quite a decent gentleman rather than that big bad boy act you've got going on,' she said softly enough that only Jax could hear it.

He grinned at her, then kissed her cheek and pulled her in for a quick hug.

'Stay safe, my one-night-only girl,' he whispered, then left.

The moment he had gone, all the girls around the table exclaimed how gorgeous he was. Everyone except for Kirsty. She shuffled along the bench to make a space for her. Bryony squished in next to her.

As the others continued talking noisily, Kirsty spoke so only Bryony could hear.

'We can drop you home if you like, or you could stay at mine. I've got a charger so you can charge your phone and let your parents know where you are.'

Bryony looked at her, noticing the tiny fleck of brown in those blue eyes.

'Joe and I broke up,' she added.

'Oh my gosh – are you guys okay?'

'Yeah, we're both fine about it. Still friends and all that. We just didn't want a romantic relationship with each other anymore. We, well, I… I guess I'm looking for something different,' she said, looking very pointedly at her.

Bryony swallowed hard.

Chapter Eighteen

She left a note for Kirsty, hastily written on the back of an envelope she found amongst the clutter on her dressing table. It was short and perfunctory, thanking her for last night and explaining she was being picked up super early by her dad because they were going on holiday in a couple of hours. Finally, she left her mobile number.

The drive home with her father was quiet. Her dad clearly hadn't had his morning coffee before he headed out, as he was barely able to function. Bryony was unable to speak because she was exhausted, hungover and had far too much running around her head to make basic small talk.

They had kissed.

Bryony had never kissed another girl before, and to paraphrase Katy Perry, she liked it. She kept running through the events from the end of last night. How, once they'd got back to Kirsty's house, Kirsty had been incredibly flirty with her; she laughed coquettishly, looked at her meaningfully, and found lots of different reasons to touch her. The sexual tension had been so thick between them that Bryony had barely been able to breathe. And then Kirsty had leant forward, her lips merely inches from her own. Waiting. Expecting. Vulnerable. Bryony closed the gap between them. She had been so nervous, so worried and anxious, and excited and wanton. That first kiss had just been a quick peck on the lips that lingered just a fraction too long for it to be an innocent mistake. They had both pulled away then to search each other's expressions, ensuring this was what they both wanted.

Kirsty slowly smiled. It was unbelievably seductive. Bryony smiled back. With the next kiss, Bryony took charge. She cupped Kirsty's face, gently pulling her closer and angling her head so she could kiss her deeper. At first, it was just soft lips against soft lips until Bryony dared to let her hot tongue venture in to explore and taste the supple and sweet depths of Kirsty's mouth. The next few moments were a hot, wet, juicy mess, which she realised, in the cold light of day, sounded disgusting, but in reality, that minute or so was the most sensuous moment of her entire life. Her whole body had responded so intensely, yet it had only been a kiss. She and Isaac had done much more than kissing, and whilst she had enjoyed it, for the most part, at the time, her responses had never been so... visceral.

And then it had ended. She wasn't sure who had pulled away; it may have been both of them as undoubtedly they both would have needed oxygen by then, but Kirsty had smiled at her, said goodnight, and lay down on her bed with her back to her.

Bryony felt like the room was spinning, and that wasn't just the alcohol. She lay for a few minutes on the bed next to her, her head and senses reeling. Once again, Kirsty had fallen asleep quickly, and once again, Bryony had been wracked by erotic thoughts that refused to let her sleep, so she went downstairs to the sofa, and by the early hours of the morning, she had managed to finally drift off. Barely a few hours later, she'd received a text from her dad saying he was coming to get her and to let him know the address. She found a letter in the hallway with the address on it, then crept back into Kirsty's room to write her the note.

She rubbed her tired eyes as she stared out the window of the car, then replayed the whole evening again.

'Are you okay?'

Her dad's voice startled her out of her reverie.

'You look... strange,' he noted, and Bryony felt herself blushing deeply, in case he could read her thoughts.

'I'm fine, Dad, just really tired,' she said quickly.

'Huh. Okay, well, snap out of it and get in the house. Pack quickly to get your mother off your case. She's not wildly impressed with the timing of your all-nighter, so don't do anything else to make her mad, like looking tired. You can sleep on the plane.'

Bryony nodded, realising with astonishment that they were home already.

Her mother greeted her at the door, looking stressed and annoyed.

'Last night was a bad time to choose to stay out all night, Bryony.'

'I know, Mum.'

'It was very selfish. Your father stayed up late, especially to pick you up, and now he's had to get up early and traipse all over town to go and get you. We've got lots to do without you holding us up.'

'I know. I'm sorry, Mum. Sorry, Dad,' she said, genuinely feeling guilty as she looked back at him. He checked that her mum wasn't looking before grinning and winking at her. Bryony edged round her mother to get up the stairs.

'The taxi is booked and coming for us in one hour. You'd better be packed and ready young lady.'

'I will, Mum,' she called down the stairs.

When she got to her bedroom, she was hit by the icy cold temperature in the room.

Isaac sat at the foot of her bed, his back to her.

Damn it! She somehow completely forgot about him for about eight hours. The last thing she needed was a big drama to stop her from getting ready. She desperately needed a shower.

'I know you're angry with me,' he began sombrely. Bryony faltered for a moment, forgetting what she was supposed to be angry with him for.

'You have every right to be,' he added, 'And with Monroe.'

Oh, of course, now she remembered.

'It is very important that you understand that she means nothing to me. Absolutely nothing. It's just like you said last night; she's a total slag. I was just using her.'

A strange feeling washed over Bryony. It took her a moment to recognise what it was, but suddenly she was able to identify it. It was revulsion. She was actually repulsed by Isaac. And she disliked him most when he was callous with other people's feelings, even Monroe's. Did he really think that by saying those awful things about her, she would forgive him? If anything, it made it worse that he would cheapen their relationship by straying with someone he didn't even like.

'Look, Isaac,' she began, not really looking at him though he had turned to face her, his expression pathetic and annoying. She pulled her suitcase out from under her bed and threw it open. 'Here's the thing about that whole situation. I don't care. I literally cannot even be bothered to think about it anymore. I do not care.'

She began piling clothes and shoes haphazardly into the suitcase and laying out the outfit she would wear to travel in. She had to admit she was really looking forward to being somewhere hot, especially as her own room was like a walk-in freezer.

'Do you care about me?' He asked quietly. 'Or am I also something you literally cannot be bothered to think about anymore as well? That certainly seemed to be the case last night. You literally ignored me completely and then snogged that guy right in front of me, in front of everyone. That guy who I knew you were having an affair with, by the way. Have you got any idea how that felt?'

Bryony sighed wearily. He clearly didn't see the irony of him having a go at her for snogging someone else in front of him after this whole thing had happened because of him doing the exact same thing. Still, she knew pointing it out would only madden him, and she just didn't have the time for that, so she forced herself to stop what she was doing, sit down and look at him.

'You're right,' she began, as genuinely as she could. 'I haven't been fair to you. We need to talk, properly talk, but now is not the right time. I have to get ready to go on holiday. I am super tired and feeling pretty rough plus I really need to get packed. These are not the right conditions in which to have this conversation. When I…'

'Let me guess, when you get back off this holiday, you'll definitely make more time for me, just like you promised to make more time for me after your exams. You're full of crap, Bryony. This holiday is just one more excuse. How many people are you going to snog on holiday, I wonder?'

'Isaac,'

'Forget it. Just go. There's nothing I can do to stop you anyway,'

So she did. She awkwardly moved around the room, collecting the items she needed whilst Isaac sulked in the corner. She had hoped that by the time she came back from the shower, he would have disappeared somewhere, but no, he was still there, giving her the evil eye as she tried to get dressed whilst still holding up the towel. She decided to forego putting on any make-up though it would definitely have improved her appearance. She simply couldn't bear being in the same room as Isaac any longer than necessary.

'Right then,' she said, finally dragging her suitcase to the bedroom door, 'See you in a couple of weeks.'

Isaac gave her a filthy look and turned away.

Bryony happily lugged her suitcase down the stairs.

Chapter Nineteen

Her happiness was short-lived. The flight was delayed for four hours, and her hangover began to really kick in as the day continued. Also, her mother was super moody with her, snapping unnecessarily and outright ignoring her occasionally. Bryony had no idea what her problem was. She looked to her dad for a clue after her mother completely snubbed her, but he merely shrugged. He noticed it, too, though, and so did Steven. It made for an uncomfortable wait. Another issue that was really bugging her was that it was now 2 pm, and Kirsty still hadn't texted her. *Had she not found the note? Had last night just been a one-off that she was totally ashamed of now?* All sorts of questions formed in her mind, each one more paranoid than the last. If she hadn't been so drunk last night, they could have exchanged numbers properly, and she could have at least stalked her on social media. As it was, she could not find any online presence for her. Admittedly, she didn't know her surname or any other nicknames or aliases she might be using, but she knew her ex-boyfriend Joe, they were friends across loads of platforms, but she couldn't find any connections using him or any of the other band members or friends at all. Frustrated, confused, angry with herself, and deeply disappointed, she lay across three chairs, covered her head with her hoodie, put her earpods in, and was asleep within minutes, despite her mother's disapproving tutting.

Her father gently nudged her awake when they were starting to board. The rest of the trip passed her by in a sleepy haze. She shuffled onto the plane, sat down next to her dad, and slept on his shoulder. She woke for snacks, drinks, and a toilet break, then went straight back to sleep again.

By the time they arrived in Tenerife, she was beginning to feel more human. The heat was delicious, and the excitement of being abroad always rallied her, regardless of her mood. Plus, they were one of the first drops on the coach transfer, which was practically unheard of for the Duglass family, and they were delighted to see that their hotel looked lovely, unlike the stop before, which everyone on the coach had been hoping was not theirs.

It was late afternoon. The sun was still blazing gloriously in the sky. Once they had checked in, they found their enormous family suite, with private bedrooms for them all and two bathrooms, as well as a common living area. They set the air conditioning unit onto freezing as the room was stifling hot and felt the immediate effect. Bryony showered and changed into a new summer dress, and they all went down to dinner.

Her mother's frostiness began to thaw, and the all-inclusive food was delicious. Bryony, who hadn't eaten anything but a bag of crisps and chocolate since yesterday, was ravenous and went up for seconds and thirds, ignoring the comments her mother made about hangover medicine. Everyone seemed to relax and unbuckle all their usual woes and baggage, easing themselves into stresslessness.

They didn't watch too much of the evening entertainment in their hotel, though it seemed good enough, but they were all exhausted, so they had an early night. The following few days were spent doing next to nothing. As a family of avid readers with very little time to read for pleasure, they all lost themselves in their books on the sunbeds, occasionally going for a dip in the pool when they got too hot, napping, and taking it in turns to go up to the pool bar to get drinks and icy refreshments.

More often than not, they skipped lunch, favouring an enormous breakfast and evening meal instead. At first, they would spend the evenings watching the entertainment that was laid on for them, but one evening Steven produced a pack of playing cards, and everything changed. From then on, their evenings were spent on their balcony playing competitive gin rummie, Black Jack, Chase the Ace, and poker using hotel matchsticks for currency.

On the fifth day, her mother had pre-booked a mother/daughter spa day. Bryony was a little wary about it as things had not yet returned to normal in their relationship, and she was worried that this spa day, without the gentle intervention of her father, would become awkward. She needn't have been concerned, though. Her mother practically bounced her way to breakfast that morning, and she grinned enthusiastically as they discussed the treatment options. As the massages did their jobs, the ladies finally felt at ease with each other, and by the time they sat down to a light lunch at the exclusive spa restaurant in their fluffy towelling robes and one-size-fits-all slippers, Bryony's concerns were a distant memory.

'I owe you an apology,' her mother began after taking a sip of ice-cold, cucumber-infused water.

'You do?'

'Yes, I do. I've treated you very unfairly.'

'Really, when?'

'You know full well when. At the beginning of this holiday, I was very curt with you. Don't pretend you didn't notice.'

'Ahh, yes, that. I figured you were angry with me for staying out the night before we came away.'

'Well, yes, I did think that was a bit selfish; I stand by that. But it was more than that. Your father pointed it out to me the other day. I had set double standards for you and Steven. If Steven had behaved the same way, I would have been a little annoyed but would have forgotten about it almost immediately. But with you, I held onto it. I couldn't let go and held a grudge about it, and I don't know why. I'm not sure if it's because you are a girl, which I'm fully aware is deeply unfair to you. I'm not sure if it's because you're usually more thoughtful and respectful than that, and therefore it felt more like a personal affront. Your father believes it's because I'm scared you'll go back to behaving the same way you did when you were with Isaac. I confess it is a worry of mine. I feel like I've only just got you back, and I know that university is just around the corner, and then I'll lose you all over again. So, I really wanted this stage in-between to be special. I obviously have been cutting off my nose to spite my face by being harsh with you the last couple of days. Not exactly what I had planned.'

She paused, blinked back tears and smiled at Bryony.

'Oh, Mum,' Bryony began, but her mother stopped her.

'The point I am trying to make is,' she said, putting her hand over Bryony's, 'That this is my issue, not yours. I am very sorry for making things uncomfortable for you. You are a young woman who is free to make her own choices, and of course, you're allowed to blow off steam after the year you've had. I will endeavour to be more understanding in the future.'

Bryony squeezed her mum's hand.

'So will I,' she said, and her mum grinned properly again. And then Bryony did something she'd had absolutely no intention of doing that morning; she confessed to her mum everything that had happened on that evening, omitting the part about Isaac being there, of course. But the part about finding the photo of Isaac with Monroe, getting drunk in the kitchen and giving Monroe hell, then kissing the boy she'd seen at the therapist's that one time, and then finally everything, including her innermost feelings about Kirsty. She had no idea why she did it, except that she felt she owed her mum a proper explanation for why she had stayed out that night. Plus, they were building bridges with their relationship, her mum was making apologies, and she was confessing secrets; what better ways are there to strengthen bonds?

To her credit, her mother listened attentively and without interruption, except a little cheer when she told her what she'd said to Monroe until Bryony had finished. Admittedly, she had smiled rather knowingly when she told her about kissing Jax, and her eyebrows then rose so high when she told her about kissing Kirsty that they disappeared behind her fringe, but that was the worst of her reactions.

'Are you shocked? Or you know… disappointed or whatever?' She ventured tentatively.

'I've told you before, and I'll tell you every single time you ask me. I will NEVER be disappointed by you, Bryony. I'll confess to being a little surprised, though; that's all. You were so very much in love with Isaac. It never occurred to me that you could be gay. Is that the right terminology? I don't want to offend.'

'Gay is fine, with me Mum. And honestly, I don't know if I am truly gay or a lesbian or whatever or if I just have feelings for Kirsty. I've never looked at other women that way before. Are you really okay with this?'

'Oh darling, when you get to my age, you begin to realise a few things. Life is made up of thousands of little moments; some are wonderful, some are awful, but truthfully, most of them are just dull and monotonous. So if this girl, this Kirsty, gives you butterflies and makes you happy, then you grab onto as many of those moments as you can get. I promise you, your father, and I only ever want you to be healthy and happy. As long as you're not hurting yourself or anyone else to do it, then have at it, my darling.'

Bryony grinned and felt truly blessed. She had been downright awful to her mum in the past, and she really had never done anything to deserve it.

'Oh my goodness. Is this a secret? Am I not allowed to tell your father? I don't know if I can do that. We tell each other everything, especially about you kids. I might just blurt it out by accident.'

'Don't worry, Mum. We'll tell him together.'

'Oh, thank you, darling. I feel so hip. My daughter, the lesbian!'

Bryony snorted into her ice-cold, cucumber-infused water, and her mother burst out laughing.

The rest of the holiday was picture postcard perfect. Bryony told her dad and Steven, as she promised her mother she would, that she was experimenting with her sexuality. Their response was a lot less effusive than her mother's. Steven had shrugged, claiming pretty much everyone did that at university anyway, and her dad had looked a little uncomfortable but simply said, "Oh, right. Okay then," and nothing more.

The only way she knew that either of them had properly absorbed this new information about her was during a family game of golf, which Bryony was humiliatingly bad at. After failing to putt the ball yet again, her brother wondered aloud whether all lesbians were this bad at sports or if she was the exception. Her father had laughed and agreed the lesbian community were likely to unite and refuse to accept her as one of their own as she was giving them such a bad name. Whilst it was all far from politically correct, their teasing of her life choice was so good-natured that it pleased her no end, and her game picked up. Slightly.

The final week consisted of more reading, pool dipping, and family sports events such as table tennis, which she was terrible at, and doubles tennis, which she was worse at. They also played pool volleyball, which she was marginally better at, and crazy golf, which she was so bad at they had to move onto the next hole several times before she putted the ball because she was holding the queue up too much. She endured them all with good humour and generally got her own back when they played cards or other games in the evening. They didn't spend the whole time at the hotel either; they did some sightseeing and shopping, and one night, after a beautiful meal in a restaurant overlooking the ocean, they managed to wander into a karaoke bar. They had intended to leave immediately, but somehow their dad convinced them all to stay, just for one drink. Three bottles of wine later, they were all on the stage singing their hearts out to "Babooshka" by Kate Bush. They had been sitting chatting to a family from Liverpool, and one of them had taken a photo of the four of them really going for it, eyes closed, fists clenched, the whole shebang. She sent the picture to her mum, who then shared it with all of them on their family WhatsApp group. Bryony saved the photo as her screensaver.

The return home was bittersweet. They all agreed that despite the luxury of their suite, they had missed their own beds and proper English teabags, but the two weeks had been incredible, and none of them had wanted it to end.

On the plane home, Bryony sat next to her mum. Mostly they were quiet, each deep into their own trashy novels, but when they stopped for snacks and drinks, her mum asked if Kirsty had texted her yet. Bryony confirmed she had not.

'Don't worry darling; there are plenty of reasons why she hasn't got in touch.'

'Yeah, one of them being she was horrified by what happened and never wants to see me again.'

'Well, yes, that is one possibility.'

'Cheers, Mum.'

'I'm sorry, darling, but maybe she is freaking out about it. You are, too, aren't you? This is a very different situation from what you had with Isaac. You cannot expect to be wooed the same way. This relationship may take a bit more patience on your side and lots of reassurance for both of you.'

'Yeah, thanks, Mum,' Bryony said distractedly. Her mum had just bought up something else she hadn't thought about all holiday. She had to deal with Isaac.

Chapter Twenty

Her bedroom was a frozen shambles. Everything that could be upturned and thrown around the room, was. She'd been here before, of course, but now she was tired, depressed, and emotional. Plus, she was fairly sure she had fallen out of love with Isaac, so she was finding it much harder to forgive him. He was sat in the same position on the bed, which was the one thing he had not moved. He was perched on the edge with his back to her, radiating icy cold air.

She slammed the door behind her and waited for an explanation. Finally, still facing the other way, he spoke up.

'Sorry about the mess. I got mad and trashed the place last week, and I haven't been able to control myself enough to put it back,' he said, sounding not even slightly remorseful.

'Get out,' she demanded, fatigue making her lose her temper.

'I thought we were gonna talk when you got back, or is this just another excuse for you to ignore me?'

'You expect us to talk with this mess? You expect me to say anything reasonable to you when I'm so angry with you right now. I was ready five minutes ago to sit and have a chat with you, but now I can't because I have to rebuild my entire room,' her anger rose with every word she uttered, as did her volume until, eventually, she was shouting.

'Is everything okay up there, darling?' She heard her mother call up.

'Everything's fine, Mum. Just me talking to myself, I forgot I'd left my room in such a mess before we went away,' she called downstairs, anxious no one should come up as she had no reasonable explanation for this utter annihilation.

'You know what, it's really nice to see you too. I can tell that you really missed me when you went away,' he grumbled moodily.

'Excuse me?'

'I'm not being funny, Bry, but you've been off sunning yourself for two weeks, and I've been stuck here all alone. And then the first thing you do is kick me out. What kind of greeting is that? What the hell has happened to you recently? You can never be nice to me anymore. Do you actually even care about me at all?'

'Nice! You want me to be nice to you after you trash all my stuff?'

'I told you I did this ages ago. I can't help it if I can't tidy up after myself. I am a ghost, you know!'

'Isaac, you really need to get out of my sight before I say something I might regret later?'

'What are you gonna do? Banish me again?'

Bryony let out a small but anguished shriek. She crossed the room and sank to her knees, gently grasping the beautiful first edition copy of *To Kill A Mockingbird* she'd received for Christmas, which had been torn in two.

'Yeah, look, about that… I really am sorry, alright. I was really, really mad at you. I couldn't control myself. Obviously, I wish I could fix it, but, you know, I just can't.'

Bryony felt the hot tears spring to her eyes and flow immediately down her cheeks as she clutched the two pieces of the same book to her chest.

'Bryony, come on, don't cry. It's just a book, for goodness sake.'

She couldn't talk. She was devastated. Not just about the book but about the whole situation. What had happened to the sweet, thoughtful boy she had first started dating? When did he turn into this vengeful monster? Was it before or after he died? Was it her fault? Did she bring out the worst in him? She didn't know. The only thing she did know was that she really didn't love him anymore, and at that very moment, she hated him.

'Just leave,' she said between sobs. He did, and she really cried her heart out. When she finally stopped, her legs had gone to sleep underneath her. She took a few minutes to stand up, trying to get the feeling back into her legs. She then hopped around like a wild animal, trying to get rid of the pins and needles in her feet.

'Dinner's ready,' her mother called up the stairs. She heard Steven respond from his bedroom.

'Coming,' she called a few seconds later, deciding not to let Isaac ruin the whole night. She washed her face in the bathroom, and even though it was obvious she'd been crying, she went downstairs anyway. She was hungry.

'Have you been crying?' Her mother asked her immediately. Bryony nodded.

'It was a really good book,' She explained, and for her family, that was all the explanation they needed. It was not at all uncommon for her to shed a few tears at a really good book. Besides, it wasn't a lie, not really.

They all ate their dinner in a far less jovial manner than they had eaten their breakfast in the hotel that morning. Occasionally, someone would compare the two places or begin reminiscing, but for the most part, they were pretty quiet.

'I'm going to do a big sort out of my room tonight, so probably best to steer clear of it. And if you hear lots of banging and shuffling, I've had an idea for a change around of the furniture, so don't worry,' she informed them, covering all her bases.

'What, tonight? Aren't you exhausted from all the travelling? Why don't you leave it for tonight and sit and watch a film with us in the sitting room instead? Your father has bought the telly in especially.'

Bryony would have loved to just chill, watching telly with her family. She was exhausted, and it would have been the perfect way to end their holiday. Angry tears burned her eyes again, but she blinked them back and smiled.

'Nope, I'm determined. I've already made a start. If I leave it till tomorrow, I won't do it.'

'Well, shall I come up and help you? Some of that furniture is really heavy,' her dad offered.

'No, no. It's fine. You have your evening planned. I'll be quite happy sorting stuff out. Come and have a look tomorrow when it's finished.'

'Okay darling, if you're sure,' her mother said. 'Just be sure to bring your washing down tonight so we can get a load in early in the morning.'

Bryony assured her she would, but after two helpings of Dad's Shepherd's pie and two of apple crumble, one with ice cream and one with custard (she was still sort of on holiday!) She found it almost impossible to summon the energy to go upstairs, let alone tackle her room.

When they all left the dining room, the others headed for the sitting room, and Bryony hauled her heavy carcass up the stairs and surveyed the mess. She rolled up her sleeves, and using the tape measure she'd bought up from the toolbox under the stairs, she measured the different areas of her room to see if the furniture would fit in the different spaces she wanted to move it to. After a couple of design tweaks, she'd finally worked out a plan and began picking everything off the floor and piling it on her bed.

She finally finished the last flourishes of her newly organised room at 3 am. She was surprisingly pleased with it, considering it had been forced upon her. Her mum had popped her head in at about midnight to check how she was getting on and let her know they were all going to bed. By that time, whilst it was still a mess, the main furniture had been moved into its new place, and it was all beginning to take shape. She had managed to hide the damaged book as her mother appraised her work and told her what a wonderful job she had done. After having a quick shower and crawling into bed, her final task was to search the internet for somewhere local that could possibly fix her beloved book. She managed to find somewhere fairly close to work and decided to go there on Monday when the buses were more regular. Tomorrow was Sunday. Tomorrow she would deal with Isaac. With that thought running through her head, she fell into a deep, dreamless sleep.

It was gone midday before she woke up. She was groggy and grumpy, and her mood was not improved by the sight of Isaac grinning at her from the armchair. She was confused and disorientated, and it took her a while to remember that she'd moved everything around last night, which explained why the armchair was there but not why Isaac was so damned chirpy.

'Good morning, wait, no, good afternoon, sleepy head. I didn't know if you would surface at all today.'

Bryony grunted in response and pulled the duvet over her head. She knew what he was doing. He used to do it all the time when they fought when he was alive. He would be all happy and smiley and positive and try to make her forget the argument or just not care that she had been mad at him. Only now did she realise how manipulative that was.

'I love what you've done with the place. Very good feng shui. This chair is much better here. I can't believe we didn't think about putting it here before.'

Bryony refused to respond but also knew she couldn't go back to sleep again. Plus, she got really claustrophobic when her head was covered. Angrily, she pushed the duvet back and sat up. Isaac came to sit next to her on the bed. She immediately drew the duvet up to her chin, tucking her exposed arms in to protect them from his chill.

'Hey Babe,' he said in a much quieter, more sincere tone, 'I'm sorry for being such a jerk. I get so crazy over you I can't control myself. I was just sitting here all the time, remembering you kiss that guy. Anyway, I know I had no right to be, but I couldn't help it. I was like, crazy jealous and mad and really hurting, I guess. That's why I did what I did. I'm sorry, babe. I guess I just love you too much. You know, if I could have tidied it all up again and fixed it, I would have.'

Bryony said nothing. She couldn't believe she had used to fall for this BS so easily before. It all sounded like pre-rehearsed, insincere crap to her now.

'Besides,' he continued in a brighter tone, 'It all turned out for the best in the end, didn't it? Look at your room now. It's fantastic. You did a much better job than anything I would have done. Brilliant work, babe, well done.'

'My book is still ripped apart,' she said through gritted teeth.

'Oh right. Yeah. I really am so sorry about that. I had no idea it meant so much to you.'

Liar, she thought. *You knew exactly how I felt about that book because that was the only one you ripped apart.*

She put her head in her hands and tried to calm down. Today she was going to tell him that she was ready to let go of him and he should move on, cross over to the other side, or whatever it was that was supposed to happen. She couldn't do that when she was mad at him; otherwise, it would come out too harsh and cruel, and she'd have to live with that for the rest of her life. Whatever her feelings were for him now, she had to remember that not so long ago, she adored this boy so much he came back from the dead for her. The very least she could do was send him off to the afterlife with kindness. With that in mind, she lifted her head and looked at him.

She felt like she hadn't really looked at him for ages. He was still, objectively, very good-looking, but she didn't feel any desire for him at all anymore. Maybe she really was a fully-fledged lesbian, or maybe because she didn't love him anymore, she didn't fancy him either.

'We need to talk.'

His positively optimistic face fell.

'That sounds ominous.'

'It's not necessarily bad.'

He stood up and began pacing. Bryony knew there was no turning back now, she would have to do this here and now, she just wished she could have gotten dressed and had breakfast first.

'Are you going to banish me again?' He finally said, looking at her with anguish in his eyes.

She softened immediately.

'No Isaac, I'm not. However, I do think that the time has come where we don't need each other anymore. I think I'm ready, and you're ready, to move on.'

'This is because of him, isn't it? Have you been texting and calling each other while you were on holiday?'

'What? No, this has absolutely nothing to do with Jax.'

'Of course, it has. You have one snog with that emo little douchebag, and suddenly you want to break up with me. What the hell else did you do with him that night? I'll bet that filthy little maggot was all over you. Well, I hope you used a condom, 'cos I can guarantee that guy has some sort of VD.'

'Isaac, enough!' Bryony interrupted sternly. Given what an absolute gentleman Jax had been to her on the night of the party, she couldn't bear to hear him being spoken of in that way. 'Jax and I only kissed that one time. We both agreed that we had no chemistry and, if anything, I was only using him to get back at you and upstage Monroe. Not that I should have to, but I am willing to show you my phone, which will prove we have had absolutely no contact since then. In fact, I haven't even got his phone number. Anyway, that's not the point,' she paused to breathe and remind herself of her objective again. She continued, much calmer, 'The point is, this has nothing to do with Jax or anyone else at all. This is about you and me.

'I think at first, when you first died, I was so lost, if you hadn't come back, I wouldn't have survived. I think that's why you had to come back, to help me get over you. To help me learn how to continue in a world without you.

'And I think that, in this form, this ghostly existence, you're changing. Your mood swings are like smacks in the face for me, and it must be even worse for you. I don't think you were meant to stay with me forever, Isaac, not the way that Veronica's granny has. I don't think this was meant to be a long-term thing at all. I think that we are both ready now for you to cross over and be at peace before you get any worse. Don't you agree?'

He looked at her for a few seconds as though not really sure how to respond.

'I don't want to be so angry all the time,' he confessed in such a small voice Bryony's heart melted.

'I know you don't.'

'But I'm scared, Bry.'

'Me too. But I think that you're supposed to be. Maybe that's the trick to getting into heaven. You have to be brave enough to overcome your fear and make that leap.'

'Do you really think I'm still going to heaven after all I've done?'

‘Absolutely. None of this was your fault Isaac, not really. I think you maybe should have gone straight to heaven but stopped to check on me. So if anything, you deserve it even more.’

‘You’re so clever, Bry. I love you so much, no matter what else happened, you need to know that. I’ll really miss you, and I will wait for you.’

Bryony couldn’t bring herself to tell him that she loved him. It wasn’t fair for the last thing she said to him to be a lie.

‘You were the most wonderful first love a girl could ever have asked for.’

They both closed their eyes and waited for him to pass over.

Chapter Twenty-One

Nothing happened. Literally nothing. They both sat there like lemons, facing each other with their eyes closed for about five minutes. Naturally, Isaac was the first to crack.

'Nothing's happening.'

'You just need to relax.'

Silence. For about forty seconds.

'Bryony, seriously, what am I supposed to do?'

'Just sit still, breathe deeply, and try to clear your mind. Patience. Just wait for a little while. Veronica said that crossing over involves being relaxed. Stop panicking about it and stay nice and calm and still, and then I'm sure something will happen.'

He was silent for a while, except for the very exaggerated deep breathing. This time he managed about two minutes.

'Are you sleeping?'

'Isaac!'

'What? I don't understand how you can just sit there doing nothing unless you are going to sleep.'

'It's called meditation, and it's not about sleeping, it's about relaxation and mindfulness. Now, let's try again, and this time, instead of being distracted by me, try to be mindful of your surroundings. Close your eyes and listen, really listen.'

'Listen for what?'

'Anything. Are there any noises you can hear? Any calls for your attention that are maybe not from this world but the next, urging you forward?'

'Err, what? No.'

‘Seriously, Isaac, shut up and try to find the passage to the next world. It has to be available to you somewhere. They could have been calling out for you for half an hour, but you wouldn’t know because you haven’t been listening!’

Quiet.

Bryony peeked a look at him to make sure he wasn’t messing around, but he was sitting opposite her with his eyes closed and an intense expression of concentration on his face.

‘Is this what Veronica told you I should do to cross over?’ He asked a few minutes later.

‘Not exactly,’ she confessed.

‘Then why are we doing it then?’

‘Because her instructions were for you to “let go of this world and move on to the next”, but I knew you would only take that as a literal instruction, so I thought I’d improvise and help you to “let go” in a more metaphysical way.’

‘So this could all be pointless?’

‘Have you got any other ideas of how you could let go of this world?’

He was quiet for a moment, thinking. She gave him a minute, and he came up with nothing.

‘Exactly, and besides, even if this doesn’t work, what harm will it do trying?’

‘You’re just trying to shut me up for ten minutes, aren’t you?’ He smiled at her.

‘Well, I can’t deny it’s a welcome side effect,’ she grinned back.

They gave up on the whole meditation method shortly after, as Bryony was starving. She dressed, left Isaac to come up with some ideas that weren’t ridiculous, and went for some lunch. In the kitchen she found a note from her mum saying they had gone shopping and Steven had gone to a friends, so as she ate her sandwich in near silence, she tried to think of something else to help him cross over as well.

Ultimately, she could think of nothing. She was either too tired or too relaxed to think properly. So, she did what she always did when her brain was unable to come up with an answer to her query, she turned to the internet. Google bought up several local mediums and psychics in her area. It also bought up links to a few websites with "spells" to help rid her of her poltergeist. She clicked on a couple, feeling sceptical immediately but trying to push it aside. They all involved burning various herbs and saying incantations. She dismissed them instantly. Scrolling down the results, she found a website called "holdingontootight.co.uk", which suggested that those who found themselves "haunted" by a ghost who wouldn't leave, ought to help them identify the unfinished business they were holding onto, which was keeping them tethered to this world. There were various "real-life" examples that Bryony wrongfully scorned considering she too had a ghost who wouldn't move on, so why she had the audacity to doubt them was pretty hypocritical. Still, other people's ghost stories seemed so unbelievable. She couldn't bring herself to identify with Mrs Patterson in Watford, who had a ghostly postman that always called at her door at 8 am every morning except Sunday because he hadn't finished his round before he died. It was so banal and un-extraordinary. Why would it ever happen? But then again, why would someone make that up? Still, the idea of unfinished business seemed to her to be the most reasonable explanation, so she put her phone away, tidied up her lunch things, and walked purposefully back up to her room.

Isaac was not helpful. And yet, it wasn't entirely his fault either.

'I don't know what you want me to say, Bryony. I just can't think of anything. Have you got any unfinished business with me?'

Bryony immediately meant to shake her head, but she stopped and thought about it for a moment. Did she have unfinished business with Isaac? Did she want to tell him that she didn't love him anymore? That he, in equal parts, irritated, bored, and scared her. Did she want to tell him that theirs couldn't be a forever love because she had very much moved on from him? And that, in fact, she liked someone else. Admittedly, that someone wasn't exactly reciprocating those feelings, but that didn't mean that she wanted Isaac any more. Did she want to tell him all that before she sent him off to his forever resting place?

No. She did not. Whatever had happened between her and Isaac since he had died could not change the fact that when he was alive, he had been, for the most part, a very good first boyfriend, and she had, even if she didn't now, loved him with her whole being. And he had loved her. She didn't want to tarnish his view of their relationship for him to have to mull it over forever more. She wanted him to find peace and be happy in the next life. And who knows, maybe when you crossed over, you could see what was still happening in your living loved ones' lives, so Isaac would be able to see that she had moved on anyway, but she didn't want to take that chance. She would protect him if she could. She did not have any unfinished business she wanted to discuss with him. It wasn't her keeping him here; she was sure of it.

But something certainly was. Days passed, and Isaac was still lingering. Bryony quizzed him again and again about anything he could be subconsciously holding on to. She insisted they attempted the meditation every day and always encouraged him to listen for someone calling to him or look for a light he could go into or a door in his mind he could go through. Some passageway, as Ronnie had said there would be.

She even bought and burned the suggested herbs and chanted mumbo jumbo latin-esque incantations, but nothing worked.

Another odd thing was Isaac's behaviour. Bryony thought he understood that they were indeed "broken up." They no longer told each other they loved each other or called each other pet names. There was no more sexual tension between them or lingering looks. In fact, there was no tension between them at all. For the last week or so, he was level-headed and good-humoured. He went off and did his own thing. Sometimes going to watch football games he knew his dad and brothers would be at because they were season ticket holders. Sometimes, he would hang out with them all day, occasionally mentioning the odd anecdote to Bryony in the evening if he wasn't going to the cinema or going to see what his mates were doing.

It relieved an awful lot of pressure to the point where they were almost just friends. He didn't say a word when Bryony said she was going to her therapy session, though he knew she might run into Jax. It didn't seem to bother him that she took on even more shifts at work, so she was practically full-time there. In fact, sometimes they only saw each other for a few minutes a day.

When Bryony arrived at work for her first shift with Joe since their respective holiday's, she was positively jubilant.

'You're in a good mood,' he observed, in his laid-back way, looking tanned. 'It must be that boyfriend of yours, giving you some good lovin',' he suggested, wiggling his eyebrows at her. The coffee shop only had a few of the regulars in, so they had the chance to catch up. Immediately her good mood began to evaporate. Joe mentioning Isaac reminded her about his ex-girlfriend, Kirsty. She had promised herself she would not ask Joe about her. It was inappropriate, insensitive, and unfair. She would not do it.

'Uh-oh. Clearly not the boyfriend then, from that reaction.'

'No,' she confessed. 'We broke up.'

'Huh, no way. So did Kirsty and me. Strange coincidence, huh?'

‘Oh no. I’m sorry, Joe,’ she said, feigning her ignorance like an Oscar winner.

‘Nah, it wasn’t meant to be. She’s totally cool, and we’re still mates. There was just no spark anymore, and both of us agreed, life’s too short for there to be no spark.’

‘So, you’re not upset at all?’

‘Nah. I’m kinda enjoying the single life, you know. I went on holiday with the boys last week, and it was nice to do some flirting and work on my dirty dancing moves, which always drive the ladies wild.’

‘Oh really. And did that work on many of the girls out there?’

‘Hey now, a gentleman never tells. But I’m no gentleman, so I’ll tell you all the sordid details. I got absolutely no action! Seriously! Spanish women have no love for skinny English nerds. Even after I told them I was in a band! What is that about? It was so much fun, though.’

Bryony laughed while inwardly fighting the urge to turn the conversation back to Kirsty. She would not do that. Wouldn’t be that girl.

‘And have you spoken to Kirsty since you guys broke up?’

Damn it!

‘Yeah, we’re both cool. Actually, we’d broken up just before that night when we met up with you. We’re still totally up for hanging out together. Not that we’ve been able to much. I got back from my holiday on Monday, and she went on her holiday with her family Friday, so we haven’t seen each other much. But talking about that night, spill the goss about that dude who was totally overprotective of you. I reckon your boyfriend might have had a bit of an issue with him, did he?’

Bryony explained the situation to Jax, and the two discussed the joys of the single life.

The coffee shop remained quiet all day, and Bryony and Joe, free from the stress of exams or partners, passed the day gossiping, playing stupid games, and setting each other even stupider challenges, such as filling a cup up to the brim and being the fastest to put on the farthest table without spilling any of it. Needless to say, they also did a lot of tidying up after themselves.

When she went on her lunch break, she saw she had a missed call from a number she recognised but didn't have saved in her contacts. She called the number back, but it was busy, so she selected the option for them to call her back when the line cleared, hoping it would be in the next twenty-five minutes whilst she had her break. It wasn't.

She and Joe waited as patiently as they could for the last lingering customer to finally finish their cup of coffee so they could close up on time and say their goodbyes. They'd had a great shift, and she was looking forward to a few more before they both went their separate ways in September. As she waited for the bus, she saw that the number had called her again. She returned it, and this time someone answered.

'Hello, Ivy Bush House Nursing Home.'

'Oh, hello, this is Bryony Duglass. I've a missed phone call from this number.'

'Oh yes, Miss Duglass. Veronica Wainswright has named you as her next of kin. As such, we have an obligation to let you know that we have placed her on end-of-life care and to let you know she may only have a few days left. If you wish to visit her, we'd advise you come as soon as you can.'

Bryony was silent for a moment. She knew Ronnie was old, she had told her herself that she was dying, but somehow, Bryony had never really thought that she would actually die. She'd only known her for a few months, but they'd really connected. She felt like family now.

'Miss Duglass?'

'Yes. Yes, I'm sorry, I'm still here. And yes, of course, I'll come and see her. Is it too late to come over tonight?'

'The general visiting hours are over now. We do make exceptions for our end-of-life clients, but if I'm being honest with you, I'd leave it till the morning. Let her get a good night's sleep, and you can see her properly tomorrow.'

'Oh, okay. Yes, tell her I'll be there first thing.'

Chapter Twenty-Two

Bryony arrived at the nursing home just after breakfast. Quite the accomplishment as she had to catch three buses and walk half a mile to get there. When she arrived, she was sweating unattractively due, in part to the already hot sun, but mainly to the speed that she had walked/jogged to get there. She vowed to begin some sort of exercise regime as soon as she started uni, just in case another emergency should crop up, God forbid.

'Hello,' she began, gasping. 'I'm here to…'

'Oh wonderful, you came, Miss Duglass. Ronnie knows you're coming. She's looking forward to seeing you,' Chloe, the receptionist, greeted her kindly.

'She is? Is she okay?'

The whole way there, Bryony had been terrified she'd be too late, that Ronnie would die without hearing her say thank you for all the wisdom she'd passed on and the friendship. She wanted to tell her she would miss her when she was gone, that someone alive in this world would be sorry and sad that she wasn't here anymore. But most importantly, she didn't want Ronnie to die alone. Of course, she knew there were nurses and carers here, but none of them actually cared about her; more specifically, Ronnie didn't care for them. But she liked Bryony, and she knew she did.

'Well, she's hanging in there. She'll be delighted you're here. Why don't you take a few minutes to cool down before you go through? Shall I fetch you some water? It wouldn't do to go rushing in and startling her. She needs calm, stillness, and serenity. Nothing too strenuous.'

Bryony was pretty desperate to see Ronnie, but the nurse had a point. She accepted the water and signed herself in. Whilst she was waiting, Sharon, one of Ronnie's main carers, walked by.

'Bryony! I'm so glad you're here.'

'Oh, hi, Sharon.'

'Has it been explained to you that Veronica is on end-of-life care?'

'Yes, that's why I'm sweating. I ran here.'

'Oh, okay. And are you prepared for this? Ronnie may look quite different from the last time you saw her.'

'I was only here a couple of weeks ago.'

'I know. But once the soul decides to leave, the body seems to … wither. Even in that short period, the change can seem extreme.'

'Oh, okay. Thank you for warning me.'

'Also, forgive me for saying this,' she looked around to make sure no one else was listening and gently guided Bryony further down the hallway to give them a little privacy, 'Please tell me if I'm overstepping the mark here, but I know the two of you often chat about the afterlife and the supernatural. If I may advise you to steer clear of these topics now. It is not uncommon for previously firmly held beliefs and ideas about what happens after death to alter considerably when in their final days.'

'I er… that's not… okay. Thank you.'

'Just something to bear in mind.'

She tapped her arm and then continued off to do her work. Bryony returned the empty glass to the reception and then made her way to Ronnie's room. She took a deep breath before entering. Even so, it didn't prepare her for the change in Ronnie. She didn't just look older, she looked old, like ancient. And frail. Her already dainty frame was suddenly brittle and delicate. One deep breath could break her ribs. Her face suddenly looked skull-like, and her hair was thin and stuck to her head. She barely looked like Ronnie at all. It was almost as if she was dead already but just hadn't completed the paperwork.

'Hi, Ronnie,' she whispered, barely audible. The nurse who had taken up full-time residence in the room as part of the end-of-life care programme double-checked her ward, then smiled at Bryony and beckoned her closer. Bryony summoned her courage with a deep breath, plastered a fake, sympathetic smile on her face, and tiptoed nearer the bed.

'Hi, Ronnie,' she repeated, only slightly louder, trying to be as respectful as possible.

'Bryony? Is that you?' She said in a surprisingly strong and loud voice. Bryony jumped, then suppressed a relieved grin. 'Where are my glasses? I can't see a damned thing without them,' Bryony located them on her bedside table and gently handed them to her. Then, at her insistence and with the nurse's subtle consent, she helped Veronica sit up.

'I'm not dead yet, you know. There's no need to whisper. Although why you'd whisper when I'm dead, I don't know, it's not like I'd be able to hear you.'

'I was just trying to be respectful, Ronnie.'

'Well, don't. Just be normal. It's bad enough with her hanging around twenty-four-seven,' she pointed to the quiet, unobtrusive nurse, who completely ignored her. 'I don't see why I can't just die in peace.'

'Hush now, Ronnie, don't be rude.'

'Why not? I'm dying. Why on Earth would I not be rude?'

'Because I don't like it.'

That shut her up. She pouted petulantly as Bryony redistributed the many pillows whilst avoiding the wires that attached Ronnie to various machines around her, so she was more comfortable. She looked and sounded so much more alive and normal again that Bryony's anxiety began to ebb away.

'How are you feeling? Do you need anything?'

'I'm dying. That's how I'm feeling.'

'Yes, but not in this very instant, Ronnie, so until you actually do shuffle off this mortal coil, as Shakespeare would say, is there anything I can get you? A drink? Some more cushions, perhaps?'

At that, Ronnie stopped pouting and grinned. She was surrounded by enough pillows to make an interior designer wet herself. It was abundantly clear that she absolutely did not need any more.

'I'm old, I need pillows,' she grinned, and Bryony returned it, both resuming their relationship as normal, despite the imminent death.

'In all seriousness though, how are you feeling? Are you in much pain?'

'They've got me pretty well drugged up,' she lifted up her left hand, which was attached by a tube to a time-release bag of liquid morphine. 'I'm just tired, always tired.'

'Well, if you want to have a little nap, you go ahead. I'm here all day, so there's plenty of time to catch up.'

'I'm not going to sleep now! I want to talk to you. Find out what's happened to make your face like that. I want to know if it's the boy in your life or the girl. And if this bloody woman would leave us alone for five minutes, we could talk properly,'

'Ronnie, enough with the rudeness. What's wrong with my face anyway?'

'Something's happened, that's what. You want to talk about something. I can tell by your eyes.'

‘What? No, don’t be silly. They called me last night to say how poorly you are. My face is only like this because I am worried about you,’ she lied.

Last night Isaac had planted the idea in her head that Veronica may know why he was unable to move on. He had been, in her opinion, horribly insensitive about the fact that these could be her last few moments on this earth, and Bryony had vowed that she would not use and abuse Veronica for information. True, that was how their relationship had begun, but since then, it had flourished into a genuine friendship, and she would not be crass enough to put that in jeopardy at the most crucial moment. And yet it would be so useful to get Ronnie’s opinion on the matter, plus it wasn’t like she had much time left to ask. No. She would not be that type of person.

‘Liar,’ Ronnie hissed at her. She may be dying, but she was as sharp as ever. Bryony blushed and lowered her eyes.

‘Can’t you leave?’ Ronnie suddenly demanded of the nurse. ‘She’s here. She can watch me. If I start dying, she’ll come and get you straight away. Leave us alone to chat in private for a while. I still have rights, you know.’

The nurse slowly rose to her feet. She checked a few things, made some notes in her little pocket notebook, and then turned to Bryony.

‘If any of these numbers change, even a tiny bit, then you press that button, and I’ll be right back in. I’ll be waiting outside your door, Miss Wainswright. Enjoy your privacy,’ and with that, she left them alone.

‘So,’ Ronnie pressed her.

‘So what? Ronnie, I’m here to see you, to talk to you about anything you want to talk about. This is your time. Tell me anything you want. Have a moan or a gossip, tell me some old memories, deep, dark secrets, whatever, I don’t mind.’

'Well, I don't have nothing to say. Moaning and gossiping is only fun if you join in, which I know you won't, 'cos you think all these nurses and carers are God's gift to the world, even when I tell you they ain't. And I don't wanna hash out any old stories, that's too depressing. I want to be interested, entertained, and useful. If you want my help with something, which I can tell you do, then ask me. If there's some drama in your life, then tell me. Don't let my final hours in this world be boring. You asked what I want to talk about, and this is it. What is it you want to tell me? I insist you tell me now.'

Bryony relented. She confessed everything to Ronnie, including the kiss she had with Kirsty and then being blanked by her. She told her about her confusion as to why Isaac was still here after they'd tried multiple times to get him to cross over and find out if there was some unfinished business. She'd even considered going to a psychic to see if they could help open a door Isaac couldn't see. Veronica listened, only occasionally interrupting to clarify something or make a rude comment. When Bryony had finished, she was quiet again. This was not uncommon, but given the proximity of death, Bryony grew more and more concerned, becoming obsessed with the readouts on the machinery, and eventually, she gently shook her foot.

'I'm still alive!' she said grumpily, 'I'm just thinking.'

'Oh right. Sorry. So what are your thoughts?'

'I don't know.'

'You don't know why he's still here, or you don't know what your thoughts are?' She joked, but Ronnie clearly wasn't in the mood.

'I don't know, and I'm tired. Leave me now to sleep.'

'Oh right. Yes, of course. Sorry, Ronnie.'

‘Don’t be sorry. Get the nurse back in here. She can watch me whilst I’m sleeping. You can go for a walk or something. Don’t go too far, though. I only need an hour.’

‘Okay, don’t worry. I won’t go far.’

Bryony did as she was told but found she could barely venture away from the hallway. Eventually, she just went to sit in Ronnie’s room again. As Veronica slept, her breathing was inconsistent, and the nurse regularly had to intervene with a gas mask or medicinal adjustments. It was crazy how different sleeping Ronnie was from waking Ronnie. It was about two hours before she woke up again. It was the longest two hours Bryony had ever experienced. Though she had pretended to be reading, in reality, she had spent the whole time just watching her friend, hoping she would wake up again. When she did wake, she had a coughing fit so violent her whole body shook, and she vomited all over herself. Bryony left the room to avoid either of them feeling uncomfortable as the nurse cleaned and changed her. When she went back in, Ronnie looked exhausted again.

‘Are you okay?’

‘Stop asking me that?’ She snapped irritably.

‘Excuse me, but you stopped breathing several times in your sleep, and you were sick when you woke up. Asking how you are feeling seems perfectly reasonable and appropriate.’

‘Bryony. I have maybe just a few hours of life left in me. Let’s take it for granted that I feel god-awful all the time. I don’t even want to think about it, let alone talk about it, so please, stop asking.’

Bryony felt properly chastised, more so by the fact that Ronnie’s voice was starting to sound as weak as her body looked, and Bryony hated being the reason she was exerting so much effort.

‘I’m sorry. Shall we do something else? Maybe I could read to you,’ she suggested. This was something she had observed happening in other rooms and thought it might be helpful or entertaining for Ronnie. She snorted derisively.

'No. I do not want you to read to me. When that happens, you'll know I'm moments from death,' she said firmly, albeit much quieter than usual. She shifted, trying to get more comfortable. 'I've been thinking about your situation,' she added eventually. 'I think there is only one logical solution.'

'There is? You'd better tell me before you die and leave me with this cliffhanger!'

Ronnie laughed, then coughed but managed to move on to her side, so when she vomited, it went into a nearby bucket, thankfully lined with a bin bag. Bryony noticed the red blood within it and deeply regretted making that stupid joke. The nurse cleared up efficiently and gave Bryony a stern look. Bryony nodded, knowing what she'd done. She moved her chair closer to Ronnie's bed, so their conversation was less likely to be overheard by the nurse, who returned to her spot in the far corner.

'I think that, if what you say is true and you are no longer in love with Isaac,' she continued as if she hadn't just been sick, 'Then there must be someone else who is holding on to him. Someone whose love has not diminished and is keeping him here.'

'But wouldn't they be able to see him, like I can?'

'Not necessarily. We were both fairly young, impressionable, and incredibly vulnerable when we first saw our ghosts. Therefore, our minds were at least open-minded about the idea of ghostly entities. The person holding on to your boyfriend may be very rigid in their beliefs, therefore unable even to entertain the possibility. My best guess is it's one of his parents.'

'Oh, God! How do I convince them to let him go if they don't even know he's here?'

'That I don't know, but you'd better figure it out fast. If not, that boy is staying with you forever,' she lay back and closed her eyes, but Bryony's brain was now racing so fast with possibilities and scenarios that she didn't notice at first.

'How will I know which one it is?'

'I don't know. Maybe whichever one looks sadder,' she mumbled.

'But what if I pick the wrong parent? They'll think I'm crazy.'

'Hmm. Probably.'

'Maybe Isaac could learn to become visible to them. Your Grandma learned how to do that, didn't she? Maybe she could try to teach him again.'

'I let her go a few weeks ago. She's crossed over now.'

'Oh, really? Sorry, that was really insensitive. Oh gosh Ronnie, are you O…' she stopped herself just in time, but Ronnie still raised an eyebrow at her. 'Maybe we don't have to talk anymore. We could just sit here quietly if you prefer.'

'I want to sit quietly, but I don't want you to. Tell me about your holiday or the girl you like or whatever.'

So, Bryony rattled on about this and that. Utter nonsense, really, occasionally making a funny remark but not enough to do much more than raise a smile. Ronnie listened quietly, sometimes smiling, sometimes raising an eyebrow or frowning. She barely said another word, though, and she would nod off occasionally. Her liquid lunch came, and they kindly bought Bryony some soup and a sandwich too. At one point, they asked Bryony to leave so they could change her catheter, but other than that, Bryony never left her side.

It was only when she was about halfway through reading her copy of *To Kill A Mockingbird*, which she kept on her at all times these days and which Ronnie confirmed she had neither read nor seen the film of, that the nurse spoke up for the first time.

'Bryony dear.' She interrupted gently, 'She's gone.'

'What? No! I didn't get to the end yet. She won't know about Boo Radley.'

'Don't worry, my dear. You'll be able to tell her when you meet again. I'll leave you for a few minutes now to say your goodbyes.'

Bryony moved to perch on the edge of the bed and took her still-warm hand in hers. She hadn't told her all the things she'd been so resolved to tell her this morning, but then, Ronnie wouldn't have wanted to hear them. At least she had been with her. She hadn't been alone.

'I hope you find peace wherever you go. And for goodness sake, try not to be rude,' she whispered. She kissed the back of her hand and stroked her hair. 'Goodbye, my dear, obnoxious friend. I will miss you.'

The nurse returned a few minutes later, knocking gently before entering to announce her return. She brought a doctor and other uniformed people with her, including Sharon, who steered Bryony towards the door. She asked Bryony if she was ready to leave Ronnie now. Bryony merely nodded, feeling rather dazed.

'We have a few things for you to sign.'

'Okay. Why me?'

'Ronnie named you her next of kin. As far as we're aware, there is no one else. We need you to sign some release forms, and I'm sure a solicitor will be in touch with you in the near future about her will. Don't worry about her funeral, she organised that herself, and it's all paid for, so we'll get the ball rolling on that one. We'll simply let you know when and where it is unless you want to go through it and make any alterations?'

‘No, no. Whatever Ronnie wants is fine.’

She took her through to a small room with a couple of chairs and a table and had her sign some papers. Refusing a cup of tea or anything else the nursing home had to offer, Bryony left feeling more than a little overwhelmed.

Her journey home was a surreal one. It felt crazy to her that Ronnie was now gone. She’d probably never make this journey again. And no one on this bus would know or care about it or her.

When she got home, she went straight to her mum, who was cooking in the kitchen, and hugged her hard.

‘Darling, what’s the matter?’

‘An old lady I knew at work died today,’ she white lied. She had no business knowing Ronnie if you didn’t factor Isaac into the equation, which she couldn’t, so this just seemed easier.

‘Oh, my darling girl. I’m so sorry. How awful. Did she have much family?’

‘No. Actually, no one really liked her except me. She was really rude and mean, but not to me. We got on really well.’

‘Oh, Bryony, I’m so sorry. It’s always the living who suffer. They are left here to mourn whilst the dead go off on the next big adventure. I’m sure, no matter how rude she was, if she managed to secure your friendship, she can’t have been that bad. Hopefully, she’s at rest now. Are you okay?’

Bryony couldn’t help smiling at the question.

‘Yeah, I’m fine. I just needed a hug.’

‘That’s what I’m here for, darling,’ she said, squeezing her tighter.

She begrudgingly released her mother and went upstairs to Isaac.

‘How did it go?’ he asked immediately.

For once, the high-blast air-conditioning effect of Isaac's presence was a welcome one. It offered relief from the heat of the day outside. If only Isaac himself offered similar relief. She sank heavily onto her bed.

'Ronnie died this afternoon,' she said. She knew this was not what he was asking, and she was setting him up for a fall, but it was an impulse she couldn't resist. She began counting in her head.

'Oh, that's terrible. Were you there? Was it horrible? Did you manage to talk to her first? Did she have any ideas about my situation?'

Fourteen seconds.

That's how long it took for him to turn the conversation about her recently deceased friend to himself. Why was she surprised? She tried not to be angry about it, but it really bugged her.

'Isaac. She literally just died like two hours ago. She was my friend. Can you not show a little empathy for someone else?'

'I'm sorry. You're right,' he said.

One.

Two.

Three.

'It's just she was our last line of enquiry, and if you didn't manage to ask her before she died, then I'm almost certainly going to turn into a monster. I'm sorry, I know I'm talking about myself again, but honestly, that thought is the only one that keeps going round and round in my head. Please, Bry. I'm sorry, I know she was your friend, but please, put me out of my misery here. Did she have any ideas?'

Bryony sighed heavily.

'She thinks, thought, someone else is holding onto you. Keeping you here, probably one of your parents.'

'My mum,' he said after barely a moment's thought. Bryony waited, knowing he had more he wanted to say.

'I see my dad and my brothers all the time. They're okay. They have their moments, their down days, or whatever, but for the most part, they're okay. Mum, though, I never see her. She doesn't leave the house, and 'cos I'm too much of a pussy, I'm too scared to go in there and see her.

'Dad moved out, and all the boys went with him, though it was supposed to be shared custody, but none of them stayed with her. Occasionally Alex goes by and checks on her, but mostly it's just Dad. He goes around every day with groceries, and every day he leaves with the same expression. Heartbroken.

'It has to be Mum who's keeping me here. What do we do about it?'

'We have to convince her to let you go… somehow.'

'What? How the hell are you going to do that?'

'Well, I can hardly go to her without some proof that you're here, so I suggest one of two ways. The first is not ideal, but at least we know you can do it. You lose your temper whilst we're over there, and you trash some stuff in front of her.'

'What? No. I can't do that. What if I totally lose it and hurt her? No way. What's option two?'

Bryony mentally noted that he only seemed to be concerned about hurting his mum and not her, and she added it to her ever-growing list of reasons she was over him.

'Number two is that you make yourself visible somehow. I know, I know before you kick off that you don't know how to do that, but we know it's possible, right? Ronnie's grandmother could do it, so maybe you can find a way. I really think you need to try because seeing you might just bring your mum the closure she needs.'

'Don't you think if I knew how to make myself seen, then I would have done it like a million times by now? I don't even know how to go about it, Bryony. I have no idea what to do or how to try.'

'Okay then, well maybe there really is only one option.'

'No! No, I'm not doing that.'

'Then what Isaac? I go and see your mother and tell her all about you and ask her just to trust me? That won't work. She'll just think I'm crazy, and you'll be stuck here forever, getting angrier and angrier.'

'There has to be another way.'

'Then maybe we need to take some time to brainstorm other ideas till we come up with another plan.' Bryony could feel her own disappointment mingling with Isaacs at the idea of prolonging his crossover. Neither of them wanted to drag this out any further. He was ready to cross over. He had been for a while now. And so was she.

'Or we could just wing it,' he suggested.

'Wing it?'

'Yeah, you know. We'll just go over there and see what happens. If it looks like she won't believe you, then I'll do something to change her mind.'

'Something like what?'

'Something like anything I can! I can't stay here much longer, Bry. It's killing me.'

Ignoring the irony of his statement, Bryony agreed. They were both getting desperate. Against her better judgement, they agreed they'd go tomorrow.

Chapter Twenty-Three

Bryony was waiting at the Spencer house. She had been waiting for over an hour. Sixty-four minutes, to be exact. She began pacing again, her nerves getting the better of her.

'Stop pacing. Dad will be here soon.'

'You said that an hour ago.'

'Well, I made us get here early, so we didn't miss him.'

'What? Why didn't you say something? Especially if you knew your mum wouldn't open the door. If I had known, I'd have bought a book or something.'

'Oh yeah, that would have been loads of fun for me, watching you read – again.'

Bryony bit her tongue. The easy-going relationship they had been enjoying for the last week or so was beginning to deteriorate. She kept reminding herself that he would be moving on soon, but she knew the truth was she was nervous. Scratch that she was terrified. She was about to reveal the deepest, darkest secret she had ever kept, one which might not only make her appear bat-shit crazy but might also deeply offend a very troubled woman whom she was really fond of.

She checked her phone again and attempted to play a sorting game, but it was no good. She hadn't the patience. She rifled through her bag for her hairbrush again.

'Here he is,' Isaac announced.

Bryony immediately forgot the hairbrush. Her whole attention was now one hundred per cent on the navy minivan heading her way. As he pulled up on the drive, a few feet in front of her, she swallowed hard and tried to steady her electric nerves. She saw the surprise in his expression before he even got out of the car. He emerged with a warm smile.

'Whatto Kid,' Rob called in an all too familiar greeting. 'I wasn't expecting to see you here, Bry. How are you doing?'

He was carrying a bag of groceries but still managed to pull her into a tight, one-armed embrace. Bryony hugged him back, suddenly overwhelmed with a million memories. When he released her, she found she couldn't speak immediately, her throat was too constricted with tears.

'How are you holding up, kid?' He asked so gently, examining her face. For a moment, all she could do was smile and nod. She composed herself, finally.

'Up until about thirty seconds ago, I was doing well. Now, seeing you and being here, I'm a bit overwhelmed,' she confessed.

'Of course you are, Bry. You're bound to be. Why don't you come in, and I'll stick the kettle on. It's really great to see you, kid. It's been too long.'

She followed him inside the too-still and too-quiet house. Isaac came in behind, his face tight and worried.

Even on the occasions when they had managed to get the house to themselves for an hour or so when he'd been alive, there was always a washing machine or a dishwasher or a dryer chugging away. Or at least there would be a mess or clutter everywhere. Now, it was just like the last time she'd been here. Clean, sterile. Unlived in.

'Wow. The house is so tidy and quiet,' she commented.

'Yeah, it's weird, isn't it,' he said. He headed straight to the kitchen to boil some water. He set out two mugs with two teabags, one with no sugar for him and one with two sugars for Bryony. She was touched, he remembered. He then turned to face her whilst he was waiting for the kettle to boil. 'So, did you know that me and the boys had moved out?' He asked.

'I had heard something to the effect,' she confessed without saying from who.

'It was all too hard for us, being here. We needed a fresh start.' The kettle clicked off, and he turned to finish the tea.

Isaac came into the kitchen, bringing in a chill. 'Mum's upstairs in bed,' he told her. 'She's not asleep, just lying there, eyes wide open,' Bryony nodded, acknowledging him silently.

'How are they, you, all getting on?' She asked aloud.

'Not too bad, actually. It's been hard, obviously, especially without Mel. But we're getting through, bit by bit. We all have our wobbles, our ups, and our downs, but we're all helping each other out. I honestly hadn't realised how sensitive the boys could be. Alex has changed completely,' he chuckled, putting the hot tea in front of her.

'And Melanie?' She ventured cautiously.

'Hmm. She's not doing as well. That's why I'm here, actually. I pop by every day just to make her something to eat and make sure she's taking the meds the doc gave her. I think, at first, she was just in shock, you know, but after a couple of months, it all just hit her. Honestly, she's completely broken, and I… I just don't know how to fix her. I wish I could stay here with her full-time, but I've gotta work to pay for the two mortgages. I know we talked about divorce and whatnot, but we didn't go through with it. I guess we still love each other. I love her, at least. But I've gotta look out for the boys. I don't know what else to do for the best,' he confessed heavily.

'You're doing a great job, Rob,' Bryony assured him.

'Ha!' He chuckled miserably. 'You haven't seen her kid. She's … unreachable.'

‘I’m sure that’s not true.’

‘Well, I can’t seem to reach her anymore,’ he took a sip of his tea and immediately pulled a face as it burnt his mouth.

Bryony was about to speak. Was about to say she might be able to help Melanie, but she hesitated too long.

‘Sorry kid, listen to me, laying all my troubles at your feet. How are you? How are you coping? How did your exams go?’

‘Yeah, okay. They were hard.’

‘Isaac would have hated sitting them. He’d have probably flunked them all, and I’d have had to pretend to be all disappointed and whatnot, so he’d do resits! When do you get your results?’

‘Next week.’

‘Oh, you’ll be fine. You’re a clever girl. Not sure what you saw in our Isaac, I must confess.’

‘I loved him,’ she said simply.

‘We all did, kid,’ he patted her hand, then turned away to pour his barely-touched tea down the sink and wipe his eyes. He turned back with a big smile.

‘So, to what do we owe this unexpected visit?’

Bryony wasn’t expecting the sudden conversation change. She faltered before finally pulling up her big girl pants.

‘Actually, I wanted to see Melanie.’

Immediately his smile dropped.

‘Oh, kid. I don’t think that’s a good idea. She’s…’

‘I know, she’s not doing too well,’ Bryony interrupted. ‘But she came to see me when I couldn’t get out of bed, and she was able to bring me round a bit. I would really like to return the favour if I can.’ When he still looked unsure, she added, ‘It’s unlikely I’ll make her any worse, isn't it? Where's the harm in letting me try?' She felt the horrible weight of these words, knowing full well what she was about to say to Melanie could make her much worse, but she desperately needed to see her alone.

'Honestly, kiddo, it's not her I'm worried about upsetting. You got all choked up when you saw me, and I'm up and walking and talking.'

'I will regret it if I go on to university and I didn't at least try to help.'

'She's not your responsibility, Bry.'

'No, I know. But I know a little bit about the desperation of her pain. I didn't get out of bed for almost a week before she came to see me, did you know that? I just… I just want her to know she's not alone. Let her know that I was there, in her place, unable to muster the strength to go on, but I did get through, and there is hope at the end of all the nothingness. Please.'

He thought about it for a full minute. Eventually, he said, 'Please just don't be too disappointed if she doesn't react at all. She's on a lot of medication, and like I said, she's unreachable.'

Bryony nodded, relieved he'd agreed to let her see her. Now she had to actually see her. She sipped her tea, stalling.

'Come on then, Bry, let's go,' Isaac hurried her on, but she ignored him, thinking about the best way to do what she had to do.

'Why don't you let me make her some lunch and get her to eat something first? That way, I can let her know that you're here,' he suggested, much more empathetic than his son. 'You finish your tea first,' Bryony nodded gratefully.

As he busied himself in the kitchen, making lunch for Melanie, he filled Bryony in on any family news she may have missed. Bryony tried to pay attention, but she was massively distracted by Isaac, who was talking to her at the same time. He kept telling her to take some of the lighter ornaments up to the bedroom with her to place strategically on the dressing table so he could knock them off without hitting anyone.

Bryony had to focus on both conversations and answer or respond appropriately, but her head was spinning, there were butterflies in her stomach, and she had her own ideas running around her brain. In the end, she ignored both of them and focussed on her tea.

'Right, I'll take this up to her. Be back down in a bit. Make yourself at home,' Bryony nodded and managed a small smile. As soon as he was out of earshot, she rounded on Isaac.

'You couldn't have waited five minutes to speak to me when your dad was out of the room?' She hissed.

'I'm sorry. I'm kind of nervous.'

'You're nervous! How the hell do you think I feel? If this doesn't work, your mum is either going to think I'm crazy or never speak to me again. And that's best case scenario!'

'I know, I know. Look, grab that picture frame over there and hide it in your bag.'

'What?'

'I can knock it over real easy when you tell me to. It's proof for you.'

Whilst she wasn't happy about it, she couldn't deny his logic. She crept around the rooms on the lower floor, hiding things in her bag to strategically place upstairs.

'Bryony, what if this doesn't work?' Isaac suddenly asked, fear and vulnerability eeking out of him.

'Then I come back and try again tomorrow and the next day and the day after that until eventually, she believes us.'

‘But what if, like you said, she refuses to see you again after today?’

Bryony faltered. She had no clue what would happen then.

‘Are you okay? I thought I heard talking,’ Isaac’s dad had been so quiet coming back down Bryony hadn’t heard him come right up behind her. She leapt about a foot in the air. She clutched her bag with all the “borrowed” items in it to her chest.

‘Oh, that,’ she paused, her brain working fast, ‘I seem to talk to myself a lot these days.’

He chuckled, ‘Well, you probably want an expert opinion,’ he joked. Bryony forced a laugh out. She noticed that he’d bought the lunch back down with barely anything gone from it.

‘I guess she wasn’t hungry?’

He sighed heavily.

‘She’s really unresponsive today. Like I said, I’m not sure if it’s the meds or if she’s just getting worse. Are you sure you want to do this?’

‘Better now than never,’ she said, quoting one of her father’s favourite sayings.

He nodded and took the lunch tray to the bin.

‘I’ll be down here if you need me.’

Now Bryony had no way of backing out. Slowly, she and Isaac walked noiselessly upstairs. She tapped on the bedroom door. As expected, she got no reply, but she went in anyway. The room was dark but undisturbed. The only sign of life was the gentle rise and fall of the huddle breathing under the duvet. Bryony remembered the feeling of believing that her bed was the only thing she could deal with and that anything outside of it would probably kill her.

‘Hi Melanie, it’s me, Bryony,’ she whispered. She wasn’t sure why. She thought about pulling the stool over from the dressing table, but then she remembered the many evenings the two of them had sat on this bed watching mindless chick-flicks on the massive telly on the wall opposite whilst the boys watched some sort of sporting event downstairs. She blushed with shame at the memory of it now, realising how heartbroken her own mother would be that she’d done such bonding with someone else’s mum. Still, she could use it to her own advantage here. She walked to the other side of the king-sized bed, placing the trinkets from downstairs in strategic places as she went, and sat down.

‘Wow. Make yourself at home, why don’t you?’ Isaac remarked, having no knowledge of her history of doing this.

‘So, I know you’re having a really difficult time at the moment,’ she began, ignoring Isaac entirely. ‘And whilst it’s obviously not the same, I know what it’s like to be unable to leave your little pit of despair.’

She looked over, but there was no movement from the other side of the bed.

‘So, I’m going to tell you a story, and all I want you to do is listen. At the end of the story, you might have some questions for me, and I promise I will answer everything to the best of my ability, okay?’

Still nothing. Bryony had to assume and hope that she would listen. To be sure, she checked with Isaac, and he confirmed she was awake.

‘Okay, so once upon a time, there was a very average princess who somehow caught the attention of the most handsome prince in all the land. The two began dating, and the handsome prince opened the princess’s eyes to a whole world filled with fun and noise and crazy romance and just general silliness, which the princess had never really experienced before. Naturally, the poor average princess didn't stand a chance. She fell so fast and so hard for the prince, she barely touched the floor.

'And then, the unthinkable happened. That beautiful, wonderful, funny, vivacious young prince was taken from her in an awful accident.'

She heard and felt a bone-shuddering sob come from Melanie, and it almost undid her. She bit her lip to stop herself from crying and took a moment to get rid of the lump in her throat. Isaac stood nearby, looking lost and helpless.

'The whole kingdom mourned for the prince, for he was adored by many, including the King, Queen, and the other princes. That is not, however, the end of the story. Just when the world felt too hard for the princess to continue in it, she saw him again. The prince had returned to her, as a ghost,' she paused, waiting for a reaction, but she heard nothing.

'She's frowning,' Isaac told her, 'So she's definitely listening.'

Bryony nodded and continued.

'Naturally, the princess thought she had lost her mind or was hallucinating or something, for no one else could see or hear the prince but her. However, many people would remark about a coldness in the air whenever the ghost was nearby.'

She signalled to Isaac and carefully pulled the duvet back to reveal Melanie's arm. Isaac placed his own icy cold hand over her arm. In less than a second, Melanie snatched her arm back under the covers, and then she turned to face Bryony, her expression showing a plethora of emotions. Bryony continued, looking Melanie directly in the eyes as she did.

'The princess was delighted, her prince was back, at least in one form, and she spent that long cold winter luxuriating in the knowledge he was here. Everything was perfect again for a little while.

'Over time, the prince grew lonely with only the princess for company, for he had always been a social butterfly, and she had other responsibilities and exams to sit. He grew restless, agitated, and eventually angry. They sought the advice of a wise old woman, who had also known ghosts, and she explained that the prince was ready to move on to his final resting place, and the princess needed to let him go. So she did, but still, the prince could not move on. Someone else was holding on too tight to the prince's soul. The Queen. She was distraught by the loss of her son, it consumed her, and she had no idea she was keeping him tethered to this world when all the prince wanted, what the prince needed, was peace in the next world.'

They were both sat up now, looking at each other.

'Now Melanie, I understand how this must sound, but please hear me out. That story is absolutely true,' she said earnestly. 'Not the prince thing, obviously. I mean, Isaac coming back as a ghost. The day of Isaac's funeral, I didn't run from the service because I was overwhelmed, I ran because I saw him and I thought I was insane. I have seen him nearly every day since then. He is really here. You can tell he is because, as you just felt, his presence makes the air around him really cold.'

Once again, Isaac moved closer to his mum, wrapping himself around her. She shivered, her face horrified.

'Also, when he's really, really angry, he can move things. We had a bit of a falling out before I went on holiday, and when I came back, he had completely trashed my room. I've bought up a couple of items, and he's going to try and move them for you now.'

She watched Isaac try and fail to move the photo frame. He tried again and again but to absolutely no avail.

'Oh no,' Bryony mumbled. She looked at Melanie, who was staring at her incredulously.

'Bryony, why would you say these things? Is this some sort of a joke? You can't really believe this.'

Bryony was horrified. 'Melanie, please, please. Just listen to me for a minute,' she begged desperately, knowing full well any second now, she would call for Rob to come and remove her. 'I know how it sounds. I know it seems impossible and, therefore, cruel. But you know me. You know the kind of person I am. Have I ever hurt you before? Do you think I would ever make up a story like this? I wouldn't. You know I wouldn't. So whilst I know what I'm suggesting seems impossible, what if it was? Just imagine, for one tiny moment, that I'm right. That Isaac is actually here, and he needs you, Melanie. You felt the coldness of his presence, I know you did. You felt him when he was close to you. All you need to know he is here is tiny bit of faith.'

At that precise moment, Isaac stopped trying to move things and just sat on the bed in front of his mum, pleading, begging with the universe itself, to let his mum see him, let her hear him.

'Please, Mum. Please know that I'm here,' he begged.

She let out a tiny gasp.

'Isaac?' She asked, looking directly at him.

For a moment, time stopped as Isaac and his mum stared at each other.

'Mum? Can you see me?' He asked, barely able to consider it a possibility.

The disbelief and utter joy on Melanie's face answered his question, and a second later, she flung herself at him.

Inevitably, she fell straight through his ghostly form and landed rather unceremoniously in Bryony's lap. She fumbled, trying to sit up again, and as Bryony helped her, she couldn't help but notice the boniness of her body.

'Sorry, I should have mentioned we cannot touch him,' she explained to Melanie, who couldn't stop staring at her son.

'What? Not even a hug?'

'I know, Mum, it sucks!'

Melanie let out a short giggle then she cautiously raised her hand as if to stroke his face. He leaned into her, and she gasped when her fingers only found cold air.

'I don't understand,' she said. 'Is it really you? Are you really here?'

'It's me, Mum. I'm just a ghost now.'

'I know it's crazy, Mel, trust me, I thought I was going insane for months.'

'And you've known about him since his funeral?' Melanie asked. Bryony felt the accusatory nature of her question.

'Yes, but like I said, I thought he was a hallucination or something. We didn't think anyone else would be able to see him. The only reason we even agreed to mention it to you is because we are convinced you are the one keeping him here. Unconsciously, of course.'

They kept staring at each other, Melanie in complete shock and Isaac with a huge grin on his face. Bryony suddenly felt uncomfortable. They didn't need or want her here for this reunion, but where else could she go? As surreptitiously as possible, she slid off the bed and sat cross-legged on the floor, trying to give them both as much privacy as possible.

'I can't believe you can see me,' he grinned. 'It's so good to be seen by you, Mum.'

'I can't believe it. I mean, I know I can see you, but still, I can't believe it.'

‘I’ve really missed you, Mum.’

‘Oh baby boy, I have missed you so much.’

She broke then, sobbing almost hysterically. Isaac kept trying to comfort her with words, but she just had to cry it out.

‘It’s so unfair that I can’t hug you,’ she finally managed to say.

‘Ugh, trust me, I know. Literally the worst part about being dead.’

She laughed then.

‘I miss that laugh,’ he stopped then, getting serious. ‘Oh, Mum, what have you been doing? I never wanted you to be like this. I know you miss me, but you can’t just stay in bed for the rest of your life. What about the boys? What about Dad? I’ve been watching them, and they’ve been doing okay, but they need you, Mum. You gotta get yourself together and help look after them.’

‘You don’t understand, Baby. Losing you… it broke me. I feel like half of myself has gone, and I can’t function without you.’

‘I know it’s sad, but look at me, I’m okay, or at least I will be when I cross over.’

‘But there’s so much you missed out on. So much of life you didn’t get to experience. You’re so young, Baby.’

‘I don’t think I’m missing out on that much. You know me, Mum, I was always the wild one. The party boy! I was never that good at responsibility, and from what I can see, all that was coming my way was a whole lot of adulting, and we both know I wouldn’t have been any good at that.’

‘You could have gone to university, got married, had babies!’

‘Ugh! Please! We both know I probably wouldn’t have got into Uni! I still think it’s a win that I didn’t have to sit my exams! As for marriage and babies, well, that sounds like a whole lot of hard work. I think I’ve had a lucky escape.’

She chuckled for a moment before getting serious.

'I know it's selfish, baby, but I don't want you to cross over or whatever it is. I want you to stay with me forever. Haunt me forever.'

Bryony heard him sigh deeply, and she knew his brain was working hard to make his mum understand.

'What's your favourite thing about me?'

'What do you mean, Baby? I love everything about you.'

'No, I know, but whenever you think about me, what personality traits come to mind? How would you describe me?'

'Oh, well, you're funny and playful and fun-loving. You're thoughtful and kind, you're a hopeless romantic, a competitive sportsman, a people person but also a real mama's boy,' she smiled at him, and he smiled back.

'They are all lovely things to be and to be remembered as. But Mum, the longer I stay here, in this form, the more I'm changing. I've done horrible things, I've been cruel and selfish, and whilst we both know I'm a spoilt brat, I've taken things to a whole new level, and my temper is horrendous. Being here, like this, is changing me into a monster. I'm becoming something I don't want to be, and I can't stop it, I can't change it, and honestly, the whole thing is terrifying.'

'But Baby, *I* can see you now. I can help you, calm you, and make you better. We could get your dad and all the boys to see, and you'll be part of the family again.'

'That's not how it works, Mum. It takes a lot of hard work to make myself seen by you. I don't think I have the strength to do it for long, and there are rules about being seen. Plus, I have seen what happens to ghosts who stay here. They become unrecognisable and violent, and they hurt people. I don't wanna… I can't be that person,

Mum. I want to be the boy that you described. I want to be remembered that way.'

'But… but I just got you back. It can't be fair that I'm only just able to see you, and I have to let you go straight away. I can't do it!' She began to sob again. Isaac waited a few minutes.

'I know it's rubbish, but maybe we're looking at this the wrong way. Maybe I was never meant to stay with you. Maybe I was never even meant to be seen by you, and this is all just an incredible bonus for us. Maybe, I was just supposed to visit you to let you know that I'm okay with all of this. I'm gonna go to a good place, and I'll just wait for you there. Maybe I was supposed to come and tell you to get your lazy ass out of bed and start looking after yourself and the boys and Dad. You would have gone crazy at me if I'd tried to stay in bed all day!'

Her sobs turned into chuckles.

'It's gonna be okay, Mum. I promise.'

She sniffed hard, but when she looked up at him, her expression was resigned. She nodded.

Suddenly the room blazed with a light that blinded them all, even Bryony, who was sitting behind the bed. She knelt up to investigate.

'Okay, I may be going out on a limb here, but I think that's my cue!'

Both his mum and his girlfriend smiled at him, tears in their eyes.

'I love you,' he said to both of them. Before either of them could say it back, the light was gone, and so was Isaac.

For a moment, the two girls sat in silence, blinking the light away, trying to adjust their eyesight to the comparable darkness.

Then they looked at each other, knowing that Isaac was officially gone for good.

Melanie howled in grief and release and reached for her. Bryony scrambled onto the bed and held her as tight as she could. A few moments later, the bedroom door flew open; Rob stood in the doorway, a tea towel in his hand.

'I heard a noise. Mel, you're… Oh, darling!'

Melanie released Bryony and reached for her husband. He crossed the bedroom in two strides and pulled her into his arms. Bryony discreetly left them to their consoling and knew that they would be okay. She left with the bittersweet knowledge that she would probably never see them again. Never see Isaac again.

Chapter Twenty-Four

The following Tuesday was the hottest day on record for August. People were advised not to travel unless it was absolutely necessary and to avoid being out in the sun for long periods.

Bryony had been sweating from the moment she got out of the shower that morning. She sweated as she got dressed in the black dress she had chosen, something as light as possible without being disrespectful. She sweated profusely on the bus journeys she had taken, regularly dowsing herself in body spray, trying to avoid smelling bad. She sweated through the overly long service in the tiny, ancient church with barely any electrical outlets, let alone air conditioning. The one fan they had seemed to just continually circulate more hot air. And now she was sweating even more, standing out in the bright, hot sun at the graveside as the vicar said his final reading.

It all seemed pointless, as, other than the vicar, there were only four people at the service, including herself. Two of the people appeared to be just devout churchgoers and probably attended every service, even the funerals of people they didn't know. The other members of this little congregation were herself and Sharon, Ronnie's main carer.

There was also a woman in a big hat and sunglasses, hovering at a distant tree, who seemed to be focused on their party but unwilling to come any closer. She was wearing black, so she must have intended to come to the funeral. Bryony couldn't help but wonder if she was a distant relative or an old friend. Maybe even a mortal enemy of Ronnie's, just checking to see if she was definitely dead! That seemed the most likely.

There were no flowers. Apparently, this was a stipulation Ronnie had made when organising her own funeral, but Bryony hadn't got the memo. She had stopped off at a supermarket to pick up a generic bouquet but then spent fifteen minutes deciding which ones to get. Admittedly, the delicious air conditioning in the supermarket may have been a factor, but she was also stumped. Lilies were beautiful and smelled amazing, but they were so depressingly linked to death, and they felt rather clichéd. Plus, the dust off the stamen stained clothes, and she had three buses to catch, so she ruled them out. The sunflowers were in full bloom, but they were her absolute favourite flower, and she didn't want to always associate them with Veronica's funeral. There were roses, but they felt too out of character for her friend, who was anything but the elegant, sophisticated flower. She decided upon a generic bouquet with lots of flowers she couldn't even name but seemed understated and appropriate for a funeral service. She stood in the queue to pay, and at the very last minute, she changed her mind. She decidedly picked up the bouquet of sunflowers. The garish, in-your-face, love-me-or-hate-me flower seemed just too perfect for the obnoxious, wonderful lady she was honouring. So what if she always thought of Ronnie when she saw them? It wasn't a bad association.

The vicar reached the end of the service and indicated she should place the flowers on the coffin before it was lowered into the grave. She was pleased with her choice now. Those bright, cheerful blooms would maybe remind Ronnie of her, and she could go into the afterlife with some brazen colour. '*That probably wasn't how it worked,*' she told her runaway imagination.

Everyone was sombre at funerals, but she was experiencing a lull in mood that bordered on depression. The relief she had expected to feel after Isaac's departure didn't come. She missed him. Her room was too hot, and she knew she'd have felt the same way if it were the middle of winter and not this endless, barren summer.

When the vicar finished, he walked over to Bryony, held her too-hot hand in his too-hot hands, and mumbled some words of condolence that she didn't really listen to, then he went back up to the church, taking his two lackeys with him. Sharon approached her awkwardly.

‘I’m sorry,’ she began, ‘Usually, when we know a patient doesn’t have much family or friends, most of the nurses and carers will attend their funeral as a mark of respect, but you know… well, it’s really hot and… well, erm… Ronnie didn’t really do much to endear herself to anyone.’

Bryony chuckled.

‘I know. She was a difficult woman to like. Thank you for making the effort. You’re a good woman and a really good carer Sharon. I appreciate all you did for her, even if she didn’t.’

They both smiled then.

‘I’m glad she met you,’ she said before leaving.

On her own, Bryony’s dark thoughts couldn’t help but consider what an unfair hand Ronnie had been dealt in life. Seeing a ghost at so young an age and being subjected to institutions pretty much her whole life. It was hardly surprising she had ended up as unpopular as she was. As she pondered this, she saw that the woman in black by the distant trees was starting to move towards her. Bryony became very aware of the fact that she was alone and pretty vulnerable. She had no idea what this woman wanted, although it was pretty clear she was headed her way. She may claim that Ronnie owed her money or something. Or maybe she was another ghost! Bryony couldn’t help but draw parallels between the only two funerals she had ever been to.

‘*Oh crap!*’ she thought uncharitably, ‘*I’ve only just got rid of one!*’

Then she noticed something familiar about the gait or the form or something. The woman was almost on top of her before she realised who she was.

‘Mum!’

‘Hello, darling,’

'What are you doing here? And you're in a dress! No wonder I didn't recognise you.'

'You left a letter with the details of the funeral open on the kitchen table. I remembered what you said about this lady not being very popular, and I thought this might be hard for you. Plus, you've been in a really low funk recently, I just wanted to make sure that you were okay, so I booked the day off work. And I'm in a dress because it's a funeral, and all my black trouser suits are at the dry cleaners.'

'Oh, Mum!'

Bryony hugged her mum hard. And there, by the graveside, on the hottest day ever, Bryony broke down. She sobbed her heart out into her mother's linen dress.

She cried for the injustice of Ronnie's life and for losing this wonderful friend who had taught her so much after only recently finding her.

She cried for the loss of Isaac, the wonderful boyfriend he had been, and the complex, difficult ghost he became.

She cried for the Spencer's and the whole family's loss.

She cried for the fact that she still really liked Kirsty, and yet she clearly didn't like her as she had never gotten in touch.

She cried because she was sure she had completely buggered up her chance to achieve the dream of going to Oxford University. All because of a boy whom she was no longer with and no longer had feelings for.

And she cried because her whole life would change after this summer. She had to go to some university that wasn't her first choice, knowing Steven wouldn't be there, leaving her family and her job and having to make it somewhere else without anyone she knew.

She wasn't ready for that level of adulting, as Isaac would say.

When she finally finished crying, her eyes were so swollen she could barely see through them, and she felt better but hot and dehydrated. Her mother didn't say a word about what must have seemed like a disproportionate amount of sadness for some unpopular lady she knew from work.

When she was ready, she led Bryony from the cemetery to her car, where she put the air conditioning on and gave her daughter an icy cold bottle of water and a pack of tissues. She really was the best mum in the world.

'You know,' her mother began, as they pulled away, 'I am absolutely convinced I know that name, Veronica Wainswright. I just cannot think where. Wouldn't it be a crazy coincidence if I do?'

'Bit of a longshot, don't you think?'

Bryony dismissed it, feeling a strange, panicky sensation rise up in case her two worlds were to collide.

'Yes, of course, but still... I know, I know that name. Maybe from work?'

'Hmm.' Bryony said vaguely. Her mother was a solicitor. She could not imagine Veronica enlisting her help for much unless it was to sue someone. Ronnie was mean sometimes, but she didn't really hold grudges, so she doubted it very much.

When they got home, barely thirty minutes later, they ordered pizza for lunch (unheard of in the Duglass household) and sat watching chick-flicks in the sitting room until her father came home.

In his habitual way, her father asked how the funeral had gone. Bryony explained how there was hardly anyone there.

'That's the problem as you get older.' He began as he searched the larder for brown onions, 'By the time it's your funeral, everyone you know is either dead or hates you.'

Veronica hushed him harshly and looked over at her daughter to see if she was upset or outraged by her father's insensitivity. Bryony merely shrugged. It was very accurate in this case.

When she was convinced Bryony was not offended, she allowed her gaze to shift, settling on the corkboard on the wall behind her daughter.

'Aha! I knew it!' she reached out and pulled down the letter she had pinned there.

The kitchen often doubled as an office for her mum when she worked at home, and on the corkboard, she would pin correspondence from perspective new clients to reply to if she had the time. One of those letters had the name and address of Ronnie at the nursing home. Her mother handed it to her, and Bryony examined it carefully. It was dated a few weeks before she had ever met Ronnie, and Bryony couldn't help but think it was too weird to be a coincidence but couldn't reconcile what else it could possibly mean.

'The world really is a strange place, isn't it?'

Bryony agreed thoughtfully as she returned the letter to the board. She knew she would mull this over for months.

The next day she went for a meeting with the solicitor dealing with Ronnie's estate. As the sole beneficiary, Bryony had to decide what to do with everything she had left. The solicitor, Fred Bowman, gave her a list of all her assets and then another list of her debts. Noticing her blank expression, he was kind enough to explain that, in Layman's terms, if they sold all the assets, as was suggested by Ronnie herself, she could pay off all the debts and would still be left with just under seven hundred thousand pounds.

Bryony's jaw dropped. She was not expecting that. She didn't want that.

'I can't accept that!'

‘There’s no accepting it, Miss Duglass. It’s yours, by law. If you were under eighteen, I would have to put it into a trust for you, but as you are officially eighteen, the money is yours.’

‘But I have no idea what to do with it. I’ve only been eighteen for a couple of months.’ Bryony’s big birthday had fallen during the exams and she had refused to even acknowledge it at the time. Instead they had celebrated it belatedly on holiday. The night of the karaoke.

‘You can put it into a savings account and wait until you do know. You could invest it, donate it to charity, or blow it on a round-the-world trip. You could stick it all on red if you want to, Miss Duglass, not that I would condone gambling at all. It is entirely up to you.’

He smiled at her and began shuffling through some more paperwork. He excused himself to go and find something, and when he returned, item in hand, Bryony had made a decision.

‘I want to give it all to charity,’ she announced.

‘All of it? Miss Duglass, it is your money, but I urge you to consider this for longer. Seek advice from family or friends before doing anything rash.’

‘No. I don’t want to involve anyone else, it will just complicate things. If I accept this money, I’ll feel like it’s sullied our friendship. It’s too much, and I neither want nor need it. I’ve made my decision. I want to donate it all to charity. Well, actually, I’d like to split it between two charities, if that’s possible?’

‘Yes, of course.’

‘The first is a charity called Mind which helps people with mental health issues. Ronnie could have used some help from them when she was a kid. Hopefully, they’ll use her money to help others.’

‘Okay, I know the one,’ he said, writing it down. ‘And the second?’

‘Marie Curie,’ she said with a smile. ‘Ronnie was so rude to the nurses who cared for her it seems only fitting that her money goes to them.’

The corners of Mr Bowman’s lips twitched as he wrote it down.

‘And you’re absolutely sure you don’t want to keep any of it? It could pay for your student fees, buy a property, a really nice car...’

‘I’m sure.’

‘Okay, well, if you insist, I will do it. There is just one more item to discuss with you. Miss Wainswright had assumed you would want to liquidate all of her assets. However, she requested that you keep one memento. It’s a family heirloom. It belonged to her grandmother, I believe, and she wanted you to keep it. Maybe pass it on to your own children when the time comes. It’s not worth much, just a couple of grand, but it’s a sentimental object.’

‘Yes, of course. What is it?’ She asked, ungraciously hoping it wasn’t some enormous eyesore of a painting or an ugly piece of furniture.

Mr Bowman handed her the small padded envelope he’d been out to collect. It was sealed.

She opened it. Inside was a long, rectangular, red velvet jewellery case. Very carefully, she opened it. Inside was a gold necklace with the most beautiful sunflower pendant she had ever seen.

Chapter Twenty-Five

She was stood in line behind a couple of lads from another class. She cursed herself for oversleeping. She had planned to be one of the first people here, get in and get out, but Steven had insisted, on the eve of exam results day, it was a rite of passage to have a few drinks. So Bryony accompanied him and a few of his uni friends, including his new girlfriend Lisa, to the pub for a drink. One drink turned into two, which became cocktails, and before she knew it, they were in a taxi to the city centre, where they danced until the early hours of this morning. To be fair, she had really enjoyed herself. She liked Lisa, and she bought the best out in her brother, who could be something of a snob. Lisa encouraged him to relax more and make a fool out of himself occasionally, and to that end, at one point last night, he had fallen to his knees as he sang his heart out to a Bon Jovi song. The crowd around him had been so impressed by his commitment to the song they had raised him above their heads and crowd-surfed him to the stage, where he performed the rest of the song with the DJ. She smiled at the memory. Then stopped immediately. Smiling made her head hurt.

Now here she was, one of the last people in her year queuing to get her exam results. It didn't help that she was super nervous. She was so pleased her mum had taken the day off. She didn't think she could handle calling up other universities if none of her chosen three would take her.

'Hello, Bry,' a familiar voice caught her attention. She looked up to see Dana, one of her former friends, before Isaac came onto the scene. One of her "clever friends," as he had always referred to them.

'Dana, hi,' she said, trying out smiling again. Not quite as painful now. 'How are you? Have you got your results already? How did you get on?'

'Yeah, I've done okay. I'm pleased, I can go to my first choice.'

'Brilliant! Well done. Just checking, Oxford is still the first choice for you, isn't it?'

'Yeah,' she smiled. 'That's actually why I wanted to say hi. I know we haven't exactly been close the last couple of years, but we were good friends before. We will probably be seeing each other more over the next four years. Well, I mean, Oxford is a big place, but you know, we'll both be studying English Lit, both be freshers. It might be nice to see a friendly face if you want?'

'Oh. Oh yeah, I mean, definitely. Obviously, I haven't got my results yet, but if I get in, then absolutely, that would be great.'

'Don't be modest, Bry. You're the cleverest person in the school. You'll definitely get in. Will it be cool if I text you sometime?'

'Cool like ice,' she smiled, more genuinely now, having used one of the little phrases they always used to say when they hung out as kids. Dana grinned at her and headed off. She wished she felt as confident about her academic achievements as her friend did. Finally, she was next in line.

Mr Greaves grinned at her, taking in the sunglasses, the late arrival, and the unhealthy pallor.

'Go celebrating a little early, did we, Miss Duglass?'

'Hardly celebrating, sir, let's call it anxiety deflection.'

'I'm sure that was an unnecessary precaution.'

'Come on, sir, we both know how little I did for two of the most important years.'

'It's true, you may have had some different priorities for a while, and I know you have always set yourself virtually unreachable targets, so I imagine even if you do fantastically, you'll still be disappointed in yourself. What you get today may not be what you wanted, but please remember, in ten years' time, the grades you get today will be insignificant compared to the memories you made at school, okay?'

'Thank you, sir.'

'Try to have a little perspective if you don't get the grades you're dreaming of.'

She nodded and smiled at him. She wanted to give him a hug, he really was the best teacher she'd ever had, but given the circumstances, that may make things a little awkward. Instead, she put her signature in the little box next to her name on a piece of paper with all the students' names on it, and Miss Pemberton handed her a sealed, A4 brown envelope. Mr Greaves made her give him a high-five.

'Good luck Miss Duglass. Tell your mum I'll be able to hear her shrieks from here!'

'Will do,' she grinned, then she walked out of school for the last time and didn't look back.

Her mum was waiting for her in the car.

'So, how did you get on?' She asked immediately, ever the eager puppy, as Mr Greaves had predicted.

'I haven't opened them yet, and I don't want to here. Can we go and get a coffee or something, please?'

Her mum almost broke the speed limit, she was so desperate to find out the results. Once they were parked up in the car park of a drive-thru Starbucks, and they'd both got their frozen macchiatos, Bryony opened the envelope and removed the piece of paper. She had taken four A' level exams: English Language, English Literature, History, and Journalism. To get into Oxford, she needed at least three A's and an A* minimum.

Journalism	A
English Lit.	A*
English Lang.	A
History	B

She had known it. Deep down in her bones, she had known she'd missed too much to catch up, but that didn't stop the heart-squeezing disappointment or the heavy tears pouring down her face.

Unable to speak, she passed the paper to her mother, who took longer to examine them than she did.

'Oh, darling! These are amazing results. You have done an incredible job. You should be so proud of yourself. Now, now, don't get too upset. There's always clearing if they won't accept these grades. Plus, you've got the right grades for the subject you want to study, so it could all be fine anyway. Oh, don't be disappointed darling, you've done marvellously. Plus, you have extenuating circumstances; you've had a much tougher year than most, they're bound to take that into account too.'

Bryony managed to control herself. She nodded at all her mum said as though in agreement, but she knew it wasn't going to happen. Oxford Uni was so sought after because it was the best; she was clearly not one of the best.

After two days spent either on the phone or waiting for a phone call or an email, Bryony and her family finally conceded that neither Oxford nor Cambridge, her first and second choice uni's would accept her with those grades, and she accepted instead a place at her third choice uni, The University of St Andrews in London.

By the time she had completed all of the necessary paperwork, she was actually quite excited by it. Still, she didn't want to be taken off guard by Dana about Oxford, so she proactively texted her:

Bryony - Hi Dana. Just FYI, I didn't get into Ox. I'm obvs a bit gutted but real chuffed for u. Hope you love it there. I'm going to St Andrew's, so we may still meet up at competitions. Gd luck. Bry xxx

Dana replied in a typically self-effacing way, and they struck up a text friendship, even planning to catch up for coffee before they both went on their separate ways. Bryony was surprisingly pleased by this turn of events. She and Dana had been best friends for about five years before she had unceremoniously dumped her for Isaac. It was very magnanimous of her to extend the olive branch of friendship after how she'd been mistreated, and Bryony only now realised how much she had missed her friendship. It was all more than she deserved.

Chapter Twenty-Six

She had her final session with Dr Will a few days after her exam results. She was sure he had planned it that way to explore her emotions about the event. By now, though, she wasn't even upset anymore. She had gotten what she deserved and nothing more. Plus, St Andrews was a fantastic University, one she was becoming more and more obsessed with. She told Dr Will as much, and he didn't question her much about it, meaning he believed her.

'You seem much calmer today.' He observed. For once, she hadn't chosen a fidget toy to play with; she just sat comfortably talking with him.

'Yeah, well, I guess now my future is sorted, it's a weight off my shoulders,' She pointed out.

'And how are you feeling about Ronnie?'

Given the client confidentiality agreement between them, Bryony had felt comfortable telling him all about Ronnie, her passing, the will, and her decision to refuse the money, well, almost everything, of course. She had naturally omitted any reference to ghosts. Watching his reaction reinforced her conviction that she was right to do what she had done.

'I'm okay with it. Actually, to be honest, I haven't thought much about Ronnie. I've been somewhat distracted by results day.'

'Naturally. And you are feeling positive about the future, university, all the big change.'

'I was obviously a bit disappointed, but honestly, now I've researched St Andrews more, it actually looks brilliant. The English department there is amazing, and did you know that's where John Cleese went to University?'

'I didn't. I only knew about Prince William and Kate.'

‘Well, yes, of course, everyone knows them, but my namesake is from a John Cleese film.’

‘Really?’

‘Yeah. My parents bonded over watching Monty Python’s Life of Brian when they were at university. They made a pact when they got together that they would name a child after that film. A few weeks before my older brother was born, my mum’s dad died, so they decided to name their son after him, but once I came along, they honoured their pact in a roundabout way.’

‘And does that make you feel more positively about the university?’

‘No, not really. Most of the rest of the cast went to Oxford or Cambridge, but I just thought it was an interesting anecdote. Everyone always asks me about my name.’

He smiled and nodded.

‘Have you anything else you would like to discuss with me in this, our last session? Any secrets burning to get out?’

She didn’t know what possessed her, but for some reason, Bryony blurted out everything about Isaac. From the moment she saw him in the cemetery to the moment he left in the bright white light. She just let it all pour out of her, unable to stop once she’d started.

Fifteen minutes later, after she had spoken constantly and finally finished her unconventional tale, she looked up at him nervously. She suddenly worried he might want to institutionalise her or something. His face was as unreadable as ever.

‘That’s very interesting.’

‘You don’t believe me?’

‘I don’t think it matters whether or not I believe you. We are not really here to discuss the existence of the supernatural. I do believe that this has been a way for you to process and come to terms with the grief you've had to face and has bought you to a rather unconventional closure.'

'You don't believe me. You think I made it all up, or it was a delusion or something.'

He paused for a minute, and Bryony started biting her nails.

'Have you ever read the book or seen the film "The Life of Pi?"'

Taken off guard by his question, Bryony confirmed that she had seen the film a while back. She couldn't remember all of it, but she had enjoyed it.

'The crux of the story is that the way it is told or rather experienced by the storyteller is so extraordinary, almost unbelievable, but it is beautiful and helps to explain the nature of the individuals involved and the journey they have been on. The reason I bring it up is because you have been on a journey this past year as well. The story you have experienced, regardless of how unbelievable it is, has made you able, willing even, to let Isaac go, and you're ready now to move on.'

'It felt very real. Other people felt his presence too. It wasn't just me and, like I said, his mum saw him too.'

'Bryony, millions of people across the globe believe there are ghosts among us. Millions more believe in a religion that endorses supernatural activity, and millions more than that believe in spirituality at some level. It would be extremely arrogant of anyone to tell you what you experienced wasn't real. It was clearly incredibly real to you, and more to the point, it helped you.'

Bryony nodded. He was right, of course, no one could prove her wrong, and the experience had changed her, so it didn't matter if anyone believed her or not. She decided not to mention that Ronnie's name and address had been in her house before she had found her, maybe it wasn't a coincidence, but she didn't really want to know for sure.

‘It’s nearly the end of our time. Are there any other secrets you’re keeping that you’d like to get off your chest?’

Bryony felt surprisingly deflated. She had expected she would have to argue her case and point out specific events to prove Isaac had really been here. He had kind of taken the wind out of her sails with his response.

‘No. Actually yes. But it’s not about me. It’s about Jax.’

She hadn’t seen him once since the eventful evening. She didn’t know if his slot had changed or if he’d stopped coming for therapy though she thought it more likely to be the former. As she knew she was never coming back again, it would be unlikely she’d ever see him, and she owed him a solid.

‘So I don’t know how friendly you are with Dr Sanders, his therapist, and I know you’re not supposed to discuss your clients at all, but I am giving you my express permission to tell her this little tidbit about her client, ‘cos I reckon most people may have a fairly negative view of him. Well, I would like to give you, and therefore her, another perspective.

‘So, I met Jax at a party about a month ago. I was very drunk and mouthing off in front of everyone. We kissed and left the party together, but then we met up with some of his friends who had some fairly wild plans for the rest of the night that I wasn’t really feeling. Now, Jax could have taken advantage of me. He could have peer-pressured me into doing something I didn’t want to do, I know it wouldn’t have taken much to make me change my mind. He could have left me, in my drunken state, to sort myself out, but he didn’t do any of those things. He bought me food to help sober me up and wanted to stay with me till my dad came to get me. He also protected me when he thought someone else may have posed a threat to me. He took pains to make sure the friends that I happened to run into were really my friends and made them promise to look after me before he’d let me go. It was one of the most chivalrous, gentlemanly experiences I’ve ever had, and I didn’t even say thank you, I don't think. He's a good guy. I mean, he's got his issues, obviously, but beneath all that swagger, he's pure gold. I just think more people need to try and see that. Credit where credit's due and all that.'

'Okay, thank you. I think it's very interesting that you chose to spend your final minutes in therapy trying to bolster the reputation of another. It's been a pleasure getting to know you, Bryony. I wish you well in your next venture. I'm sure you're going to flourish.'

Bizarrely, instead of shaking the outstretched hand he offered, Bryony hugged him. Only when she let go did she realise that was kind of awkward and inappropriate. She left blushing like a lobster.

Chapter Twenty-Seven

Her last shift at the coffee shop was with Joe. She had been looking forward to it until she found out there was some sort of comicon event happening nearby, and these people liked their coffee.

Bryony couldn't remember any other shift ever being so busy. They had to call Vee in on her day off to help them, as they simply couldn't manage it, just the two of them.

Vee came in happily, after all, it was great for business. Joe too seemed quite happy to be working this crazy busy shift, but she later understood why, when he explained, most dramatically in front of a few customers dressed as Vikings, "These are my brethren" in an awful accent she couldn't place. The Vikings had promptly cheered Joe, and he went to the other side of the counter to chest bump them and perform some elaborate salute. They did tip generously, though, so she couldn't complain.

She didn't notice *her* until she was cleaning tables. She'd bought a coffee and was sat at one of the tiny tables alone. Joe must have served her whilst she was on her break 'cos Bryony definitely would have remembered seeing her, no matter how busy it was.

'Hi,' she said, walking up to her table, though there were no empty cups or rubbish on there, like many of the others.

'Oh, hi,' Kirsty replied. She looked so normal compared to all the other customers who were in fancy dress. Scratch that, she looked beautiful. Bryony felt the butterflies all over again.

'How are you?' She asked, just to have something to say.

'I'm okay. I wondered if we could talk? Joe said it was your last shift.'

‘Yeah, definitely, it’s just, it’s super busy.’ In her mind, Bryony cursed all of the comicon goers to hell.

‘Yeah, I can see. Maybe on your lunch break?’

‘I… I’m sorry, I’ve already had it.’

‘Right. Okay then. No worries,’ Bryony could tell she thought she was avoiding her.

‘I might be able to wrangle a ten-minute tea break. You know, when it quietens down later. If you can hang around? You’re coffee’s on me.’

‘Um… yeah, okay then. I’ll just wait here.’

‘Okay.’

‘Cool.’

‘Bryony! A little help,’ Joe called. The queue was out the door. She cursed quietly, smiled quickly at Kirsty, and rushed off.

It was 3 hours before the queue eased off. Bryony constantly checked to see if Kirsty was still sitting there, and apart from one time when she’d gone to the toilet, Kirsty didn’t move from her spot.

‘Okay, who wants a tea break first?’ Vee asked as they were serving the last people in the queue.

‘Me.’ Bryony shouted quickly. The others were clearly surprised but said nothing.

Before going to Kirsty’s table, she escaped to the loo to try to do some damage control. She chided herself for not washing her hair that morning. She cleared the mascara that had smudged beneath her eyes and refreshed her lip gloss. It wasn’t great, but it would have to do.

‘Hi, thanks for waiting,’ she said as she placed their coffees on the table and she pulled a chair over. ‘It’s crazy in here today.’

‘I know. Joe’s loving it, I see.’

‘Of course, he is,’ they both smiled, but an awkwardness fell over them, and neither of them knew what to say.

‘So, how have you been?’

‘Good.’ Bryony answered too enthusiastically. ‘How ‘bout you?’

‘Yep. Good too.’

‘Did you get your exam results?’

‘I did, yeah. I was really pleased. I got my first choice uni.’

‘Oh, brilliant. Well done you.’

‘How about you?’

‘Not as well as I’d hoped, but I managed to get my third choice uni, so I’m still happy.’

‘Oh good. Okay.’

‘Well, my first choice was Oxford, so it was a long shot anyway,’

‘Let me guess, second choice Cambridge?’

‘Naturally.’

They laughed, and then it was silent again.

‘Okay, we’re running out of time here,’ Kirsty began, sitting forward now. ‘I have to ask you, or I’ll forever be wondering, why did you give me a wrong number?’

‘I’m sorry, what?’

‘After that night when you stayed at mine and we kissed,’ she began. ‘I get that you had to go early, but you could have woken me up instead of sneaking off, I could always have gone back to sleep, I can literally fall asleep anywhere, anytime. And why even leave a number if you didn’t want me to get in touch? You could have just said in your note that you didn't want to do it again. I'd have totally understood.'

'I... I didn't leave you a wrong number. I have been waiting for you to call me ever since that night. I don't have your number, or I'd have called you.'

Kirsty reached into her bag and pulled out a very dog-eared, folded paper, and placed it in front of Bryony. She opened it and realised it was the note she had left. She checked out the number she had written and saw straight away the error she had made. She had been so hungover, so tired, and rushed that one of the sevens in her number looked like a two. There was no denying it.

She pointed it out to Kirsty and explained how it had happened.

'So all this time, you had actually wanted me to call?'

'Yes, desperately. You can ask my mum if you don't believe me. I told her all about you.'

'Really?'

Bryony nodded. They went quiet.

'I guess that maybe we've missed our chance here.' Kirsty said sadly.

'I guess. I'm not really one for long distance. I don't think I could make that work.'

'Me neither,' Kirsty agreed. She looked as gutted as Bryony felt. 'What uni are you going to anyway?'

Bryony told her.

Kirsty stopped lifting her coffee mid-air. She stared at Bryony in disbelief, and then her beautiful face split into an enormous grin.

Acknowledgement

This book would not have happened without the help of a few fantastic people. I'd first like to thank Lucy Mills for her guidance and expertise.

The members of 'The More Exclusive Book club' deserve my unwavering thanks for their opinions, thoughts, encouragement, and knowledge, specifically Mitchell, Jake, Maddie, and Ellie.

And then there's Lee, Dan and Faye. Their encouragement, belief, emotional, mental, and financial support, not to mention essential babysitting duties, have enabled me to do this. Thanks for everything, guys, and if this takes off, your story ideas will definitely (probably) be my next project.

I'd also like to express my apologies to Wolfie for any time his pleas for attention, food, drink, or assistance were completely ignored due to my preoccupation with this novel. I hope it doesn't stunt your growth.

Finally, and possibly most importantly, I'd like to say a big 'Well Done' to me. I did it, at last. Go me. #acknowledgeandbeproud

Printed in Great Britain
by Amazon